A triple explosion rattled the guts of the freighter

The ensuing shudder that passed through the hold shook Bolan as he held on to a metal strut for support. One of the diesels died, the silence that dropped around him weighing as heavily on the senses as the engine's constant chugging.

The warrior felt the big ship listing to one side, and realized the freighter would slip into the merciless sea within minutes. It was time to get out.

His hands caught at the short ladder leading to the overhead hatch, and the Executioner forced himself upward. With one hand reaching out to push the hatch, he was unprepared for the ship's sudden movement.

Bolan fell, slamming backward onto a strut with stunning force. Gasping for breath, he fought against the flood of water that swept into the hold.

MACK BOLAN®

The Executioner

DON PENDLETON's EXECUTIONER

MACK BOLAN ®

Death Wind

A GOLD EAGLE BOOK FROM

WORLDWIDE ®

TORONTO • NEW YORK • LONDON • PARIS
AMSTERDAM • STOCKHOLM • HAMBURG
ATHENS • MILAN • TOKYO • SYDNEY

First edition June 1989

ISBN 0-373-61126-9

Special thanks and acknowledgment to
Mel Odom for his contribution to this work.

Such as have followed the wars are despised of every man until a very pinch of need doth come.

—Author unknown
17th Century

A warrior never knows his limits and capabilities until they are tested, exhausted. I'll give completely of myself whenever and wherever I'm needed. Until I'm no longer needed. Or until there's nothing left to give.

—Mack Bolan

To the men and women
of the Drug Enforcement Administration
who fight an endless battle in the war against drugs

PROLOGUE

Fyodor Ivanovitch watched the lights of Dzerzhinsky Square fade away as the Mi-24 Hind rose from the helipad. He felt a longing and a sense of loss that he hadn't experienced since his father died decades ago when Fyodor was a child. Even then, while holding his father's hand and waiting for the cancer-ridden lungs to gasp their last breath, Ivanovitch had remembered the strength that had been part of the man.

The same feeling was evoked when he gazed upon the city below him, the city he'd given so much of his life to. He'd served the KGB faithfully for over twenty years, following orders blindly as he risked his life or took the lives of others.

Now he was being forced to leave.

He turned from the receding lights and laid his head back against the seat, closing his eyes as he locked in his emotions. The weight of the handcuffs and chains shackling his hands and ankles discouraged any movement. The rasp and tinkle of the links sounded as loud and threatening as tank treads rolling down a city street. The way they had in Afghanistan when he served there as a younger man.

The three remaining seats behind the pilot's compartment were occupied by the guards who had been assigned to him during transport. They were young, like so many in the Soviet army now, unaware of the history of conflict that fired men such as Ivanovitch, treating stories of the Cold War and America's efforts to keep Russia from becoming a superpower in the fifties and sixties like child-hood fairy tales.

That would be their undoing, Ivanovitch thought as he looked into the soft face of the young lieutenant in charge of the transport mission.

The man stared back at him, blinking rapidly.

A boy, Ivanovitch realized as he watched the lieutenant tighten his grip on the machine pistol in his lap, a boy with no true understanding of war. Or of dying. He noticed the lieutenant had the weapon's safety engaged.

"What are you looking at, Comrade?" the young man asked.

"Nothing," Ivanovitch replied, and wondered if the man would be intelligent enough to feel insulted.

The lieutenant's lips thinned out in response, but Ivanovitch sensed the reaction was more from discomfort than anger. "You will look elsewhere, Comrade."

The threat was almost nonexistent, and Ivanovitch disregarded it. "Why should I?"

"Because I say so."

Ivanovitch flashed a small, disarming grin. He raised his shackled hands in front of him, letting the links play through the cuffs. "What harm can I cause, Lieutenant? The state has already taken my freedom from me. Can you tell me now they take away my eyesight as well?"

"You will not speak again," the lieutenant snapped. "Your politics have already gotten you into trouble. You should keep your mouth shut and not make things worse for yourself."

Ivanovitch shrugged, and the chains rattled. He brought his wrists together, leaving a doubled length of almost ten inches dangling between his knees. The desire for action burned feverishly inside him, and he had to force himself to remain seated. His superiors should have known better than to send him off with this ridiculous child for a guard.

"What can make matters worse, Comrade?" Ivano-vitch asked. "I'm already being sent to one of the camps where I will in all probability die of sickness or the cold.

That's one area in which we still differ from the Americans. Our political enemies are still consigned to their deaths, no matter how lingering that death may be. The Americans merely put up with them until they are no longer popular. Maybe my criticism of the politburo met with more support than anyone was led to believe."

"You're an old man," the lieutenant scoffed. "Your views of world politics are dated, no longer true. A new world dawns out there, awaiting all of us. The Americans realize this too. Already we have amassed too many nuclear weapons to assure ourselves of any future if we aren't careful. The third world has the bomb now, and none of us are safe."

Ivanovitch pushed aside his rising anger, keeping his voice level. The two guards were watching with interest. "That's why Russia needs to remain strong, to remain aggressive. The Americans have dissidents within their own country that are willing to sacrifice themselves to perverse causes, becoming a cancer that will eat away their backbone in time. If we wait, if we remain strong, we will eventually triumph over them."

"You are wrong, old man," the lieutenant replied. "The old world, the one driven by political needs and restrictions, is a dinosaur, dying to make way for a new world."

"You believe in the dreams Gorbachev offers us?"

"He's a good leader for the times. He thinks ahead."

"Gorbachev is my age," Ivanovitch said. "How can his views be any different than my own? We were both raised in the same environment."

"Gorbachev knows the Americans and Russians will have to learn to live together before we destroy each other. Space has become important again. The economic ties between our two countries are too strong to ignore anymore."

"You mean we would starve if not for the American wheat."

A sad smile touched the lieutenant's lips, and Ivanovitch felt as if the man thought he was lecturing a child.

"No, we would not starve, Comrade, but things would be considerably harder here. Wouldn't you agree?"

Ivanovitch remained silent, feeling the pitch and yaw of the Hind as it sailed through the gathering storm. Had his superior, Kulik, been aware of the storm front moving in? Or had he simply ignored it, thinking all those months in the KGB prison had broken his spirit?

"You think the Americans are willing to keep all their activities peaceful?" Ivanovitch asked.

The lieutenant started to speak, but Ivanovitch didn't give him a chance.

"You should examine American involvement in Central America more closely, Comrade. They disclaim any active measures against Communist forces within the countries there, deny any military aid to the Contra rebels, yet keep monies publicly set aside for just that purpose. And isn't it amazing the number of ex-CIA pilots and operatives that seem to keep getting trapped or shot down over there? You are a fool, Comrade. A pathetic child with no sense of the real world that surrounds you. One day you will be extending your hand in friendship to some American and he will cut if off and throw it in your face."

"Shut up!" the lieutenant shouted as he got to his feet. He leveled the machine pistol in front of him but didn't flip the safety off.

Ivanovitch glared down the barrel of the weapon. A dull, oily sheen glinted from it in the dim interior lights of the gunship. A lightning bolt sizzled through the night behind the KGB agent, reflecting off the lieutenant's eyes. Before the clap of thunder had a chance to follow, Ivanovitch made his move, hurling himself full-tilt at the lieutenant.

The soldier's knuckle whitened on the trigger as he tried to fire a burst from his weapon, despair dawning in his eyes as he realized the safety was still on. He dropped the machine pistol and tried to unholster his Tokarev, his fingers scarcely touching the butt before Ivanovitch smashed into him and knocked them both to the floor.

Levering his shoulder into the lieutenant's chin, Ivanovitch sought the pistol with both hands. His adversary was quicker than he gave him credit for, and more committed. The younger man's fist rocketed into Ivanovitch's temple, blurring the big man's vision.

Ripping the Tokarev free of its holster, Ivanovitch fired point-blank into the lieutenant's face. Blood spattered both of them as the younger man's features exploded.

Then the KGB man rolled from the corpse, blood-slick fingers gripping the pistol, seeking a target to lock onto.

The two remaining guards had risen to their feet, surprise and fear blazing in their eyes as they clawed for their weapons.

Wasting no time, Ivanovitch drilled two shots into each man. Children, Ivanovitch thought disgustedly as he pointed the Tokarev at the chain binding his feet, children playing soldier.

Two shots later, he was free to stand and walk. He hesitated for a moment, sending a final round through the lieutenant's skull to ensure no further trouble from that quarter, then grabbed the machine pistol from the floor as he headed for the pilot's cabin. Doubtless the pilot and co-pilot had heard the shots and would be expecting the worst.

For the first time in months, since he'd been deemed dangerous to the KGB and had been locked up as a political prisoner, Fyodor Ivanovitch felt in control of his life. Clutching the machine pistol in his hands, his breath rattling between his teeth, he knew this was what freedom was about—holding a weapon in your hands and facing your enemies, even if you had once called them friends.

He rapped his knuckles against the closed door. "Open up," he ordered, knowing his voice would be unrecognizable over the roar of the rotors.

"Who is it?"

"Open the door, Comrade. I need to talk to my superiors. The prisoner tried to escape and I had to kill him. I need instructions on what to do next. Surely they won't want a dead man delivered to the camps."

There was a muffled conversation Ivanovitch couldn't hear, then a lock snicked back, followed by another.

"It's just as well you had to kill him," a voice said. "Tonight is no time for anyone to have to go out in the cold."

Inner alarms jangling loudly, Ivanovitch watched as the cabin door popped open. They were giving in too easily. He was sure the pilots would know of the directions Kulik would have given the backup gunship. They would be aware that once the other Hind knew something was going wrong, its pilots would shoot them down. The pilots of this craft would try to take care of any problems themselves and not alert their sister ship.

When the door inched open, Ivanovitch kicked it inward, never giving the co-pilot the chance to aim his side arm. The man fell back hard against the instrument panel, and the machine pistol stitched him from groin to throat in a single burst.

Ivanovitch grabbed the dead man and pulled him through the doorway to drop in a heap beside the slain guards.

Then Ivanovitch was inside the cabin. He set the machine pistol on selective fire and burned a round through the pilot's head, catching the body before it had a chance to fall forward onto the blood-spattered controls.

Ivanovitch sat in the empty seat, shifted the pilot's corpse to the floor and seized the stick. He tugged gently, feeling the gunship respond to his touch.

Static broke across the incoming radio transmission as the other Hind tried to raise the pilot. Ivanovitch ignored the call, nosing the chopper downward into the night. As he banked to the left, he caught sight of the other Hind plunging after him, its passage marked only by its running lights. The transmissions from the other copter had ceased, and he was sure the pursuing pilot was now engaged for the kill. Bright ignition sparks peeled from the other side of the attacking chopper, indicating that the pilot had released at least two missiles.

Jerking the stick, Ivanovitch felt the Mi-24 leap upward, seizing the empty air space above him in a frenzy of effort. The missiles shot by harmlessly. He brought the Hind around in a rotor-straining maneuver and released a missile of his own, knowing it would expend itself uselessly above his attacker. Then he was moving again, tracking his pursuer through the storm-darkened sky.

The other pilot tried to lose Ivanovitch, tried to use the black clouds as cover, losing and gaining altitude. But it was all in vain. In Ivanovitch, the KGB had created a warrior geared for survival.

Turbines whining, he pursued the other craft, closing the distance until he was within effective missile range. He ran his tongue over his lips in anticipation of the kill. How many times over the years had he felt like this, the almost sexual fulfillment he seemed to reach when death itself infused and inspired him?

Kulik knew about the feelings. The headmaster would often dangle an assignment before Ivanovitch's eyes, waiting to give the word to start the killhunt. Yes, Kulik knew him better than anyone.

Even as that thought filled his mind, Ivanovitch knew his former mentor Kulik would never rest until he had him tracked down and killed.

But Fyodor Ivanovitch had too many plans to die now. There would be retribution, and he knew how to get it, how to strike back at this new America groveling for international acceptance, how to force Russia to be more independent in global politics once more. He'd thought about it for months in his solitary cell. Planning the event had become as much a part of his daily routine as the exercises he performed to keep his body in shape, the meals he ate to keep up his strength.

Gorbachev would regret ordering his incarceration, and Russia would regain some of her greatness, the fear she inspired before Gorbachev succumbed to the American media and became a symbol of the USSR's weakness.

Caressing the trigger, Ivanovitch released twin death-birds. Scarlet streaks followed in the other Hind's wake. The Mi-24 transformed immediately into a white-hot nova that flared briefly before being absorbed by the storm clouds.

1

Mack Bolan perched high among the crooked branches of the old cypress, cloaked in darkness. Shifting quietly on the rough bark, he raised his infrared night glasses and scanned the drop zone. In the off-color view afforded by the glasses, the swamp area appeared even more forbidding and primordial.

Oil-black muddy water lapped sluggishly at the knobby knees of the cypress. Bolan knew the swamp wasn't deep here by observing the guards as they slogged through it in waders. Maybe eight inches at best. Farther out into the lagoon area proper, he was sure the depth reached several feet. It had to in order to provide a suitable landing area for the small Cessna that would be coming in at any moment.

Settling back against the bole of the tree, the warrior listened to the swamp sounds, thinking how little it had probably changed since the days of the dinosaurs. The occasional deep gruntings of alligators and the slapping of their tails echoed hollowly across the flat water, seeming to come from everywhere at once. They weren't the only menace that hid in the night. The swamp came alive at dusk, its denizens searching hungrily for the weak or the unwary.

Not like the men Bolan hunted. Sure, they preyed on the weak and unwary too, but theirs wasn't a hunger Nature had built into her food chain.

There were at least ten roving sentries below Bolan. They had come at different times, in different modes of transportation, including boats and four-wheel-drive vehicles. And all of them were waiting on the cargo the small plane had to deliver.

According to Bolan's informant, the cargo would be worth several million dollars—and was some of the purest cocaine Hal Brognola's DEA liaison had ever seen. That allowed the drug brokers plenty of room to "step" on it before the stuff hit the streets.

Bolan had come seeking the source.

Reaching behind and below him, the warrior retrieved a black rifle bag from the spike he'd driven there earlier. He opened the Velcro closures and removed the weapon. The pale moonlight streaming down barely touched the black matte finish of the Galil. The automatic rifle was chambered for a 7.62 mm round, and Bolan had extra clips for it secured in the weapons belt strapped around his waist. The Beretta 93-R rode in a quick-draw shoulder holster, and his .44 Desert Eagle was a comfortable weight on his right hip. A Ka-bar fighting knife hid in a sheath on his left.

It had to be a strictly hit-and-git strike. With the darkness, the openness of the swamp and the size of the group he was stalking, the numbers on this one would be falling fast.

He had one hell of a demoralizer for an opening play though. The bag holding the Armbrust Disposable Anti-Tank Weapon had to be specially designed and had been a bitch to carry through the swamp.

Bolan checked the Armbrust as carefully as he had all of his weapons. It was an armful trying to maneuver it in the cypress, but he had chosen his perch with care. The strike zone was dead ahead, already marked off in his mind.

The plane would be the first target if everything went as planned. Bolan needed the pilot alive if possible. At least long enough to finger the next link in the chain he'd been following for the past week.

Hal Brognola, Bolan's contact in the Justice Department, had requested help last Thursday, pushing the warrior into the ranks of the Atlanta, Georgia, police department until Bolan branched off on his own for a blitz that yielded more information in one thunder-filled night than the city's vice squad had turned up after months of investigations. The matter had been personal to the big Fed. One of the vice cops who'd been shot down while trying to close the drug pipeline on the Eastern Seaboard had been a friend for several years.

The network was bigger than the Atlanta vice detectives had thought, reaching from the Georgia metropolitan area to the northern Florida swamps. Bolan had found that out quickly. The further he chased the string, the tighter the security became, until it came down to seizing a prisoner and forcing the information he needed out of the guy.

Like now.

A sentry stopped below Bolan's tree, and the warrior drew his silenced Beretta. He knew he would be hidden from the man even if the guy decided to look up. With the Spanish moss hanging over the sentry's head, Bolan was sure he couldn't be silhouetted against the moon's weak glow. But he fisted the pistol just in case.

The guard let his rifle drop to the length of its strap, the barrel hanging mere inches above the murky water, and lit a cigarette. In the brief flare of orange light, Bolan saw that the guy was big and beefy, with a full beard that ran down onto a barrel chest. A cowboy hat with a floppy brim hid the rest of the guy's face.

"Put that goddamned cigarette out, Jonesy," a voice hissed from only a few feet away.

The big man below the tree ignored the order, shielding the cigarette's ember in his cupped hand.

"Put it out, you stupid son of a bitch."

Craning his neck, Bolan tried to find the other guard, finally spotting him hunkered down amid the knees of a cypress about thirty feet away. The man was willow slim and wore combat cosmetics, blending into the rough exterior of the tree behind him. The M-16 in the guard's arms seemed to be an extension of the man himself.

Definitely not an amateur, Bolan told himself when he realized this new guard wasn't one of the ten he'd counted previously. This guy had slipped in later under the cover of darkness. How many more had been with him?

Sliding back a sleeve of his blacksuit, Bolan checked the time. A little after one. The Cessna was late. For a moment he wondered if the gunners below were expecting trouble on the delivery tonight. Bolan's informant was still safely cached with Justice agents acting under Brognola's orders. There was no reason for them to think security had been breached.

He lifted the night glasses and scouted the marshy terrain again, adjusting the head count to around twenty.

"Put out the goddamned cigarette, Jonesy," the hidden man repeated.

"Man, you're too tense. There ain't nobody around who's going to try any shit with us. I can't even remember how many bodies we got scattered around this area. Hell, I think the gators are starting to look forward to these little visits of ours." Jonesy took another hit off the cigarette.

"Either put it out now or I'll shoot you myself, you stupid bastard."

Jonesy muttered something Bolan couldn't hear, but flipped the cigarette into the swamp water. He hoisted the rifle back into position and moved off.

Some of the shadows at the base of the cypress shifted form and the Executioner knew the other man had changed positions too.

As the strong hum of approaching aircraft engines filled the still night air, Bolan could detect more movement below him with the naked eye. He stored the night glasses in a pouch and tied it around a nearby limb. If he had time later he would pick it up.

The running lights of the small plane came into view, only inches from the tree line. Bolan knew the pilot had to be good to put the Cessna down in the small landing area of the lagoon.

He pulled a length of nylon rope from an overhead branch, placing the coil in front of him so he could kick it to the ground when the time came for him to leave the tree. Then he strapped the Galil over his shoulder, muzzle pointing downward so he could pull it up into target acquisition quickly. The Beretta and Desert Eagle were within reach if he needed them.

Taking the Armbrust onto his shoulder, Bolan sighted with his right eye, then opened his left to track the Cessna's progress toward the lagoon. He let the heavy antitank weapon become a part of his body, opening his senses until it became as operational as a finger on his hand.

Someone set off a flare at ground level, its greenish glow spreading across the brackish swamp waters and loamy ground. The plane wiggled its wings in response and angled downward.

Bolan could make out the dark bulk of the pontoons below the Cessna, and he tracked the Armbrust on a point directly between and above them. Even if things did go wrong, the Executioner didn't intend for the cargo to leave the plane.

The pilot landed easily, the running lights bobbing with the motion of the water under the pontoons. A small outboard revved to life and sped from under a low overhang of branches, angling toward the floating airplane.

The pilot opened the cockpit and threw out a small anchor before climbing out to stand on one of the pontoons. In the dim glow of the plane's interior lights, Bolan saw that the pilot wore a baseball cap and a Chicago Cubs windbreaker. It wasn't much, but it was enough to set the guy apart from the other men.

The outboard bumped into the pontoons, and for a moment Bolan thought the pilot was going to fall in. Then he heard the man's curses as he stepped into the boat and sat down. The engine revved up again and sped toward the nearby bank. A powerboat swung into the swamp and headed for the Cessna. To unload the cocaine, Bolan figured as he squeezed his left eye shut and focused the Armbrust on the plane.

An instant before he touched off the first round, a swarm of bullets chopped into the branches around him, sending splinters into his face.

"Raid!" someone yelled. "Raid, goddammit!"

Bolan didn't waste time looking for the sniper. He bent low over the branch he was sitting on, holding tightly on to it and the antitank gun. Muzzle-flashes sparking from the top of a tree almost fifty yards away marked the guy's position. A solid rain of 5.56 mm tumblers hacked into the tree above Bolan's head, tearing into the cypress's tough hide in hollow thumps.

Elevating the Armbrust, Bolan brought the big weapon to bear on the man in the tree, knowing other guns would be joining in once everyone knew what the guy was shooting at. He touched off the round, counting on the firing pistons at either end of the weapon to seal in the expended flash and gases and not give his position away.

The 67 mm warhead streaked through the night, eliminating the gunner and the top of the tree in a single explosion. Loading another round, Bolan raised up on one elbow to deliver another 67 mm bomb to an area of concentrated fire on the other side of the lagoon. The warhead screamed its detonation, evaporating two men and blowing a crater in the oozing muck of the swamp.

"That isn't cops," a man shouted. "What the hell is going on?"

"Bastard's up in that tree."

"Which one?"

Knowing the numbers had almost run out on his current position, Bolan reloaded the Armbrust and sighted on the Cessna. A double explosion erupted from the plane: the first when the warhead hit, the second when the gas tanks blew. Flames roiled into the night, illuminating the lagoon.

Automatic fire raked the trees in every direction as the men hunted Bolan. So far, less than a handful had discovered his location. Loading the final round, he launched it into another pocket of concentrated fire, then dropped the Armbrust and kicked the rope from the branch.

Drawing the big .44, Bolan held it tightly on his right gloved fist and slid down the nylon, anchored by his other hand and his feet. He touched down and felt the mud suck at his feet, as if trying to pull him under.

He reholstered the .44, slid the Galil forward and started angling through the creeper-tangled land toward the spot he had last seen the pilot.

Echoes of gunfire rang out in an occasional burst around Bolan as the guards began to get control of the situation. They'd be looking for him soon, and the few hours he had had earlier that afternoon to set up the strike couldn't equal his enemy's knowledge of the swamp.

Leaping over a fallen tree covered with fungus, Bolan kept the Galil up and forward, shielding his face from branches and thorns with his forearms and the rifle stock. Something heavy moved in the nearby scrub, and for a moment the warrior thought it might be an alligator. He swung his rifle around, stopping himself just short of blasting a raccoon and giving his position away.

The animal raced back into the shelter of a dead tree, making angry chattering noises. Bolan crouched behind a stand of brush as he heard men approaching his position, dropping to one knee as he held the Galil at waist-level.

"Who is this guy?" one of the men asked.

"Who the hell cares, Billy? I just want to know where the son of a bitch is. You got any idea how much that cargo was worth? That goddamned bastard deserves to be gut-shot and left for gator bait."

"I don't care what you guys say," a third man said. "I'm for getting the hell out of here."

Once they'd passed by, Bolan resumed his search. Zeroing in on the sound of the outboard, he checked his bearings and angled toward the boat. It had been the last place he'd seen the pilot, and the warhead from the Arm-

brust hadn't left the guy a whole lot of choices about where
to go.

The outboard pulled into view slowly, only a few feet
from shore. Four men, including the pilot, occupied the
small seats. Reflections of the dying flames devouring the
plane played across their faces. The pilot was young, Bolan saw, with a headful of red hair under the baseball cap.
His hands shook on a long-barreled .38, and he kept adjusting the cap nervously.

The other three were hired muscle. Built big and blocky,
they would be intimidating under the right circumstances.
At the moment they were just bigger targets.

Without warning, Bolan stepped from hiding and raked
the outboard on full automatic. The two men holding the
shotguns were knocked backward out of the craft, slipping into the water soundlessly. The rest of the clip went
for the tiller man and the engine.

"Drop the gun," Bolan ordered as the pilot tried to
bring the .38 into play.

The guy hesitated for a moment as his hands shook
around the pistol. Then he glanced past his shoulder at the
man hanging over the rudder. When he turned to face Bolan again, the .38 made a wet plop as it hit the swamp water. The pilot started to raise his hands behind his neck.

"Get out of the boat," Bolan said as other voices drew
attention to the outboard. Bullets thudded into the trees
behind the Executioner, whipping through the water as
they tracked toward the outboard.

Without hesitation the warrior stepped into the water,
sliding in the greasy mud for a moment as he propelled
himself toward the pilot. Before he knew it, Bolan was in
water almost up to his chest. He leaned over the side of the
boat and grabbed a fistful of the pilot's windbreaker and
jerked him out.

The guy came up spluttering, eyes wide with fear. He
breathed raggedly, trying to empty brackish water out of
his lungs.

Hollow pinging sounded from the outboard, sparks flashing as bullets ricocheted from the metal hull. Bolan tightened his grip on the pilot's jacket, and started pulling him toward shore.

"Be careful, goddammit," someone yelled, "or you're going to hit Frank."

"Frank's already dead," a voice shouted back. "The bastard already killed him."

The rate of fire picked up. Sharp points dug for his skin under the blacksuit, and he heard the pilot cry out in pain.

"Keep your head down," Bolan growled, "or your buddies are going to take it off." He pushed the guy behind a tree thick enough to provide shelter for both of them and reached into the ammo pouch at his waist. He changed clips in the Galil then removed two Misra MU-50 hand grenades.

Bolan lobbed both grenades at the formation of men moving toward his position. He didn't wait to see the twin explosions, knowing that the resultant flashes would hamper his night vision. The Misras had an effective kill-radius of fifteen yards. Total carnage within that area. Those who weren't killed would think twice about continuing any pursuit blindly.

"Move," Bolan said, shoving the pilot forward.

The warrior knew their progress through the night-blackened swamp would have looked comical if they hadn't been within the perimeters of a hot killzone. Repeatedly the pilot fell over cypress knees and had trouble getting back on his feet. Bolan could hear the angry yells of their pursuers as the men worked themselves into a frenzy of boldness, like the baying of human blood-hounds.

Keeping an eye on his backtrail, Bolan spotted amber beams of flashlights bobbing. A sudden snapping in the underbrush drew Bolan's attention. The pilot had fallen again and was trying to get up when a dark mass separated itself from the shore and came at him.

"Gator," the pilot screamed through a mouthful of swamp water. "Gator. Oh, Jesus."

Pulling the Galil around in a tight arc, Bolan squeezed off a burst, zipping the alligator from the two small eyes set high on its forehead to halfway down the length of its body. For a moment the warrior thought the slugs weren't going to stop the creature. It glided silently toward the pilot, opening its mouth as it neared its prey.

Bolan hauled the Desert Eagle from his hip, stepping toward the pilot, the dark water lapping around his upper thighs. Were there any more of them? he asked himself as he triggered the first round into the alligator. He could hear the meaty smack of the .44 hitting the reptile's flesh even after the booming report of the Magnum.

The pilot stood paralyzed, eyes locked on the gaping jaws that were only an arm's length away, watching helplessly as the distance diminished.

Bolan finished off the rest of the clip in the big handgun, centering his shots in the alligator's head. The brain had to be in there somewhere. He willed the creature to die, knowing he was in danger of losing his only lead to the next link in the drug ring.

The Executioner shoved his booted feet hard into the black mud of the swamp bed, wishing he was closer, mentally commanding the flyer to get the hell out of the way. For a moment he thought it was too late. He was already ramming a fresh clip into the .44 when the alligator's jaws abruptly closed.

The creature continued to glide toward its prey. When it bumped lifelessly into the pilot's chest, Bolan thought the guy was going to pass out.

"Get up," Bolan told the man as he kicked the dead alligator away and pulled the guy out of the water. He shoved the man north again, toward the Blazer and escape.

A few yards farther the ground became more solid. The pilot made better time, shoving his way through the low-hanging brush with both arms. Bolan kept his prisoner on course, consulting the compass strapped to his right wrist. Listening intently, the Executioner could still hear muted sounds of pursuit over the flyer's labored breathing, but they were dying out as the men tried to reorganize from the unexpected blitz.

Bolan paused a moment to holster the Desert Eagle and shove another clip in the Galil. Then he was pacing the pilot again, jogging easily out of the killzone, satisfied that if the operation hadn't gone exactly as he had planned, it had at least produced the desired results. And that was all a warrior could ask for most of the time.

2

Yuri Mikhailin studied his companion as he drove down the twisting road leading from Rzhev. The old man didn't look like a master KGB agent, yet that was how Yuri's immediate supervisor had introduced the man three days ago.

Dressed as he was in neutral-colored clothing and wearing a gray hat only a little darker than the beard that covered his lower face, Kirov would have looked more natural seated in a rocker dandling grandchildren on his knees than checking the safety on the black automatic pistol he'd taken from his shoulder holster.

"The man we're going to see is very dangerous," Kirov said. "But at one time he was a friend of Fyodor Ivanovitch. And he still remains one of the best forgers our country has ever seen." He holstered the automatic, loosening the buttons on his jacket so he could get at it easier. "He free-lances when the KGB doesn't have work for him."

As he made the turn onto the dirt road that would take them to the forger's house, Yuri asked, "But why would he help someone like Ivanovitch, someone who's an enemy of the state? Doesn't he know the consequences he faces?"

Kirov shrugged and again the younger man noted how out of place the man seemed in the present circumstances. "There are many reasons why a man does the things he does, young Mikhailin." The older man's eyes seemed to sift through their surroundings, and Yuri had the impression Kirov would know trouble was coming long before it arrived.

Dangerous, Yuri's superior had warned when Mikhailin was told of his new partner, but the man needed to find Ivanovitch.

Yuri could accept Ivanovitch as a threat. He'd studied the ex-agent's file and found that the man had been involved in covert activities around the globe, affecting geopolitics in many third world countries. Fyodor Ivanovitch had a file full of past violence—even during the time he'd spent in the KGB prison, where he'd killed two fellow prisoners he'd sworn attacked him. Then there was the wreckage of the two Hinds not far from Moscow that Yuri had inspected only three days ago. Nine men were dead. Nine men who had been warned that even handcuffed their prisoner was a threat. Ivanovitch was a killer, and the pictures Yuri had seen of the big, blocky man bore that statement out. You could read it in the man's face.

Not so with Kirov, Yuri's partner, the man he'd be working with to capture or kill Ivanovitch. The man Yuri would be trusting his back to.

Yuri's hands gripped the steering wheel tighter as the old clapboard house came into view.

There was no file on Kirov's past service. Yuri had checked after the assignment had been made. At least not a file he could get into, which was surprising since he had access to almost everything in KGB headquarters. Yuri was one of the top agents covering the United States, having spent a handful of years in his early twenties at Berkeley. Now, at thirty, he was someone to be trusted with the affairs of state. Then why did he need Kirov?

"Slow down," Kirov demanded.

Yuri barely heard the older man over the crunch of the tires across the frozen mud. He wanted to remind Kirov who was in charge of the mission, but knew that now wasn't the time. Later. After they had talked to the forger. He braked, intending to wheel the Volvo to a stop in front of the house, beside the ancient car already waiting there.

"Don't stop," Kirov hissed.

Yuri checked his impulse to tell his companion to stop ordering him around as if he were a boy. Instead he released the brake and coasted around the gentle curve the road took, running beside a tree-filled pasture covered with yellow grass.

"I tried to explain to you," Kirov said, "that our man is very dangerous. He'd kill you in a moment if he thought you meant him harm. And he doesn't live alone. His four sons are with him."

Angrily Yuri said, "Then what would you have us do, Comrade? According to your way of thinking, Petrovsky is just the man we need to talk to."

Kirov nodded in a condescending manner that Yuri found offensive. "He *is* just the man. Ivanovitch and Petrovsky go back many years. The forger owes our quarry his life. They were agents together a long time ago, before Petrovsky lost the use of his legs." He motioned to the side of the road with a gloved hand. "Stop the car here. We will walk back to the house."

Yuri checked the rearview mirror and made sure no one was following them, then pulled the car off the road and parked in a stand of trees. When he turned to speak to Kirov, he found that the man had already left the vehicle.

By the time Yuri had switched off the engine and retrieved his Skorpion machine pistol from under the seat, Kirov was already deep among the trees of the pasture, a nearly invisible wraith.

Strapping the Skorpion to his shoulder, Yuri concealed the weapon under the long coat he wore and jogged over to the older man.

"You should have waited for me, Comrade."

Kirov looked at him and smiled faintly. "You are in the prime of your life, Mikhailin. Surely you have no trouble catching up to an old man?"

Ignoring the agent's words, Yuri matched his steps to Kirov's. "When we have finished our business here, you and I need to talk."

"You think I'm overstepping my authority, and you are angered that your superior saw fit to pair you with such an old man, an old man who doesn't even know his place."

"Kulik had his reasons."

"But you don't know what they were."

"No."

"And you were even more surprised to learn you could not find a file on me in your computers."

Yuri remained silent.

"I know you checked, Comrade. I would have done the same in your shoes. In fact I did. Your record is most impressive, but you are still young. Still an unknown in some areas."

"How did you get into my file? That is restricted information."

"Kulik showed it to me as an enticement to get me to work with you."

"To get *you* to work with *me*?" Yuri didn't believe it. Who was this old man that Kulik would show him so much courtesy?

Kirov smiled again, his eyes crinkling in grandfatherly lines. "Perhaps I should feel the anger you are feeling. It is true that I've been away for the past seven years, but even so, ten years ago they would have trusted me to do this by myself."

Yuri knew Kirov was speaking of the directorate, Kulik's bosses, and spoke of them as if he knew them personally.

"So you see, my young friend, we both have reasons to be incensed over our pairing on this project. My question is, are you professional enough to overcome your feelings and attend to the assignment at hand? Both of our lives surely depend on it."

Gripping the Skorpion tightly, Yuri shifted it to a more comfortable position under the coat. Before he had a chance to say anything further, Kirov motioned him to silence, coming to a stop behind a tree.

The house was ahead of them, looking incongruous in its surroundings. A small barn occupied space behind the house, and two cows stood just inside the open frame, trying to stay out of the chill wind that swept across the cleared section of land between the pasture and house.

"A picture of pastoral Russia," Kirov said softly. He reached inside his jacket and took out his Tokarev, jacking a live round into the chamber. Keeping it at his side, the old man started in a circuitous route that would take him to the barn behind the house.

Yuri followed, feeling more caught up in the events that were happening around him than in control of them. He had to work at reaching the point of stealth Kirov seemed to fall into naturally. The old man was almost soundless as he moved.

"It will all happen quickly when we enter the house," Kirov said as he stood with his back pressed to the barn. "If Petrovsky has seen and helped Ivanovitch, he will know why I'm here."

Yuri nodded.

"Don't be careless in there. If a man in that house points a weapon at you, kill him. Do not ask for his surrender, because you will only be wasting your breath. Do you understand?"

"Yes." But a worm of indecision squirmed through Yuri's stomach, reminding him of the other two times he'd been forced to kill. After the last one, a female Mossad agent who had discovered his real identity, he didn't think he'd be able to pull the trigger on a human being again. Intelligence work was supposed to be just that: gathering intelligence to nullify the oppressor's advantage. Not executions.

"Good."

The way Kirov replied made Yuri think there might have been more in Kulik's personal file on agent Mikhailin than he would have liked. But if there were any doubts about his abilities, what was he doing stalking Ivanovitch?

The old man took the lead, moving more quickly than Yuri would have thought possible. Standing to one side of the wooden door, Kirov raised the Tokarev to a ready position level to his head, left arm hanging loose at his side.

"Kick it in," Kirov whispered.

Yuri stood with his back to the wall on the other side of the door. "Won't Petrovsky run?" he asked.

"The man is in a wheelchair. Weren't you listening when I was talking earlier?"

Yuri nodded tightly, angry at himself for forgetting. He shifted positions.

"But remember, young Mikhailin, Petrovsky might be crippled, but he still has his fangs. We need him alive if we can get him. Dead if he poses a threat. Take no chances with your life."

Yuri's foot connected solidly with the door, splitting it from its hinges.

Without waiting for Yuri to regain his balance, Kirov charged inside the house, his pistol thrust before him, as sensitive as a snake's tongue. Yuri followed, both hands wrapped around the Skorpion.

The house was modestly furnished and dimly lit, not at all what Yuri would have expected of a master forger. Where, then, did the man keep his earnings?

No one was in the small kitchen at the rear of the house. The dining room was also empty, though a handful of plates covered the small wooden table, still bearing the remains of a recent breakfast.

Walking crabwise, Yuri closed the distance between himself and Kirov, wishing the old man would slow down and take things one step at a time.

Movement shadowed an open doorway leading to a bedroom. Yuri caught the brief flash of light on gunmetal and swung the Skorpion down, tracking a target he couldn't yet see. His mind screamed at him, refusing to pull the trigger on the weapon. He saw the woman Mossad agent again, face and neck burned and blackened from his bullets.

The man who stepped through the door had no compunction about killing. Bearded and young, his eyes were flat obelisks above the snout of the automatic weapon he held. Yuri could already feel the line of bullets that would issue forth in only another heartbeat or two, but he still couldn't pull the trigger. Yuri knew he was going to be the death of himself and Kirov.

Then the Tokarev barked once, its harsh voice numbing Yuri's right ear. The young man was jerked back into the bedroom headfirst.

"Anton." Kirov's tone held more underlying steel than Yuri would have thought possible. "Anton, it's Boris. I've killed one of your sons. Would you have me kill more?"

Yuri watched the dead man, hypnotized by the still-quivering legs. Why, he wanted to ask Kirov, did death have to be so vulgar? Then he looked back for his partner, finding the man already striding into the living room.

Yuri pressed back into the short hallway, taking advantage of the cover it offered. He peered around the door frame, watching as Kirov crossed the living room to come to a halt facing a man who looked even older. The other man sat amid a pile of blankets on a worn couch, well within reach of the heat of the fireplace.

Petrovsky was bald, wrinkled, with watery, blue eyes sunk in a permanent yellow glare. "You killed my son?" he asked in a steady voice.

Kirov nodded. "He would have killed my companion."

Petrovsky switched his gaze to Yuri. "Is he that important to you, Boris?"

"He is with me," Kirov said simply. "You know I take care of everyone who works with me. Even you at one time."

Petrovsky nodded and looked at Kirov again.

Kirov was quiet for a moment, and Yuri watched the older man carefully search the room with his eyes. "You know why I have come here."

"Yes. Fyodor told me they would probably send you."

Kirov's voice was gentler this time. "Where is he, Anton?"

Tears filled Petrovsky's eyes as he glared up at Kirov. Yuri watched the forger's hands, waiting to make sure they didn't disappear under the blankets for even an instant. If he had to, he would shoot the man.

"What has Fyodor Ivanovitch done that is so evil, Boris? Said a few things about the way our country is governed? He yearns for the Russia he fought for all these years. He wants our country to be strong again."

"Times change," Kirov said. "It's a new world out there. Not like it was when we were young."

"You're wrong, Boris. It may look different, but it's the same. The predators are still there. They just hide better now. Do you think for a moment that the Americans would let any sign of weakness pass unnoticed? They would be on us in a moment if they thought they would keep the upper hand."

"I didn't come here to argue with you. I came here seeking a dangerous man, one whose life may threaten Russia's relations with many of her allies. Fyodor can do a lot of harm in only a short time if he goes unchecked."

"And what will you do with him once you find him?" Petrovsky asked.

Kirov said nothing.

"He was once like the son you lost as a baby, Boris. You told me that yourself. Have your feelings changed?"

Yuri studied Kirov, looking for an emotion that surely must be there. But the man still presented the same hard and neutral facade he'd worn since Yuri had been introduced to him.

Kirov raised the Tokarev and pointed it at the forger. "Tell me what you know." His voice was hard and flat, as if it had been squeezed from the nether reaches of frozen Siberia. Yuri was glad he wasn't on the other end of the pistol.

"Or you will shoot me? I'm an old man, Boris. The KGB seldom uses me anymore. I'd been forgotten until the past few days. Just like you."

Kirov remained silent. The pistol never wavered.

"What will happen to you once this is over?" Petrovsky asked. "I can tell you what, Boris. They will forget about you again if you're lucky. Or perhaps they will kill you so one less person knows about this."

"If you don't tell me," Kirov said, "I will put a bullet through each of your hands. Then, even the small amount of money you have been able to make at your trade will be cut off. You will be a burden to your sons. You will truly be old then. And useless. Is that what you want?"

Yuri felt sick to his stomach. This was the kind of espionage work he didn't want to be exposed to. The kind he tried to forget about when he found himself face-to-face with it, knowing it would come back as nightmares.

The forger's face seemed to be poised on the knife point of uncertainty. The yellowed eyes searched Kirov's face.

The click of the Tokarev's hammer being thumbed back was as ominous as thunder in the small room, though it wasn't much louder than the crack and pop of the logs in the fireplace.

Tears fell from Petrovsky's eyes. "Damn you, Boris Kirov. Damn you for coming here and killing one of my sons, and damn you for making me feel so helpless." Then he began to talk, telling Kirov of the night Ivanovitch had appeared on his doorstep and of the documents that had been forged.

As Yuri listened, he found himself almost numb to the situation, in awe of the coldness that Kirov could exude. Not at all like the grandfatherly type Yuri had mistaken him for. The man was an animal, bred by the KGB to kill on command, feeling no remorse afterward. Not even now, when he was stalking someone he'd once thought of as a son. Yuri wanted to ask Kulik why he'd been paired with this man. But deep down he knew. Kulik wanted someone to monitor Kirov, to make sure he accomplished the task they'd set out for him. Was Kulik afraid that Kirov would join Ivanovitch in whatever plan the man was putting together? To fight for the Russia that used to be?

From the list of documents Petrovsky gave them, Yuri knew Ivanovitch wasn't just rushing into anything. The different passports would give the man access to many different countries, different routes of getting to whatever his ultimate destination was.

Kirov knew it too. Yuri could tell from the tightening of the man's lips.

Holding the Skorpion tightly, Yuri studied his partner through new eyes, widened with the knowledge of what Kirov could do. He was sure the man had noticed his hesitation to kill earlier. How, Yuri asked himself as he looked at Kirov, was he supposed to prevent the man from joining Ivanovitch if that was what Kirov wanted? Or was he slated to die under Kirov's Tokarev as well? The lack of answers gave birth to a hard, cold knot in the center of his stomach.

3

Perspiration trickled down Ivanovitch's cheeks as he stared at the man across the small table. Only the proximity of the occupied tables around them kept the big Russian from striking the man.

Averting his eyes, Ivanovitch looked down the slope leading from the outside café, past the white sands of the shoreline and toward the evening sun. It would be dark soon. The clouds had already purpled against the broken red sky, reflecting harshly against the blue of the Caribbean.

They made an odd couple, sitting at the white wrought-iron table. Ivanovitch could tell from the furtive looks the other patrons had given them. The tall Russian with broad shoulders and closely clipped light brown hair dwarfed the smaller man, who was clearly a native of the island country. Both wore suits, but the small man seemed more comfortable in his, less susceptible to the humid heat that lingered in the evening air.

Ivanovitch leaned forward, lacing the fingers of his hands around the drink in front of him. "When will I see Diaz?"

The other man shifted uneasily, and Ivanovitch knew the anger he held in check was noticeable to the man. Good. As long as no one else at the café became interested in what was going on.

"Tomorrow."

"Where will I meet him?"

"He will call for you," the contact replied, "at your motel."

Sliding his dark glasses down his nose, Ivanovitch fixed the messenger with a stare that had loosened tongues halfway around the world. "I'm not a man to be kept so easily waiting, Miguel."

"Señor Diaz knows this and extends his apologies, but there are certain things he must ascertain before recognizing you for who you say you represent. These are not safe times in this country. American agents remain in place around this city and others."

Ivanovitch drained his glass of Finlandia vodka, leaving the icy skeleton to melt in the heat.

Miguel's fingers twitched uncontrollably at the edge of the table, as if they were itching to reach for the butt of the weapon he had concealed under his jacket.

The Russian felt the wet leather of his own shoulder holster chafing against his skin, but it was too dangerous to go unarmed, even with the false trails he'd laid since leaving Moscow. It had been years since he'd last been on Grenada, but there were people living here who would recognize him for who he was—Americans as well as countrymen.

And how far behind him could the hounds be? How much time did he have to set the operation into motion, push it past the point of no return? So much of it depended on Ramon Diaz and the man's greed. Yet Diaz was now acting like a frightened child.

"Tell Diaz I'll wait until tomorrow afternoon. If I still haven't heard from him personally, I'll go looking for someone else. My country doesn't have time to attend to the petty ego Diaz is displaying. Tell him Castro is already gathering troops. More than twice as many as the last time. Do you understand?"

The man nodded.

Ivanovitch slid his glasses back into place and stood. He left the café, walking briskly along the narrow road that

led to the bungalow he'd rented under one of the aliases
Petrovsky had created for him.

If Diaz hadn't been so necessary to Ivanovitch's plans,
if Russia had truly been supportive of the coup the ex-KGB
agent was putting together, things could proceed more
quickly. With a greater margin of success.

But men of his own country would be coming for him
soon, to bury him in an unmarked grave despite his record of service. Anger burned the length of Ivanovitch's
hard muscled frame as he thought of Gorbachev and the
new policies that were in effect. Russia was a bear, Ivanovitch thought as he walked, meant to overcome all of her
foes in time. She deserved more from the world than Gorbachev and his aides intended to get for her.

The crunch of his footstep on the sand drew Ivanovitch's mind back into the present, tensing the skin across
his shoulders. You were too long in prison, he chided
himself as he resisted the impulse to turn around. You kept
the mind and body in shape but your skills have dulled.

Who was following him?

Kulik had no one who could locate him this fast, considering the wealth of misinformation Ivanovitch had left
behind him over the past few days.

One of Diaz's men?

Maybe, but why?

Refusing to be drawn any further into the game his mind
had started, Ivanovitch quickened his pace, glad the night
was closing around him and his pursuer.

He drew the American .357 Magnum he'd purchased
from a black market dealer in St. Croix. As he reached the
end of the nearest bungalow, Ivanovitch slid to a stop
around the corner and double-timed it around the cabin in
an effort to flank his pursuer.

Keeping below the windows, Ivanovitch moved silently,
once more a shadow player in his shadow world. The .357
was a solid weight at the end of his arm. As he cleared the
last corner, he saw the man who had been following him
and studied the unknown profile.

The ex-KGB agent had no doubt that the man was an American. The flowered shirt, shorts, and the way the man wore them spoke volumes to his trained eye. The man had also been at the café where Ivanovitch had met with Diaz's lieutenant. He had occupied a rear table by himself with a clear view of the ex-KGB agent.

Ivanovitch stepped from the darkness, thumbing the hammer back on the Magnum as he closed in on his quarry, pressing the muzzle of the big handgun into the man's back when he was within arm's reach. Using the weapon and his own bulk, the Russian shoved his prisoner into the darkness at the side of another cabin.

"Turn around," Ivanovitch ordered.

The man turned, lifting his arms away from his body mechanically. He was younger than the Russian had at first assumed, perhaps middle twenties with the same sort of unlined and unworried face the lieutenant in the Hind had possessed.

"Hold on, man," the American said with a slightly perceptible quaver. "I didn't mean no harm."

CIA? Ivanovitch asked himself as he patted his prisoner down. If so, even *they* were using children now. Satisfied the man was carrying nothing more than a wallet and a camera, the Russian took a quick glance at the visa. William March, American, twenty-six years old, a salesman from New York City.

"Hey," March said, "if it's money you want, I got some more in my room. Just be careful with that gun, okay?"

"What were you doing following me?"

March swallowed as he gagged on the pistol at his throat. Ivanovitch released some of the pressure so the man could speak. "I wasn't following you. We just happened to be going the same way, that's all."

"If you don't start telling me the truth, I'm going to just happen to pull the trigger on this pistol," Ivanovitch said. "Most of your head is going to be spread over that wall behind you."

March nodded.

"Where's your backup?"

"There's nobody but me, man."

Ivanovitch remained silent, letting the tension build instead of using more threats.

"Nobody, man, I swear on my mother's grave."

"Then you're a fool."

"I'm not a cop."

Ivanovitch's voice was soft. "I know. You're a salesman on holiday who likes to follow complete strangers at night. That kind of hobby can get you killed fast in certain parts of the world."

March nodded again.

"How did you find me?" Ivanovitch asked.

"I don't even know who you are."

"How did you know to be at the café at that time?"

"I was just there, man, that's all. It was just a coincidence."

Ivanovitch dropped the visa and grabbed a fistful of the man's hair, jerking his head back against the wall. The hollow thump seemed to echo inside the other man's skull.

Groaning, March almost dropped to his knees, suspended only by the pistol and the handful of hair the Russian held.

"Who are you working for?"

"Nobody."

"Are you CIA?"

"I don't know what you're talking about."

"You were following me."

When March refused to answer, Ivanovitch slammed his head against the bungalow again. Blood ran freely down the man's chin from a bitten tongue; he sagged heavier in the Russian's grasp.

"Who are you working for?"

March shook his head.

"How many are in your group?"

March shook his head again.

"Who knows about me?"

March was a limp weight at the end of Ivanovitch's arms. Without warning the man spit a glob of blood into his captor's face, shoving himself forcefully at the larger man.

"Fuck you," March screamed as he swung his right fist.

Ivanovitch blocked the blow effortlessly, stepped back and drilled a round between March's eyes.

The younger man flew back against the bungalow, a dying scream locked in his throat. He fell in a crumpled heap, a bloody line smearing the wall behind him from the crater that had been the back of his head.

Ivanovitch knelt to retrieve the camera but before he could remove it from the man's body, a voice split the heavy night air.

"What the hell is going on there?"

The speaker was a grizzled man holding a flashlight. The beam fell weakly on March's corpse.

Letting go of the camera strap, Ivanovitch wheeled around the corner of the building, knowing the shot and the man's bellow would attract attention quickly. He didn't need the local authorities looking for him as well.

Ivanovitch ran, holstering the .357, embracing the shadow world once again. But now he was a pawn, a player without rank or privilege. And the shadow was growing smaller every day.

THE YACHT WAS SLEEK and expensive, springing above the waterline of the blue Caribbean Sea like a flexed muscle. *Lady's Desire* was scrolled in lighter blue on her prow, matching the rest of her trim. A rich man's weekend toy, like many of the other vessels that called this area of Key West home.

But Mack Bolan knew that in the case of the *Lady's Desire*, appearances were definitely deceiving. Her crew had a reputation of violence all over Key West. She was off-limits to civilians and even the women who stayed aboard her for short times weren't local. Nobody would say who owned the vessel, but there were several rumors that it was nobody who lived in the Keys.

Yeah, Bolan thought, the yacht was strictly a business operation. Just as the captured pilot had told him four days ago, before Brognola's boys from Justice picked the man up and put him on ice.

He raised the Nikon 35 mm and sought to focus the powerful telephoto lens once more. The images blurred, winking into perfection and sharpness in less than a heartbeat, then out again just as quickly. If he had the telescopic sights of the old Weatherby Mark V, he thought, the surveillance attempt would have been much simpler. The reflexes honed to handle the big gun were ingrained, part of his life. Raking the yacht from stem to stern would have required a concentrated effort, sure, but it would have been infinitely more rewarding than struggling with the heavy and sensitive lens.

But to say the least, that would have blown his cover as Mike McKay, a free-lance travel writer who was doing a piece on Key West for a New York based magazine.

The shuffling footsteps of the old charter captain approached from behind.

"Having any luck, Mr. McKay?" the captain asked. He was a short, chunky man with a pug nose and a black puma tattoo winding around his left forearm.

"Not a hell of a lot," Bolan admitted. He tried focusing the Nikon again, ignoring the growing ache in his back and shoulders.

Captain Rigaberto came to a halt at the railing and leaned on it heavily. The breeze, carrying the jasmine scent from Crawfish Key, ruffled the man's iron-gray hair. "Isn't that *Lady's Desire*?"

The sea calmed for a moment, allowing Bolan to track the camera on target. "Not sure," he lied, "I haven't been able to get set up long enough to get a shot."

"Yeah, that's her," Rigaberto said. "I can tell from the cut of her even from here." He gave Bolan a grin that showed tobacco-stained teeth. "A sailing man gets to know these things after a while, Mr. McKay. Like one of those preppies back on the beach can tell which school a girl goes to by the cut of her bikini.'' He spit a thick gob of brown juice over the side.

Bolan grinned, marveling at the difference in their thoughts even though they were looking at the same subject. The charter captain was placing the yacht in his mental files, while the Executioner was figuring wind velocities and trajectories. It all depended on the field of reference.

He let the Nikon drift back from the prow, bringing each man into focus as he found them. There were only three, but from the head count he'd been able to establish over the past few days, five men constituted the yacht's crew. Four hardguys and a man named Ruffino Marino who was the lieutenant in the drug-trafficking operation. The pilot hadn't known any names higher up in the organization than Marino's.

During the past three days Bolan had heard a lot about the *Lady's Desire*, enough to be sure she was the target he was after. According to the stories Bolan had garnered in different bars around the key, Marino ruled the yacht with an iron fist. Rumor had it that when Marino replaced a man in the operation it was because he'd killed the man himself. A real tough.

Rigaberto spit into the sea again and wiped his mouth with the back of his hand. "A bad ship, that one. You would do well to stay away from her."

"So I've heard," Bolan said.

He zoomed in on the two men lying on lounge chairs on the forward deck. Both wore swimming trunks and sunglasses, bodies smeared with suntan lotion. It was a harmless scene to the casual observer, but Bolan could see the barrel of an automatic weapon stick up when the sea pitched the yacht.

And the guy helming the vessel, the newest crew member from what Bolan had learned, had been cleaning a pistol two days ago while piloting the yacht. But Marino had put a stop to that practice, jerking the pistol away from the guy and whipping him across the face with it.

Through the long eye of the telephoto lens, Bolan could make out a bandage covering the pilot's left eyebrow and the dark circle beneath the eye. He shifted the camera back to the two men on deck, wondering where Marino was.

"Young Ruffi," Rigaberto stated, "has become something of a hero to the younger people living here. He lives a life of daring and ease, defying the police, the Drug Enforcement Administration, the elements, as well as other men who would take from him. It is no secret Ruffi guards much money, and that knowledge brings braveness to some men at times. He's been attacked at least a handful of times that I know of. Never has he lost what he protects. Like some young dragon caring for his nest, breathing fire and death when he is threatened. A very hard young man on all counts, Mr. McKay."

Bolan let the Nikon hang by its strap. "Is there some reason you think I need to know this?" he asked easily, realizing the charter boat captain had been paying more attention to his activities than he thought.

Rigaberto answered without looking at him. "I see the dragon in young Ruffi, Mr. McKay, but in you I see the wolf. There is a hardness about you. I've seen men such as yourself upon occasion. Hard men, full of a fire that only they can control. Your kind lives life to the fullest, Mr. McKay, safe only if they can contain the inferno that propels them."

Living life to the fullest, Bolan repeated to himself as he brought the Nikon to his eye again. To the largest.

"So you think I'm after the *Lady's Desire*?"

"It's in my mind. During the time we've gone out together, I've come across her three times. Once, I dismissed. Twice, I began to get my suspicions. At first I had thought you were a drug agent. I knew you were no writer. You used your camera, yes, but basically only for the yacht. And you did no writing at all. The bag you bring with you each day sits there undisturbed." The man pointed toward the leather camera bag near the railing. "I don't think it holds only extra film."

Which was true enough. The camera bag held the Beretta and Desert Eagle, as well as spare clips for both. Even then he had cached a .38 Chief's Special in the elastic band at the back of his boat pants. The tank top he wore fell loosely, effectively covering the pistol and giving him easy access to it at the same time.

"Is there a reason you're telling me this?" Bolan asked in a soft voice. Was the old man trying to warn him away? Maybe Rigaberto felt if something happened to Bolan his own life would be in jeopardy as well.

When the captain looked at him, Bolan could see the hidden sorrow buried deep in the rheumy hazel eyes. "I don't think you're a government agent, Mr. McKay, or I wouldn't have taken you out again after I started getting suspicious. Ruffi can pick up an agent's scent too easily. I'm an old man, but I'm not ready to die yet."

Rigaberto went back to watching the yacht. His voice was old, tired, when he spoke. "Like I was saying, Mr. McKay, there are those young ones in Key West who believe young Ruffi to be a hero. I see the shine of respect in their eyes. They watch eagerly as the police bend from Ruffi's way. They see him eat at the finest restaurants with some of the most expensive, imported whores dirty money can buy." He sighed. "The young girls are the worst to watch. They see this invulnerable image Ruffi casts about him, the unapproachable air that is so like a challenge to them. If he wanted, he could have them hanging off him just as surely as the gold chains he wears around his neck."

Looking through the telephoto lens once again, Bolan saw the helmsman reach for a phone fastened to the wall beside him. The man spoke briefly, nodded, then hung up and lighted a cigarette.

"They forget," Rigaberto went on. "The children forget Ruffi makes his money buying drugs and smuggling them into the mainland to other children who kill themselves with it."

"If everyone knows he's a trafficker," Bolan said, "why don't the locals do something about it?"

The old captain shrugged and spit into the sea. He leaned on the railing with his elbows. "There's nothing the police can do. Ruffi pays his informants well. Every time the police or the DEA make a move toward him, he always knows. More than one lawman has vanished at Ruffi's orders. Some who tried to go undercover and trap him, and some who refused to be bought off. Whoever Ruffi's master is, he's either a very rich man or one who's feared." The captain paused. "I believe it to be both or Ruffi would kill him as well."

Who had the helmsman called? A warning itch started high between Bolan's shoulders, winding down his spine like an ice serpent.

He tracked the Nikon across the yacht again, picking up the two men in the lounge chairs, the helmsman. A small eddy knocked his aim off for a moment, swirling the mixture of blue sky and deeper blue sea into a kaleidoscope for a dizzying moment.

When he focused on the *Lady's Desire* again, he found Ruffino Marino standing in the stern. The cross hairs of the telephoto lens centered on the twin circles of the binoculars the drug lord held. As Bolan watched, a mirthless smile twisted Marino's mouth and exposed white teeth against the dark skin of his face. Bolan scooted the focus back, taking in all of the man instead of just the head shot.

The lieutenant was wearing a brightly colored sport shirt, a lightweight white jacket, and matching white pants. The afternoon sunlight splintered from the gold chains around Marino's neck, from the two jeweled rings, one on either hand holding the binoculars. The short black hair was lacquered in place.

Marino dropped the binoculars, allowing Bolan to look him full in the face.

"We've been noticed," Bolan said.

"Eh?" Rigaberto glanced up from his contemplation of the sea. "Ruffi?"

"Yeah." Bolan never looked away from Marino though the other man looked no larger than his forefinger to the unaided eye. He felt Marino would know if he did, through some animal sense predators develop over years of killing.

He watched the drug lord signal the helmsman with a wave. The yacht obediently swung to port and came toward the small charter boat.

"He's coming to meet us," Rigaberto said.

Bolan felt his combat sense flare into life, sending out its special antenna, analyzing, figuring odds for offense and defense. He was plugged in again, living life on the heartbeat and by the numbers. As much a part of the world around him as the violent storm that could erupt between him and the crew of the yacht.

"Shall I pull around and head away?" Rigaberto asked.

"Can you outrun her?" Bolan asked, though he knew the answer.

"Never. Not on this tub's best day. Oh, the *Marilou* is reliable enough, but she's never been a thoroughbred. We could at least show them we're willing to shove off."

White water spumed off the sharp prow of the *Lady's Desire* as she cut toward them. The two men on deck had gotten up from their chairs and buckled on shoulder holsters. The helmsman, Bolan was sure, had gotten a piece for himself during the time he'd dropped out of sight behind the wheel.

"I don't think that would help."

"Neither do I. Ruffi's a smart man. He's noticed you spying on him before. Now he comes to see how much trouble you might be to him."

Yeah, Bolan thought. To see. And to intimidate. The Chief's Special was a comfortable weight against his back.

"*Will* there be any trouble?" Rigaberto asked. Bolan heard fire in the old captain's words. "I have a double-barreled shotgun below."

Bolan shook his head. No, there wouldn't be any trouble now. He was on a scouting mission to find out when

Marino's next shipment would be. Anything premature could defeat his chances of getting the needed information, and break his trace on the cocaine supplier he wanted. As well as bring harm to Rigaberto and his boat.

The Executioner let the strap of the Nikon slide down his shoulder as he took it off, holding it in his left fist, freeing his right to grab the .38 if it came down to that. Then he waited, watching the yacht come closer.

4

Lady's Desire came to a buoyant halt fifteen feet from the charter boat. As low-slung as the yacht was, Marino and his crew still looked down on Bolan.

The lieutenant stood in the stern and stared at Bolan across the agitated expanse of blue Caribbean between them. As the breeze blew, it ruffled his jacket and revealed the H&K 9 mm pistol in its shoulder holster.

Marino's voice was harsh and biting when he spoke. "Who are you?"

"The name's McKay," Bolan said. "I'm a free-lance travel writer doing a piece on Key West for *Penthouse*."

The mirthless grin reappeared on Marino's face. "If you're doing something on Key West, shouldn't you be taking more pictures of the scenic beauty around you instead of showing so much interest in me?"

Bolan shrugged and flashed the guy a grin of his own. "Since I've been here I've heard a lot about Ruffino Marino. Somebody even called you the last pirate working the Keys. It didn't seem right to finish my work and leave you out of it."

"There are many pirates in the Keys, McKay. As I'm sure Rigaberto has informed you."

Despite the man's arrogance and tough demeanor, Bolan heard education and culture in Marino's voice. Somebody was grooming him. The trafficking operation was just a proving ground for the man. Which made Marino more dangerous. He wasn't only defending his cargo, he was protecting his future as well.

Bolan felt the sun beating down on him, the perspiration gathering in the small of his back that made the tank top cling to him, threatening to expose the outlines of the .38.

"It seemed a real waste not to mention such a colorful personality," Bolan repeated.

"Have you got any credentials showing that you work for that magazine?"

Bolan felt the jaws of a trap closing in on him. At his side he heard Rigaberto's sharp hiss of drawn breath.

Bolan shook his head. "Don't have any. I free-lance. That means I work for myself. I offer different editors ideas, different concepts. If they like them I get the job. If they don't, I move on to the next guy and give him a different pitch."

Marino took the H&K from his shoulder holster and pointed it at Bolan. "From time to time, I've had annoying trouble from undercover agents. You understand my position." He thumbed the safety off his weapon.

Bolan shifted his weight with the pitch of the charter boat, moving his center of gravity forward until it rested on the balls of his feet. He waited, watching Marino's face for any sign that the man was going to pull the trigger.

"Rigaberto," Marino called.

"Yes?"

Marino kept the gun centered on Bolan's midsection. The two men behind him made no move toward their own weapons, waiting to see what was going to happen. "Rigaberto, is this man what he says he is? Or is he a federal agent?"

"That I cannot say, Ruffi. I've been hired by him for the past three days. In that time I've seen him take a great many pictures and speak into the small tape recorder he keeps in his camera case."

The captain was one cool customer, Bolan realized after the man gave him the opportunity to reach into the camera case if Marino demanded it. With the big Desert Eagle, the Executioner could lay down a pattern of fire that could save them both. And the helmsman with the Uzi would definitely be history.

"Has he shown any undue interest in the activities of the *Lady's Desire*?"

"From the questions he asked me, I could tell he has been listening to the gossip they spread in the bars. A curiosity, perhaps, but nothing more. He wanted to know what the chances were of interviewing you, and I laughed at him."

The shark's smile returned to Marino's mouth, but this time Bolan could see honest amusement there also. "You, reporter, hold your camera up so I can see it clearly."

Bolan raised the Nikon until his hand was even with his shoulder at his side. The camera swayed a few inches either way with the motion of the charter boat. He saw the barrel of the H&K track the movement and wondered if Marino was that good or just thought he was.

"I *am* a pirate," Marino admitted, "if you want to call it that. A smuggler. But I'm also a businessman, McKay. A professional. If you were a cop, I would know. I can smell them. Trust me, I've proved myself many times over. I don't know exactly what you are, but I don't think you're some free-lance writer who's taken a passing interest in me. No, you're after something else."

The camera grew heavier in Bolan's grasp.

"If I thought you were a true threat to me," Marino continued, "I would eliminate you now and leave your body in chains here. But I think you're like some of the others who've tried to take from me. I've left their bodies scattered all over these islands. And one more won't make a fucking bit of difference to me."

The 9 mm exploded a split second before the Nikon shattered and blew away behind Bolan. The Executioner dropped the useless strap, never taking his eyes from Marino's.

"That camera cost over six hundred dollars," Bolan said, feigning anger.

The smile Marino flashed him was genuine. "You're a professional. You know the risks of working for yourself. Consider it a business loss and find someone else to profit from. You mess with me, you're not going to be able to cover the opening bid." Marino shoved the gun back into the breakaway shoulder rig and waved to the helmsman.

The yacht's giant turbines gave a full-throated roar as the vessel pulled away.

"Quite the speech maker, our Ruffi," Rigaberto observed once the rocking of the boat had subsided.

Yeah, Bolan had to give Marino that. Impressive in his own way, too. Marino liked the power he wielded, and he kept it totally for himself. By keeping his men apart from the mainlanders, Marino reinforced the division between them and himself as well.

The guy definitely had potential for leadership, and Bolan wondered who was sponsoring him. Perhaps later, after he'd traced the cocaine back to its source, the Executioner would pay a return visit to Miami. But for now he had to stalk the octopus one tentacle at a time.

"You'll need to watch your back from now until you leave Key West," Rigaberto said. "Ruffi won't forget you. Nor will he dismiss you so easily after the way you stood up to him. You showed no fear of him, and he knows his men saw that. He's not used to being treated so."

"I've been watching my backtrail for a long time," Bolan said. "At least in this case I know where to look."

The captain nodded. "Are you here to kill Ruffi?"

"Not unless I have to."

"I thought maybe someone had hired you to kill him," Rigaberto said, "from the first time I saw you take an interest in him. There are many who would pay to see him dead. You are very precise in your movements, even in the way you had me searching for his ship without my knowledge. The boots you wear and the way you wear them tell me you're a military man. And, like Ruffi, you are a hunter."

"Thanks for saying what you did back there," Bolan said.

Rigaberto nodded. "Will you be wanting to go anywhere else today?"

"No."

The captain hesitated. "Would it help you to know where Ruffi will make his pickup tomorrow night?"

Bolan turned toward the man. Was it a trick? Had some unseen signal passed between the charter boat captain and Marino?

Rigaberto paused before speaking, as if wondering if he had said too much. "I had a daughter. A fine girl. Pretty, like her mother, God rest her soul, but I had to raise her by myself so she lacked a woman's attention and a sense of things. As she grew older, we drifted apart as a parent and child will. She fell in with a bad group, like the ones who wait for Ruffi's goods on street corners. We fought for months. Then one day she could stand her life no longer. She hanged herself, and I had to cut her down when I found her that morning. She hadn't even reached her sixteenth birthday."

Bolan saw the tears in the old captain's eyes, felt some of the old hurt echo in familiar shadows of his own soul.

"I have no reason to protect Ruffi or his men. I've watched them for the past year, since Gayle died, searching for some way to break him down. I want to see him destroyed. I know his business occasionally, where he meets with his contact at times, and when. Once I called a policeman and told him Ruffi's ship was full of contraband. A few moments later some of Ruffi's men arrived at the pay phone I'd used and I knew then that I could trust no one." Rigaberto paused. "I'm trusting you now because I sense only good about you. And because of the way you stood up to Ruffi. If you fail and Ruffi finds out who told you this information, I'm a dead man with no one to avenge my daughter."

Bolan felt the honesty of the captain's words. If the old man trusted him he could at least do the same.

"Yeah," Bolan said, "I could use that."

"I'll get the map. You don't mind if I hope you have to kill him when the time comes, do you?"

Bolan gave him a wry smile. "Maybe it will be the other way around."

Rigaberto shook his head. "I don't think so. Whoever you really are, I think you're more than a match for Ruffi." He disappeared inside the cabin.

Turning back to the railing, Bolan placed his hands on the sun-warmed metal and stared at the broken pieces of the Nikon at his feet. He thought briefly about the need for another camera then decided against it. The recon work was done. Now it was time to kick the opening numbers into play.

BOLAN FOUND Murphy's Copter Service in a small office that looked like it had been tacked onto the open-air restaurant in front of it.

Pausing at the door of the office, he pressed a button and heard a soft tinkling echo inside.

"Come in," a man's voice called.

As he opened the door, Bolan found that someone was watching him. He'd had an itch on the back of his neck that told him he was being followed. He'd been right.

The reflection of the area behind him came sliding into view as the door angled inward. The man was dressed in a T-shirt and slacks, and wore a jacket that hadn't been tailored to conceal the shoulder holster beneath it. As Bolan stared back via the pane, the man suddenly found the need to use the phone by a fruit drink stand across the narrow street.

"Something wrong with the door?"

"Just kicking the sand off my shoes," Bolan replied.

"Don't worry about it. If the cleaning lady gripes I'll tell her I did it. She's going to hate me after today anyway."

The air inside the small office was cooled by an ancient ceiling fan whirling sluggishly overhead and creating a steady drone that was barely audible over Bruce Springsteen's heartfelt deliverance of "Born in the U.S.A." The disc player sat on the scarred and often repainted desk at the far end of the room. Maps and charts covered the paneled walls, many of them in color, some in parchment and sepia brown.

Bolan closed the door behind him and positioned himself so that he could look out the office's only window. The man talked animatedly into the phone by the fruit drink stand.

The guy sitting in the middle of the floor had parts from a stripped-down Harley Roadster on both sides of him. He was younger than Bolan had expected, even though Jack Grimaldi had called him a kid. Twenty-four or -five, Bolan guessed.

"Something I can help you with? Or are you here to sell me an interior decorating package?" He never looked up from trying to install a set of bearings in the rear wheel.

"Chase Murphy?"

"That's me."

Murphy looked up. His corn-yellow hair looked out of place against the deep tan of his face, and his eyes belonged on some big cat. Hard and bright, shifting constantly somewhere between a handful of light greens. The rest of the guy was lean, like a rapier, sheathed in faded Levi's; he wore Asics Tigers that had been white once and had possessed a full complement of red stripes, and a tank top that bore a picture of Huey Lewis and the News. The headband that kept his long hair out of his face bore Confederate markings.

"Should I know you?" Murphy asked as he reached for an oily rag and made a futile attempt to wipe the grease from his arms.

"No, but we have a mutual friend."

Murphy grinned benignly. "Well, that's surprising. I usually run kind of light on mutual friends."

Though the younger man's manner was still easygoing, Bolan could detect an edge of steel in his voice. Grimaldi had warned him about that, too. The kid had a hot temper, the ex-Mafia copter jockey had informed Bolan, and when Murphy blew, it was best to stand back or take him out fast.

"The guy I know said to mention Crystal Key."

A look of chagrin filled Murphy's face as he pushed himself up from the floor. He palmed the Walther that had been hidden under his right thigh and slid it into the belly holster concealed by the tank top.

"Jack Grimaldi," Murphy said. He walked around to the back of the desk. "Like to sit?"

Bolan shook his head. From his vantage point he could maintain his surveillance of the man who'd been following him.

"Did Jack tell you why you were supposed to say that?" Murphy asked as he sat in the creaky swivel chair behind the desk. He turned the volume down on the disc player and Springsteen became part of the background.

"No. Just that it would identify me to you."

"Yeah, well, Crystal Key was a glowing example of Murphy's Flaw." Murphy shifted in the seat to place grime-encrusted elbows on the plastic desktop. "So what do you need me for?"

"An hour's work."

The green eyes shifted color again as they hardened. "The fact that you thought it best to okay me through Jack Grimaldi tells me this little caper isn't exactly on the up and up, Mr... ?"

"McKay."

Murphy's face took on a look of disbelieving amusement. "Yeah, well, it beats the hell out of Smith or Jones."

Bolan had trouble keeping a grin back, already liking the younger man. Murphy was battle-hardened, too, in his own way, and used to playing his own hand.

"Your being a friend of Jack's doesn't cut a whole lot of ice with me. Dad and I never talked about it, but we both knew what business Jack Grimaldi was involved with. We figured it was his affair. We didn't bring it up because Jack was a real friend to us when friends were scarce. There were a couple of years we might not have been able to pull this business out if it hadn't been for Jack. But Dad and I never flew transport for anybody involved with drugs or running guns. Did Jack mention how Dad died last year?''

"No."

Murphy nodded. "I wasn't sure if he knew. You had to know my old man to appreciate him. He was an abrasive kind of guy and didn't mind showing it. A trafficker tried to hire us one time and Dad refused. Threw the son of a bitch out on his ass, actually, when the guy got around to threatening us. The guy came back with a friend later and forced Dad at gunpoint to fly them to a place in Dade county. Then they killed him."

Bolan didn't say anything, holding Murphy's gaze. He had the impression that if he moved wrong the younger man would pull the short-barreled automatic and start shooting. Hotheaded, like Grimaldi had said, but with plenty of reason.

"I killed the guy who pulled the trigger," Murphy said. "And another guy in between who tried to stop me from getting the second man. It took me four months, and I almost lost this business, but at the time it didn't matter. The cops still don't know who zapped those guys, and neither do the people they did business with."

Murphy leaned back in the chair, and Bolan noticed the way the man kept his hands on the arms of the chair.

"I'm telling you this so you know where I stand, in case you got business like that on your mind. And if you take offense, grab a number and stand in line. A lot of people on these Keys would like a piece of me."

Bolan nodded. "You're familiar with Ruffino Marino?"

"Our paths have crossed a time or three," Murphy admitted. "I got the distinct pleasure of breaking the arm of one of his pretty boys a couple of months ago in a bar fight. You could say we're not real fond of each other."

"Marino's making a buy tomorrow night. I got the in-tel and the coordinates. I need somebody to fly me in and pick me up when it's over."

Murphy's eyes glittered dangerously. "You're after the dope?"

"No. I'm after the operation. How long has the *Lady's Desire* been working out of Key West?"

Murphy remained silent.

"And nobody's been able to shut it down yet. I'm the guy who can."

"You a cop?"

"No."

"Then what kind of interest do you have in this?"

"Personal," Bolan said, thinking of Brognola's friend and Rigaberto's daughter.

"And if I say no?"

"I find another way."

Adjusting the rebel flag headband, Murphy said, "Marino's got a lot of guys backing him up on that boat."

Bolan held up a hand with outstretched fingers. "Five guys."

"You figure on going in there, in the dark, and taking on six guys by yourself?"

"Plus the crew of the rendezvous ship." Bolan smiled grimly. "Could be you'll end up with nothing to show for your time."

"It could be that I'd consider helping to put Marino and his shitheels out of business my contribution to helping the current social condition. Hell, it might even improve the tourist trade and boost the local economy."

"I want you to stay out of it. I do things my own way. I don't want to have to look over my shoulder when I make my play. If anyone does shake loose from this operation, I don't want you tied to it. Not by Marino and not by the local authorities."

"I can hold my own when it comes to cops. I've had some experience."

"Marino's going to be waiting for something to happen tomorrow night because he's already made me." Bolan glanced out the window at the telephone where his tail was still hanging around. "On the way over here I picked up this guy." He indicated the man. "You know him?"

Murphy crossed the floor and knelt by the window. "Yeah, I know him. That guy means more trouble than you already got."

5

The transition from sleep to wakefulness happened with the suddenness of a wire strand snapping in the jaws of bolt cutters.

Yuri Mikhailin kept his eyes closed and regulated his breathing to the same slow speed as in sleep, even though his lungs screamed out for more to offset the adrenaline rush he experienced. The faint and warm pressure of his wife's breath still fell on his right cheek. Her body still draped across his, her palm in its accustomed place over his heart.

What had disturbed his sleep?

Earlier, nightmares had plagued him, drowning him in their intensity until Natasha had shaken him awake and held him while he sobbed and shook. Old phantoms and new, joined by Petrovsky's son now. His wife no longer asked him to talk about the nightmares. At one time it had been a source of discomfort in their marriage. Natasha was six years younger than Yuri, and the times she had to spend alone not knowing where he was had been much harder on her at the beginning. Now, even though he did not know where she found the strength, she seemed content to have him home, to let those mysteries remain unsolved.

Breathing normally, he searched the air for any lingering scents that did not belong. Natasha's perfume was almost dissipated from their earlier lovemaking, and he could smell the sweat over his own body. He heard nothing but the steady ticking of the antique clock that hung over the bed, a wedding gift from Natasha's mother three years earlier.

Satisfied nothing was in the bedroom with them, Yuri opened his eyes, staring at the dark ceiling. Had it been little Tanya, then?

He shifted in bed, edging off quietly so he wouldn't disturb Natasha's sleep, knowing that she would wake anyway.

"Yuri?" Natasha's hand was on his shoulder.

He gathered her fingers from his shoulder and kissed them gently, standing to look down at her. "It's nothing, my love. I'm only going to check Tanya."

"Is anything wrong?"

"No. Go back to sleep. I'll only be gone a few minutes."

"You don't have to leave now, do you?"

"No, Tasha." But later, when Kirov called, Yuri knew he would be leaving, unsure of when he would return to Moscow. He hadn't told her that yet, and he felt guilty. But it would've been like bringing a dead rat to the beautiful dinner table she had fixed last night. He and Kirov hadn't finished with Kulik until late evening, and Natasha had kept the dinner waiting. And later there had been no time. Little Tanya had gone to sleep and they had made love on the living-room floor as if they were teenagers. Then he'd carried her to the bedroom, Yuri making faces as if she had gained too much weight with this new pregnancy.

In truth, Natasha was only starting to show. She was lean and trim, standing almost as tall as Yuri. Her dark hair was a black river down her back, almost disappearing against the black lace nightgown he'd brought her from Paris the previous year. It was contraband, he knew, but contraband of an elegant sort.

Padding noiselessly down the short hallway, Yuri poked his head inside his daughter's bedroom, searching her crib with an expert eye. Tanya slept fitfully, almost swimming through the blankets Natasha had so carefully placed on her. A mop of unruly red hair peeked through at one end.

Moving silently across the tiny room, Yuri came to a stop at the edge of the crib and looked down at his child. In only a few months she would be two years old. It was hard for him to believe.

Touching his daughter's cheek softly, Yuri listened to the sound of her breathing. He'd had mixed feelings about becoming a father. He'd been a ward of the state at an early age, too early to have any memories of a father or mother, and hadn't thought he would know what to do. Natasha had only laughed at him then and, afterward, told him he doted on their daughter too much.

Instead of returning to the bedroom and his wife, Yuri went to the kitchen, pausing to make a sandwich out of the leftover black bread Natasha had baked for dinner. Then he pulled the false wall from the back of the kitchen broom closet and turned on the small computer he'd cached there a few years ago. With as many illegal access lines as there were for different Party members to check on the KGB, it was a wonder any intelligence was kept secret at all. Of course, Yuri thought wryly, it helped if you knew how much of what could be accessed was false.

He sat in front of the computer and broke into the case files again, this time searching for Ivanovitch's name instead of Kirov's.

He bit into the sandwich as the program ran its course, scrolling forward at his command. Once at Ivanovitch's file, he accessed the past information, digging for Boris Kirov's name. There was enough discrepancy in the files to make him sure someone had purged Kirov's name from the text, but Yuri knew enough now to fill in some of the blank spaces the document left.

Kirov had trained Ivanovitch for the KGB. Yuri was convinced of that. Which was why Kulik had brought the old man out of retirement. But how had someone like Kirov managed to go into a semblance of retirement anyway? Surely someone would have killed him rather than take the chance of the CIA getting their hands on him.

A cold chill spilled through Yuri when he couldn't help but ask himself if that was the same kind of future he could expect for himself. Ivanovitch had outgrown his usefulness as well, Yuri thought as he stared at the green-and-white monitor, and look where the man was now.

He finished the sandwich and tried another angle, opening the file on the current activity concerning Ivanovitch. He found his name mentioned, as well as Kulik's, but again the absence of Kirov's name was as obvious as a broken tooth.

How did Kirov rate this kind of power?

Angrily he switched off the computer and glared at the empty screen. A secondary flicker let him know someone had been monitoring the transmission.

Who?

And, more importantly, why?

Yuri couldn't accept the coincidence that whoever had been on-line with him had only just discovered his computer link.

Kirov?

Somehow Yuri couldn't imagine the old man sitting somewhere at a computer console. Yet Boris Kirov was the only new wrinkle in Yuri's routines.

He was now more frightened than the nightmares could ever have made him, and he walled the computer up again and retreated to the bedroom. He broke his own house rules about firearms before he crawled back into bed, taking his service pistol from the locked drawer in his desk and placing it between the mattresses.

He closed his arms around his wife and held her tightly, agonizing over every imagined sound he heard, amazed at how easily he could lose the feeling of security in his own house.

ROCKING BACK on his heels, Chase Murphy said, "His name is Peter Vincent. He's the local DEA field agent. Is there any paper circulating on you?"

"No."

Murphy grunted and stood. "Which means somebody put him onto you." The pilot readjusted the Walther in the belly holster.

"How much do you know about Vincent?"

"You mean what are the chances Marino has him in his pocket?"

"Yeah."

"I really couldn't say. At least not before today. Vincent is a low-key operator." Murphy reached into his back pants pocket and pulled out a tin of Copenhagen. Thumbing some into his lower lip, he asked, "So what now?"

The numbers on this one were in free-fall, Bolan thought as he watched the DEA guy, able to drop anywhere without warning. He hadn't wanted the authorities in on his attack on the cocaine ring because he knew there would have been too much red tape involved. Brognola had figured that too, which was why he'd asked Bolan to step in. But now it looked like the DEA was going to be involved anyway. One way or another.

"If you're hesitating because of me," Murphy said, "don't. It's worth the risk to me to be rid of Marino."

"We do it," Bolan told him, "as long as we can outmaneuver the local law."

"Suits me. What are you going to do about Vincent?"

"I'll play follow-the-leader for now. When I get around to it, losing him won't be that hard."

"And if Marino tries to take you out in the meantime?"

"Maybe you should worry about yourself since he knows I've been here."

Murphy smiled. "Not that simple, my friend. These are my islands. I was raised here. When this rabbit decides to run, he has plenty of holes to drop into. If I stay visible it'll be in the midst of friends. A lot of them. And when I get ready, nobody will be able to find me."

Bolan believed him. Since meeting the man, his assessment of Murphy's skills had risen considerably. Hell,

Grimaldi would probably be surprised to see the man the boy had grown into. Murphy was sharper than he let show at first, and a hell of a lot harder than the devil-may-care gleam in his eye advertised.

"When you're looking over your shoulder," Murphy said, "you might want to look twice. I know some of the punks Marino keeps on the dole for local leg-breaking. I'll be watching. If it starts getting too heavy, I'll be there."

Bolan nodded.

Murphy looked out the window. "Your date looks lonely."

"Yeah," Bolan drawled as he walked toward the door. "Wait until he finds out we're going dutch."

BOLAN FIGURED the boy couldn't have been more than seven or eight.

Dressed in shorts cut from a brilliantly colored flower print, barefoot and shirtless, the youngster stood outside the room, three doors down and across the hall from Bolan's.

Eight years old tops, and locked out.

After making sure the broken toothpick he'd left at the top corner of the door hadn't been disturbed, Bolan dropped his room key back in his pocket and walked toward the boy.

The youngster looked up at his approach and fear widened his blue eyes. The boy's left hand swiped at the dark hair hanging straight and loose in his eyes. The thin lips compressed into an even thinner line.

Dropping into a squatting position so he could look the boy in the eyes, Bolan asked, "You need some help?"

The boy shook his head.

"Are you locked out?"

At first the boy didn't say anything, didn't even look back at Bolan. Then, "Yes. I left the key in my other pants and I don't want to wake my mom. She hasn't slept good for a couple of days and the medicine the doctor gave her really makes her tired. I wasn't supposed to go outside, but I got bored.''

"And now you've got a problem."

The boy nodded.

"There's two solutions," Bolan decided. "Either we wake your mom up and you get back inside, or we wait out here until she wakes on her own."

"I'll wait. She's been really tired and upset."

"That's pretty thoughtful of you. But won't you get bored sitting out here, too?"

The boy shrugged, a quick lifting and dropping of thin shoulders that Bolan found comical.

"I was about to go downstairs and get something to eat. Are you hungry?"

"Yeah, but I don't have any money. It's in my other pants."

"That's okay. I'll buy this time and you can buy next time."

A frown creased the small face. "Mom said I shouldn't go anywhere with strangers."

Bolan smiled. "Your mother is a smart lady. You should listen to her. But we'll leave a note for your mom. While I'm leaving it, you can take the elevator down to the restaurant and I'll meet you there. Does that sound okay?"

The boy still hesitated. Then, "Okay." He pushed himself up from the floor. He started toward the elevator then stopped and looked at Bolan. "You will come, won't you?"

"As soon as I leave the note."

"Okay." The boy started to walk away again then stopped. "My name's Jason, but you can call me Jase. Everybody does."

Bolan smiled. "I'm Mike."

He'd planned to catch a few hours of sleep in the early part of the evening and spend at least part of the night cruising the bars to pick up information concerning *Lady's Desire*. It would have kept Vincent busy and maybe allowed something else to break loose. But the warrior knew he couldn't have turned his back on the boy.

VINCENT PICKED Bolan up again in the lobby, remaining a discreet distance behind as he walked into the small, dimly lit restaurant.

Bolan found Jase sitting at a corner table, studying a large menu with a frown on his face. The boy looked up as Bolan sat across from him.

"I can't read it," Jase said. "I recognize the letters and everything, but none of them make any sense."

Bolan scanned the columns. "It's in French. What do you want?"

"A hamburger." Jase held his fingers open about an inch. "This thick with lots of mayonnaise. And a Coke."

The waitress came and Bolan gave her the order, feeling the boy's eyes on him the whole time.

"Where did you learn to talk French?"

"In a war a long time ago."

"Vietnam?"

"Yes."

"We talked about that in history." Jase's hands captured the vase in the center of the table, and he traced with his fingers the petals of the red rose it contained. "Our teacher taught us some French words last year but I wasn't any good at it. She was from France and told us nearly everybody over there knows two languages. They're bi-something." His mouth compressed as he searched for the word.

"Bilingual."

"Yeah, that's it."

The waitress brought their Cokes and food and put them on the table.

Bolan scanned the room and saw Vincent sitting at a table with a coffee and a newspaper, seemingly absorbed with world affairs.

As they ate, the conversation became more animated. Jase told Bolan about his home in Miami, his school. Bolan enjoyed the conversation. For a while it was almost like having a little brother again. But the part of him that was the warrior kept him mentally cataloging everything that went on around him, kept track of Vincent's movements, even when the DEA agent got a message for a telephone call and returned only a few minutes later. He listened to Jase intently, but a separate consciousness wondered if the vultures had started to gather.

When the elevator doors opened and Bolan stepped out with Jase at his side, they found a woman waiting to get in.

Jase said, "Hi, Mom," and went to her.

The woman looked into Bolan's eyes, and he felt as if he was being searched and analyzed at the same time. Her relief was evident by the way she held the boy to her, dropping to a crouch that revealed a lot of healthy leg.

"I found your note," she said to Bolan, "but I was still worried."

Bolan nodded.

The woman was a knockout. She was blond, a shade over five and a half feet tall, with full breasts and rounded buttocks. A knockout, except for the bloodshot brown eyes and the tiredness that seemed to cling to her like fog.

She stood to face him and smoothed down her dress. "Was Jase any trouble?"

"Not at all. I think I got more enjoyment out of the time we spent together than he did. I wasn't much of a conversationalist."

The woman smiled and it came off, despite her exhaustion. "Jase has never had a problem holding up both ends of a conversation."

Another elevator opened down the hall and Vincent stepped out. The man did a quick double take and acted like he'd gotten off on the wrong floor, then reentered the elevator.

Bolan wondered how many men were involved in the surveillance. Surely there were two or three others. If Marino was as sharp as Bolan thought he was, there would have to be at least two outside the building, one more inside, and another team waiting in the wings to take over.

"Jase knows he's not supposed to leave the hotel room," the woman said. She glanced meaningfully at the boy.

"That's what he told me. I caused my mother a lot of worry when I was his age. I was an explorer myself."

She smiled, but it was more reflex than anything else. He recalled what Jase had mentioned about the medication his mother was taking and wondered what was wrong with her.

The woman smoothed her son's hair.

"His name is Mike," Jase announced.

Offering a hand to Bolan, she said, "I'm sorry. My name is Abby Nichols."

"Mike McKay." Her hand felt warm and smooth in his.

"I want to thank you for what you did," Abby said. "I guess I was more tired than I thought."

"I'm glad I was around. It was a more pleasant evening than I had planned." And what diverting surprise was Vincent working up? Bolan wondered. But he kept his smile in place while he watched for any of the man's handiwork.

Abby checked her watch and made an apologizing face. "I wish I had more time to talk, but if I don't hurry, I'm going to be late for an appointment."

Bolan nodded.

She took Jase by the hand and said goodbye. Bolan watched her go, returning Jase's wave when the boy twisted around to look back.

Layers of life, Bolan thought as he walked to his door, fascinated by the way the lives of people sometimes touched in odd, fleeting moments, sharing a common goal but having no common background.

His combat sense washed over him quietly when he saw that the toothpick was gone, pushing the flesh and blood man out of the way for the warrior. The Executioner reached inside his jacket for the Beretta.

6

The party aboard the houseboat was in full swing, and more than once Chase Murphy found his hands momentarily filled with resilient, bikini-clad flesh as the big boat rocked to the beat of the waves and the heavy metal bands. The *Bobby's Inferno* was known all over Key West as the place to go for a blowout.

Murphy was an often invited but seldom present guest. Tonight was different, though. Tonight the pilot had surfaced at the party to occupy the attention of the man following him.

Murphy took another drink of the imported beer that was among the large selection the host, Bobby Drake, kept on board, and he watched the girls dancing in the middle of the floor. There had to be over sixty people on board. The houseboat was still tied up to shore, so the pilot knew the man keeping him under surveillance was lounging back somewhere in the shadows that gathered along the white sands. Murphy had someone else watching the man who watched him, so he wasn't worried the man would get on board unannounced. Even if it was possible for him to get past Drake's bouncers.

"Hell of a party, isn't it, Sky King?" Drake's voice boomed into Murphy's ear.

Murphy looked over the small bar and found Bobby Drake leaning on the expensive wooden top. Drake stood over six feet tall, was lean and muscled, with sandy-colored hair and boyish freckles. It was hard to tell how old Drake was, even for Murphy, who figured he knew the man as well or better than anyone on the Key.

Robert W. Drake had been an investigative reporter in years past, stinging several political and big business names with his barbed prose. He'd been called a muckraker at first, but then he started breaking stories that grabbed the attention of a majority of America, stories Drake had had to risk his life for on several occasions. A hit man from an embittered congressional aide almost succeeded in killing Drake when he first came to Key West. The man would have finished the job if Murphy hadn't stepped in.

Murphy raised his bottle in response to Drake's question. "I can hardly hear myself think."

A disparaging smile appeared on Drake's face. "Okay, so maybe it's a little slow now, but I promise it'll pick up."

Murphy laughed.

The DJ in the Plexiglas booth at the other end of the dance floor changed disks and introduced a number by Whitesnake.

"I like this singer," Drake said. "He's an older guy. Like me. You want another beer, Chase?"

Murphy nodded and took the neck of the bottle being offered. He twisted the cap off and left it in the deep dish ashtray set into the wood of the bar top.

"So what brings you to the *Inferno*?" Drake asked. "We usually don't find ourselves on your agenda unless you're feeling sorry for yourself and want to get shit-faced."

Turning from the crowd gyrating to the heavy metal beat, Murphy faced Drake. "I got a guy following me around tonight."

"Personal business?"

Murphy shook his head. "It belongs to somebody else, but I've been asked to take a hand."

"And you accepted?"

"Just doing my bit for the human condition."

Drake made a face. "Why don't you try buying Girl Scout cookies?"

"There's no personal satisfaction that way."

"My ass," Drake said. "How long you known this 'somebody else'?"

"Just met him today."

Drake looked incredulous. He poured himself a couple fingers of brandy and downed it. "Tell me you're joking."

"Impressive guy, Bobby. Trust me."

Drake swirled the liquor in his glass, falling silent as a handful of young women made their way to the bar for fresh drinks.

Murphy watched the ex-newsman meet and greet each one by name amid a chorus of "Hi, Bobby," and "Great party, Bobby." He liked Drake's style and the honest appreciation the man generated for everyone who knew him. It wasn't hard to picture Drake as someone people could talk to, even as a newsman in media-troubled times.

Murphy's own life was that of a loner. He kept to himself, got to know women on a one-to-one basis before allowing any sort of relationship to develop. He did that now, he corrected himself as he gazed at the stressed bikinis at the bar. It hadn't necessarily been that way in the past. Murphy's Flaw.

He grinned sourly to himself as he sipped more beer. Maybe that was why he wanted to help McKay. Because he sensed the same kind of nature in the big man. And because Marino was scum that needed to be taken out.

"Kiley told me one of Marino's local hardcases was hanging around out there," Drake said, speaking of his chief of security for the houseboat. "He's the one that belongs to you?"

"Yep."

Drake was silent for a moment. "You make me nervous, kid. Do you know that?"

"Sometimes, Bobby, I make myself nervous."

"Terrific."

"How about another beer?"

Drake handed him one.

"Did Kiley happen to see Sloan out there too?"

"Sloan's out there?"

"Yep. Keeping an eye on the guy keeping an eye on me."

Drake poured himself another brandy. "You know as well as I do nobody could find that Seminole in the dark, even if he was within arm's reach."

"Which is why he's out there now."

"And you're here because of Kiley."

Murphy grinned. "You give good security, Bobby. Everybody on the island knows that. And you've got a telephone and a quiet way out of here if I need it."

"Plus you get to soak up all the free beer you want."

Murphy hoisted his bottle in a mock salute.

"You son of a bitch," Drake said affably as he seated himself on the bar and looked out at the crowd. "How much trouble are you in, Chase?"

"None yet. Marino's boy is just out there to make sure I don't get into any."

"But you're not going to let him stop you."

"No."

Drake sighed. "I always liked you, kid. Even if you hadn't saved my life that time, I'd have liked you. But you're biting off a lot if you're planning on moving against Marino."

"You haven't seen my hole card."

"This guy you're helping out, is he connected?"

"I don't think he is, not to the regular channels, but it feels like he's got a hardwire to hell."

"Sounds like an impressive guy."

"That's what I said."

"Are Marino's boys playing pin-the-tail-on-the-jackass with him, too?"

"Yep. Only he rated Vincent as a dance partner."

"Ruffi must've been pretty impressed with your man too if he's pulling out his heavy guns."

"That's why I don't think he's regular government issue. Evidently Marino can't find a handle on him, either."

"How many guys does he have with him?"

Murphy smiled and drained his beer, then looked at Drake and said, "Me."

"You're kidding."

"No."

"You're a fucking lunatic, kid." Drake looked over his shoulder at the bartender. "Give this guy another beer. He's been sitting on his brains again."

Murphy accepted the chilled bottle, telling himself he needed to slow down with Marino's man still waiting in the shadows for him. Maybe he should have backed out of the operation after McKay made the offer. It would have been the smartest thing to do. Marino had a lot of pull on the island. But there had been something about the big man that had convinced Murphy if anyone could bust the cocaine pipeline it was McKay.

Drake excused himself and went to rejoin the party, promising Murphy one of the best eulogies ever written.

Without warning, a very blond and very tanned young woman stopped in front of Murphy, her lean flesh still jiggling in all the right places from the sudden halt.

"Hi," she breathed.

"Hi back."

"I couldn't help but notice you look kind of over-dressed for this party."

Murphy knew she referred to his T-shirt and jeans, but the loose folds of material kept the Walther out of sight. "I just had an impulse to stop in while I was passing by."

"I'm Jennifer."

"Chase Murphy."

Grinning in a mischievous way, Jennifer said, "Are you into doing impulsive things, Chase?"

"Sometimes," he replied, wondering if Drake had arranged for the girl to meet him.

"I couldn't help but notice you're alone."

"It's a good night for it."

"It's a good night for a lot of things."

Murphy sipped his beer, using the movement to check around for Drake. It was impossible to find the man in the cramped confines of the houseboat.

"Somebody told me you fly helicopters."

"A mutual friend?"

Jennifer grinned. "Something like that."

Murphy raised his eyebrows as he studied her. "Usually I run kind of light on mutual friends." A chill dawned inside the pilot's head as he looked at her again. The magenta bikini didn't leave a lot of places to hide things, but Murphy felt suddenly threatened. He'd had women come on to him before. Hell, that had been happening since he started going to bars when he was seventeen. But this was different. He felt like the blonde was stalking him, gauging his depth and measure.

She reached out to stroke the back of his hand with her fingers. "I've never made it in a helicopter before."

"Neither have I."

"It might be interesting to try. I'm not doing anything tonight."

"Couldn't make it tonight, but I wouldn't mind taking a rain check."

The blonde made a pout that took ten years off her age. She kept stroking his hand. "You have something else planned?" She stepped closer, planting her pelvis next to his thigh.

Murphy felt himself respond, felt the moist inner heat of her. The chill had spread down over his shoulders.

Her hand strayed from his hand to his chest, and he found himself looking down into her eyes. He knew if he tried to kiss her she wouldn't resist.

No one else seemed to notice anything. The same scene was being played in different areas of the dance floor. Party business as usual as two people got to know each other.

The blonde's voice was soft and husky when she spoke. "You seem nervous. Haven't you ever seen an aggressive woman who knows what she wants?"

Murphy captured her wandering hand as it traveled gently toward his crotch, weaving his fingers in hers. He knew she must have touched the automatic, but she gave no sign of it. He gave her a crooked grin. "The name's Chase, lady, not chaste." He took a step forward, which caused her to stumble backward.

An uncertain look rippled over the women's face, and she seemed to be searching for something else to say.

Before she could open her mouth, Murphy left her and angled across the dance floor to the head. Pulling the door closed behind him, he relieved himself, washing the accumulation of beers out of his system.

The Walther should have frightened her, he told himself. He checked his hair in the small mirror. Somebody had sent her to keep him occupied. The "who" seemed fairly simple to deduce. But why?

As he looked in the mirror, Murphy saw the door behind him open. He started to turn around as the other man stepped in. The new arrival raised his hand, filled with a small, silenced automatic.

Moving instinctively with the speed that had saved him in other sudden encounters, Murphy spun to the far corner of the small room, little more than an arm's length away. His fingers found the light switch, plunging the room into complete darkness except for what came from the dance floor down the hall.

The DJ had switched the strobe lights on while Murphy was in the head, and the stuttering flashes impacted on the pilot's senses, creating nightmarish images of the man with the gun.

Two silent flashes darted toward Murphy as he threw himself down and forward. His outstretched arms connected with his attacker's legs, and they went down together.

The gunman fired three more rounds as Murphy clawed his way to a sitting position on the guy's chest. His left hand wrapped around the gun barrel, his thumb sliding neatly under the hammer and keeping it from firing. He jerked out his Walther and lodged it under the man's Adam's apple.

Murphy's voice was ice-cold, and he struggled to keep from pulling the trigger.

The man fought to get away, still trying to fire the gun.

"The only thing that's keeping me from killing you now, asshole, is that a friend of mine paid good money for the carpet you'd bleed all over. If you don't relax, I'm just going to owe it to him. He'll understand."

The man froze.

"Let go of the gun," Murphy commanded.

The automatic fell with a muffled thud and Murphy picked it up, shoving it into the back of his jeans.

"Colt Woodsman .22," Murphy said, keeping his seat on the man's chest. The Walther was jammed so deeply into the man's neck that the pilot could feel the heart beating a rapid tempo. "That tells me you're not exactly a novice at this. I don't know you. That tells me you're new to the Key. Want to tell me why Marino sent for you, or do you want me to kind of figure it out on my own?"

"You're a dead man, motherfucker," the man said through gritted teeth.

Murphy backhanded the man across the face with his free hand, splitting the guy's lip. "Maybe I should go ahead and pull this trigger. After all, a dead man doesn't have to worry about murder charges. Want to try to encourage me some more?"

The man didn't reply.

"Marino didn't tell you very much about me, did he? I got a reputation for doing crazy things. He might not know about the men I killed, so I'll give him that." Murphy relaxed the pressure on the gun so his prisoner could speak. "You a city boy, or do you know anything about the ocean?"

"You're gonna die."

Murphy nodded wearily. "Sooner or later. But it won't be because of a two-bit hardass like you. Do you know anything about sand crabs, or are you just into your Murder, Inc. routine?'' The pilot shifted but kept the pistol in place. ''Let me tell you about them. You see, crabs like meat. Especially fresh meat. I've found bodies of people your boss probably had killed. Sometimes the crabs in the area where the bodies turned up were still feeding on them. There are places around here that I know I could put a man, tied up, of course, and leave him for a few days. Sort of an appetizer for the local sand crabs. I could even use a location where the crabs have already developed a taste for human flesh.''

''You wouldn't do that.''

''Like I said, guy, you weren't told squat about me. And right now, the way I figure it, I own your ass.'' Murphy made slow pincer movements with his left hand.

The man stared at his hand as if mesmerized. ''Marino hired me this afternoon. He figured you'd end up on Drake's houseboat before the evening was over, and he knew I could get on board through Jennifer. She's been hanging around here for months just keeping up with what Drake does.''

''Why did Marino hire you?''

''To get you out of the way. He said you were mixing in where you didn't belong.''

''I could have told me that,'' Murphy said in disgust.

''It's all I know, man.''

''Yeah, yeah. You know anything about the guy waiting outside?''

''Marino sent him in case I needed any help getting out of the area.''

Drake's voice bellowed down the short hallway behind Murphy. ''Hey, Sky King, I don't know what the hell you said to that little blond bombshell I saw you talking with a minute ago, but she lit out of here without looking back. And Cochise is on the phone. He says it's important.''

Murphy stepped back and motioned his prisoner up with the gun.

When Drake appeared, he was carrying a drink in one hand and a beer in the other.

Murphy took the beer and shoved the Colt Woodsman into the ex-newsman's empty hand. "You want to do me a favor, Bobby, and watch this son of a bitch?"

Drake shrugged. "I don't mind doing it for a little bit, I guess, but hell, Chase, I'm trying to throw a party here. I don't have time for this cops-and-robbers shit. If you see Kiley standing around up there, send him down. That's what I pay him for."

Murphy headed back to the dance floor, holstering the Walther and twisting the cap off the beer. "I need you to sit on him for a couple of hours if you can, Bobby. At least until I can figure out what's going on."

"Tell Kiley. I think I've got a pair of twins set up for tonight. How did this guy get on board?"

"He was with the girl you saw me talking to. They both work for Marino."

"My ass. I should have known there was something wrong with that girl when she wouldn't come across," Drake said. "What did this guy do?"

"He shot up your bathroom."

Drake glared at his prisoner. "You're a cold bastard, you know that?"

Out on the dance floor, Murphy threaded his way through the gyrating torsos and arms, finally reaching the phone on the bar. "Murphy," he said as he covered one ear with the receiver and the other with a hand.

Sloan's deep bass voice was almost drowned in the steady roll of heavy metal. Murphy barely recognized the song as an old Ratt number.

"The *Lady's Desire* just put out to sea five minutes ago."

Murphy put his beer down and dug out the number McKay had given him. "You still got my shadow covered?"

"Yeah. Do you want me to take him out?"

Murphy smoothed the paper out on the counter so he could read the number. "No. I'm going to need a diversion, though, in case Marino's paid cops are looking for me too. Can you fix this guy's car? Just leave the box on my bike. I gotta set up a couple more things.''

"Okay." Sloan broke the connection.

Murphy dialed the number McKay had left, thinking Marino had evidently seen something in the big man as well. Something that had convinced Marino to make the drop early. Or was something else going on that none of them knew about? He counted six rings, wondering if McKay was in his room or if Marino had made some sort of arrangement for him as well. Seven rings. Maybe the man was already dead, as Murphy might have been if things had turned out differently. Eight rings.

Silently he willed McKay to pick up the phone.

7

After making sure no one else was in the hallway, Mack Bolan eased his key into the lock and turned it. At his touch the door swung open and the Executioner let the Beretta lead him into the dark room.

Clothing lay discarded on the floor. The bed sheets lay draped across open bureau drawers. The mirror in the bathroom had been levered out of its frame, and the broken pieces stabbed into the sink.

Whoever Vincent had assigned to do the job had been thorough, Bolan thought as he holstered the Beretta. He stepped up onto the edge of the bathtub and pried the heat vent loose. Reaching into the dark cavity inside, he removed his combat harness and Desert Eagle.

He returned to the bedroom and took a small pair of binoculars from the bureau. They didn't look much different than a regular pair, but the lenses were the same as those in a Starlite scope, designed to take in any available light and make better use of it.

He shrugged out of his jacket and walked to the window. He'd chosen the room because of the view it afforded him of the docking area on the south side of the island. And because of the proximity to the slip that held the *Lady's Desire*.

Adjusting the glasses, the warrior scanned across the dark waters of the Caribbean, skipping across the bows of boats he'd become familiar with over the past two nights.

People still wandered up and down the beach and along the docking area singly and in groups. Gaily colored lanterns burned on various houseboats and cabin cruisers, rocking gently with the motion of the sea. Bolan could almost feel the cool breeze that swam in from the sea, twining in through the palms.

His sweep of the docks ended at the slip Marino's boat usually occupied. It was empty. Had Rigaberto's information been wrong? Or had something else happened?

Chastising himself for not keeping a closer watch on Marino's activities, Bolan put the binoculars away and took out the card Chase Murphy had given him. He switched on the small lamp next to the telephone by the bed and picked up the receiver. Suddenly the room's window exploded, showering him with glass.

He dived automatically, hurling himself over the bed, knowing the thin mattress and box spring wouldn't offer much protection, but at least he'd be out of sight while he planned his next move.

The Beretta filled his right hand as he edged himself around the bed on knees and elbows. A quick grab with his left hand netted him the combat harness and the .44.

The sniper laid down a pattern of fire that raked the wall, the room alive with flat, slapping noises as the heavy-caliber bullets drilled the paneling.

Bolan fired a silenced round from the Beretta that shattered the lamp and plunged the room into darkness. Then he was in a crouch, sprinting for the window in an effort to see the flashes made by the shooter's weapon and triangulate the guy's position.

Then, as suddenly as it started, the shooting stopped. Bolan wondered if the assassin was only changing clips or if the man thought he'd scored on his target. He stepped away from the window, trying to estimate the angle of fire from the holes in the wall. Before he took two steps, the door to his room ripped free of its hinges and two men charged inside.

Bolan's Beretta was up and firing, a 3-round burst stitching the lead guy's chest. The man rocked back on his heels, then righted himself, flailing with both arms.

"Goddamn, that hurt," the man growled in a muffled voice.

With the hallway light behind them, Bolan could only see the two men as bulky shadows, misshapen wraiths that rushed at him. The lead man's pistol hissed and the Executioner felt a bullet burn along the inside of his thigh.

Raising the 93-R, Bolan loosed another burst at the man's head, seeing it jerk back as the bullets scored. The man sank to his knees, then started pushing himself up again. With an ear-splitting screech, the man stood his ground and raised his weapon.

Kevlar, the Executioner reasoned as he raked the two men with the rest of the Beretta's clip. Body armor and helmets. Then he pushed himself out the window, rolling on the fire escape in case the rifleman was still in position. Bullets from the guns inside the hotel room hit the metal railings, creating sparks before careering off into the night.

Bolan holstered the Beretta and fisted the Desert Eagle. Kevlar or no Kevlar, a guy couldn't wear enough body armor to stop one of the big 240-grain boattails the Magnum spit. He knew he'd be sacrificing silence and generating a lot of sudden interest in the area, drawing friendlies, as well as whatever people Marino and Vincent had stationed nearby. But it couldn't be helped.

The first guy came vaulting through the window, certain Bolan would be more interested in trying to escape than returning fire that wouldn't do any good.

Bolan triggered the .44 as the man raised his pistol in both gloved hands, its foot-long muzzle-flash nearly touching its target. The 240-grain slug cored through the Kevlar helmet, splitting the material and shredding the brain matter underneath. The impact knocked the man backward, toppling him over the low railing of the fire escape.

The heavy recoil gave the remaining man caution. Bullets pinged against the fire escape in such rapid succession that Bolan figured the guy was holding an Uzi.

Using the butt of the Desert Eagle, the Executioner broke the window glass of the room next to his, clearing the remnants out of the way with an elbow. He found the inside lock and released it. He passed by the empty bed and made his way to the hallway. When he reached the door to his room, Bolan found the other assassin gingerly approaching the window, the Uzi out before him.

"Hey," Bolan called softly as he lined up the .44.

The man turned quickly, despite the bulkiness of the body armor, bullets from the machine pistol spitting out to kick splinters from the walls.

The first round drilled into the man's chest, and the Executioner rode the bounce of the heavy Magnum, triggering off the second round to crunch into the guy's chin.

The Executioner stepped into the room, still holding the .44 up and ready. Cordite from the expended cartridges hung heavily in the room, for the moment masking the smell of sudden death.

Bolan moved with an economy of motion, shrugging into the combat harness and reloading both guns. He pulled on a jacket to cover the weapons, not bothering to take anything else. There was nothing in the room that would incriminate him later. He'd been living his kind of life far too long to make a mistake like that. As it was now, he had the yacht to find, the night and a whole ocean to find it in, and no time at all.

The phone rang when he was out on the fire escape. He debated briefly, remembering only Brognola and Murphy had the number. Unless Vincent had somehow gotten it. Then he went back into the room and picked up the receiver.

"Yeah?" Bolan could hear people moving out in the hallway now, voices growing louder as they became more curious.

"McKay, it's Murphy."

"We're going to have to chat later, kid. I'm about to have a whole room full of uninvited company. How soon can you have that chopper warmed up?"

"I was on my way now. I just called to let you know our pigeon flew the coop."

"I noticed. Things have gotten a lot hotter on this end of the operation. I've got a dead man inside my room and one outside, three stories down. You might want to reconsider your involvement."

"Marino tried to have me seduced and iced tonight. I'm in for the duration."

"Good enough. Where can we meet?"

"I'll pick you up at the back of the hotel in five minutes. It's easier than trying to give you directions to the helicopter."

Bolan said okay and broke the connection, stepping quickly through the shattered window. The Desert Eagle filled his right hand and he held it low, covering it with his legs. Behind him he could hear surprised curses and the sound of retching. The curious had become bold enough to enter his room.

Knowing someone would risk looking down the fire escape within seconds, Bolan chose a darkened room on the second floor and broke in. "Get your clothes on," he told the startled couple as he opened the hallway door. "There's a fire upstairs. Tell as many of the other guests as you can."

The man nodded and reached for his pants.

Bolan closed the door and took the stairs down to the first floor. With everyone on the second floor in an uproar about a fire, he figured the chances of his getting away unnoticed were improving all the time.

It would take five or ten minutes for the local law to react to a call from the hotel. And another five or ten minutes for them to decide what kind of problem they were dealing with. By the time the patrol cars and the fire department arrived, more people would be drawn to the area, confusing things even further.

At the first floor, he slid the Desert Eagle under his jacket. He kept his steps measured as he angled for the rear

exit. So far, no one in the lobby seemed to know anything
was happening upstairs.

As he passed by the open restaurant, a shock of blond
hair caught his eye. He paused behind an artificial palm
tree. Abby Nichols sat at one of the tables with a man in a
three-piece suit who carried the stamp of officialdom. Jase
sat at another table behind his mother, occupied with a
stack of comic books.

Before the warrior could melt away, a hotel employee
rushed past him, heading for Abby's table. The man
apologized for interrupting. Bolan couldn't hear the conversation, but he could tell from the guy's movements that
he was telling Abby's acquaintance about the activities
upstairs.

When the man stood up, Bolan noticed the holstered
revolver on his hip and the shine of a badge next to it. After giving the hotel employee instructions, the man moved
toward the elevators.

Bolan watched him go, wondering what Abby was involved in. Jase had mentioned that he and his mother lived
in Miami, and Abby Nichols didn't look like a woman on
vacation. Which meant she was in some kind of trouble.

The thought bothered Bolan as he watched her turn
around to talk briefly with Jase. Evidently the guy she was
talking to wasn't a friend, or she would have met with him
in her room.

When Abby turned back, her eyes locked momentarily
with his. Even across the dimly lit interior of the restaurant, Bolan could sense a loss within her. Tossing her a
small wave, he continued toward the exit and hoped the
guy she'd been talking with could help her.

THE MUGGY NIGHT AIR clung as tightly to Bolan as the
shadows covering the exterior of the hotel. He heard the
high keening of the fire trucks as they approached, saw the
red flashing lights as the vehicles turned around a corner
farther down the street.

Firemen spread out from the three trucks that had arrived as the police set up a barricade. Men in yellow slickers ran toward the hotel, trailing heavy hoses behind them.

The dull roar of a motorcycle cut above the confusion of voices and emergency vehicles, drawing Bolan's attention to the side street behind the hotel. A single light, bobbing with the unevenness of the road, came at the Executioner, purposefully. Behind it were a set of car lights, trailing just far enough behind to let Bolan know the car was following the motorcycle.

Murphy brought the motorcycle to a stop in front of Bolan, holding the bike upright with both legs. The pilot gave him a grin as he revved the Suzuki's engine.

"Get on."

"Don't you think it's a tad conspicuous?" Bolan asked as he threw a leg over the seat.

"Can't beat it for maneuverability, though," Murphy shouted over the roar of the engine as they shot away from the curb.

Bolan glanced over his shoulder and saw the car move into position behind them. "You've got a tail."

Murphy nodded. "It's been my day for them. You and I must be the two most popular guys on the island." He threaded the motorcycle through the gathering crowd, earning a curse from a policeman.

The driver pushed his vehicle through the momentary opening after them. Bolan did a quick head count. There were at least four guys in the car.

"I started out with one guy," Murphy said as he shifted gears and the Suzuki plunged ahead at increased speed. "He picked up three more on the way. I figure they were in radio contact with one another. Luckily they took my guy's car."

Bolan freed the .44 as Murphy ran a red light, keeping it out of sight between their bodies. He didn't want a firefight in the street, and the motorcycle afforded little protection. Maneuverability be damned. The Executioner was more at ease behind something big and heavy. "Can you outrun them?"

Murphy glanced in the mirrors, increasing his speed until Bolan felt weightless when they hit a bump. "Probably, but that's not what I intend to do." He downshifted as he guided the Suzuki around a corner, the tires squealing frantically as they clawed for traction. "Don't worry. These clowns are the least of your problems tonight." The pilot released his hold on the left handlebar and reached under the gas tank, producing a remote control device Bolan was familiar with.

Murphy flipped the protective cover off the toggle, then triggered the electronic impulse.

Bolan looked back at the car as four explosions sounded so closely together they made a small roll of thunder. He got a vague impression of the tires being blown away from the wheel wells. Then the car was skidding out of control, sparks showering in its wake.

Murphy replaced the remote control under the gas tank. "The guy I know does really nice work."

Bolan slid the .44 back under his jacket.

BOLAN CHECKED HIS WEAPONS in the back of the helicopter as Murphy navigated across the black emptiness of the ocean. He wore a headset that allowed him to talk freely with the pilot as he worked, but both of them were silent, concentrating on what was coming up.

Dressed in his blacksuit now, with his face covered with combat cosmetics, Bolan stuffed his gear into a black, watertight bag that had been designed with enough built-in buoyancy to offset the weight it contained. Besides the Beretta and the Desert Eagle, he carried smoke grenades, tear gas and inert packages of C-4 with electronic-delay detonators. He examined the MAC-10 that would be his head weapon for the assault, then packed it as well. Then he went forward to sit by Murphy.

"Doesn't it bother you that Marino and his crew are probably expecting you?" Murphy asked.

"Yeah, but let's hope it ends up bothering them more than it bothers me."

"Only one way to find out. The hard part's going to be trying to save somebody who can give me the information I need."

"Why don't you give it a rest? Marino's going to be around for a while. Hit him another time when he lets his guard down again."

Bolan shook his head. "A lot of men have died to get me this far. You could have been another casualty for the good guys tonight if you hadn't been watching your ass so closely. Tonight's the night. If I wait, it'll give these guys a chance to work out something new, to tighten up their organization."

"But shit, you're doing this alone."

"It's the way I work best. Sometimes it gets harder trying to take care of your partners. You can blow it for yourself at a critical time by looking over your shoulder."

Murphy pulled the stick and banked the helicopter. "You've done this sort of thing before?"

"Yeah."

"So I shouldn't worry, right?"

"Only if you want to."

"Terrific," Murphy said dryly. "We should be coming up on the drop zone within a couple of minutes."

Bolan leaned forward in the seat, touching the handles of the knives he had strapped to his legs. Below the whirling blades of the helicopter, the black water looked endless.

"How will I know when to come back in for you?"

"I'll set off a flare. Don't look for it around the boats. I should be well clear."

Murphy nodded, concentrating on the ocean. A faint gleam of running lights appeared on the horizon and the pilot said, "There she is now." He made adjustments with the controls, taking the chopper down, charting a course that would run parallel to both vessels.

Bolan removed the headset and left the seat, holding the straps of the bag in his right hand. He poised on the pontoon halfway out of the cockpit, getting ready for the jump. The wind from the rotors churned the surface of the water, making it hard to hear.

"Good luck," Murphy called.

Bolan flipped the pilot a thumb's-up as he released his hold and dropped into the waiting ocean.

8

Major General Vladimir Kulik stood at his office window and stared out through the early-morning darkness at the Kremlin. The magnificence of the dome almost disappeared against the backwash of the starless sky. He had observed it many times during his three-year tenure in the office.

Still dressed in the same uniform he'd put on fresh the previous morning, Kulik carried himself with the same military bearing that had sustained him throughout his adult life. In the washed-out reflection presented by the windowpane, he could see the gray stubble across his lower face. From time to time he had rubbed his fingers across his chin and considered using the electric razor in the bottom drawer of his desk. But within seconds he would put it out of his mind again as his thoughts turned to other subjects.

Fyodor Ivanovitch was of the ultimate concern, even though Kulik was certain he knew where the renegade agent would turn up. He had worked with the man for years, had gotten to know how the man's mind worked better than anyone.

Except for Boris Kirov, late of the KGB.

The anger Kulik had experienced when the politburo recommended pulling Kirov out of retirement still burned. If Gorbachev and his aides had been kept clear of the matter, Kulik thought as he stared out the window, the affair would have taken care of itself. Eventually the things Ivanovitch planned to do would be looked on as acts of heroism. Luckily Kulik had been able to restrain himself from telling that to the pacifistic bastards.

Retreating to the small hot plate on a corner table, the KGB general poured the dregs from the coffeepot into his cup. He switched the heat off and looked out over his office, proud of its Spartan appointments. Efficient, economical, some said. But the lack of frills permitted Kulik to keep his mind focused where he needed it to be.

And tonight it needed to be on Boris Kirov and Yuri Mikhailin.

Kirov had trained Ivanovitch in his early days with the KGB. Kulik didn't need the files to tell him that. He'd been there with them. But Ivanovitch's politics since Kirov had left the active list closely coincided with Kulik's own.

The major general was almost certain Ivanovitch hadn't known he'd been manipulated. It didn't matter if he did, because Ivanovitch was already moving in the direction Kulik wanted. Kulik's informant had notified him of that. Even if Ivanovitch didn't take the next few steps by himself, the team Kulik was sending after him would. They were a small, handpicked army, loyal to Kulik even over the politburo. For months he'd worked to bring them together, to be able to drop them from the roster at a moment's notice without anyone being the wiser.

Today would bring about that moment, Kulik thought. A small glow of satisfaction filled him, making even the bitter coffee taste good.

Boris Kirov was the only fly in the ointment.

Seeing the old man in his office those days ago had put to flesh Kulik's thoughts that Russia had grown weak. If Ivanovitch had seen his old mentor, the major general was sure he would have agreed. Once, Kirov had been a man to fear. A killer with a heart of stone as he destroyed American and British attempts to hold the Soviet Union in check after World War II. Now he was just another old man, fit for nothing more than sitting in the sun and waiting for death.

From his early conversations with Kirov on behalf of the politburo, Kulik had been surprised to find that Kirov didn't share his convictions. The man had seemed more interested in the hunt for Ivanovitch, more interested in the chance to kill again. Already he had killed one of Petrovsky's sons while gathering information about Ivanovitch. Yuri Mikhailin had come to Kulik and complained of the shooting, sure some other course of action could have presented itself. Kulik wished he could have removed Kirov from the operation.

But the politburo wouldn't hear of it. Boris Kirov was a master spy, they said, a force to be reckoned with. Someone who could save Russia from the embarrassment Ivanovitch would have the country suffer.

So Kulik had had to resort to other plans—in case Kirov located Ivanovitch too early and spoiled everything.

The major general rubbed at his chin again, hearing the snap and crackle of the stubble under his fingers.

A soft knock on his door drew his attention. He turned on his heel, sitting the cup down so he would have both hands free to go for the pistol belted at his waist. It was possible that one of the righteous fools in the politburo had happened on to what he was planning.

"Enter," Kulik said curtly.

The aide who walked into the room was one of the men Kulik had worked into position over the past few months, even before the major general had reassigned the young lieutenant and his men to the guard detail over Ivanovitch's transportation. The aide was young and strong, the way Kulik often wished he still was, and totally loyal to Kulik.

"You have a report?"

"Yes, Major General."

"Concerning agent Mikhailin's activities?"

"Mikhailin broke into the files again tonight, Comrade."

"Could you tell what he was looking for?"

"He searched through Ivanovitch's files again, as though looking for something that was missing."

Kulik, intrigued by the mysteries of the computer age that had seemed to become so much of the espionage world he lived in, asked, "How could you tell this?"

"By the way he searched. Mikhailin covered the information several times before disengaging from the file."

Kulik swirled the remnants of the coffee in his cup. "You did alter Ivanovitch's files as I ordered?"

"Yes."

"And negated the report of Ivanovitch's service with the Cubans in 1982 and 1983?"

"Yes. I filled those times in with standard assignments. He won't know about that objective through KGB files."

"Mikhailin doesn't know you found his connection to the computer?"

"I'm not sure, Comrade General. He dropped off-line more quickly than I had anticipated tonight. Usually he's very careful about entering and departing the program."

"You think he discovered he was being watched?"

"I couldn't say for sure."

Kulik nodded. He felt angry that the aide had gotten caught, but knew it was a worthless anger because it was too late to alter the circumstances. Yuri Mikhailin wasn't as dangerous as Kirov, but the younger man was certainly more resourceful, more at ease with the new technologies that permitted espionage activities than Kulik could ever hope to be.

But it was the willingness to kill for the cause that made a successful agent. Kulik knew that from the men he'd trained, from the men whose sole loyalty lay to him and the vision he offered. There was a moment just right for death, the major general had told many of them. The agent had to be poised right on the cusp of it. Too hesitant or too willing, either way was unacceptable.

Kulik knew more about Mikhailin than the agent was probably aware of. The Mossad woman had been a turning point for Mikhailin. Killing her had removed the serpent's teeth KGB trainers had sought to instill in the young agent. It was that way with many agents who spent formative years in America. Mikhailin had made friends in California, embraced life-styles that seemed to hold room for personal dreams and designs.

In the end those dreams had robbed him of his commitment to the state. If it hadn't been for Ivanovitch, Kulik would have taken Mikhailin off active duty and disposed of him properly. His weakness about killing had made him the perfect choice for pursuing Ivanovitch, though. The politburo knew only of the spotless record Mikhailin had maintained over the past few years. They weren't privy to the speculations made by the major general. They readily agreed to place Mikhailin in charge of the effort. It would have been perfect if Kirov hadn't been added.

But ultimately, Kulik thought, Mikhailin's squeamishness would be the death of Boris Kirov. The old man would be overconfident of his own abilities, never knowing he didn't have a solid backup until it was far too late.

The aide stood awaiting orders.

Kulik sat his empty cup on the desk. "Return to your duties, Comrade. Keep an eye on Mikhailin's activities as you have been. I need to know everything he's planning."

"Yes, Major General."

"Also, send for Gronsky. I have some information I want the CIA to believe they have stolen from us."

"Yes, Comrade."

Kulik walked back to the window. "Summon Kalinin to my office. I have further orders to relay to him before he begins following Kirov and Mikhailin's movements in the morning."

"Yes, Comrade."

"And bring another pot of coffee." Kulik heard the door shut as he stared out over the Kremlin. The sun was just starting to rise behind the girth of the dome. The major general watched it come with anticipation. The next handful of days would be hectic, Kulik thought as he studied the crimson-stained clouds. But everything was accounted for, every possibility carefully planned for. With only the dying to be done.

MACK BOLAN SWAM with powerful strokes, getting the most out of the flippers he wore. The weapons bag floated behind him, held prisoner by the strap around his chest. The water was more chill than he'd expected, but the exertion warmed him quickly and the blacksuit trapped most of the heat against his body.

Two dark ships were directly ahead of him. The *Lady's Desire* and a larger boat sat side by side with only minimal running lights showing. If it hadn't been for Murphy's sharp eyes, they might have missed Bolan's target. Sounds of men's voices drifted across the uneven planes of the ocean's surface.

As Bolan entered the fire-zone, he concentrated on keeping his strokes beneath the water so the guards wouldn't hear him. He gave the yacht a wide berth and closed in on the freighter. He paused with one hand on the barnacled hull, listening but hearing only the lap of waves against the metal. Vibrations of the powerful turbines housed within the freighter echoed through his fingertips and palm.

Treading water, he unzipped the weapons bag and reached inside for a prepped block of C-4. After closing the bag, he took a deep breath and dived, arcing to reach a vulnerable area on the freighter well below the waterline.

His lungs strained against the pressure of the ocean around him and from his recent exertions swimming to the drop site. Using his left hand to anchor himself to the ship, he placed the explosive carefully, making sure the electronic detonator was working properly. Then he surfaced, swallowing the impulse to gasp for air. He made two more trips underwater, setting one charge on the other side of the freighter and the remaining one on the outside of the engine compartment.

The yacht received only one at the bow, but the warrior knew it would be enough. When all the plastique had been placed, he was confident that neither the freighter nor the yacht would have a prayer of staying afloat if he chose to detonate the charges. The thing to do now was to make certain there were no innocents aboard.

Bolan kicked free of the flippers and they gently floated to the surface. Taking a small, collapsible grappling hook from one of the pouches of his web belt, he fanned out the hook and tossed it over the railing above. The padding on the hook allowed only a muffled thud. He pulled the nylon line taut, testing the hold.

Satisfied, the Executioner slid into his combat harness, keeping himself above the water by clinging to the rope so none of his weapons would be immersed for even a short time. Both the .44 and the Beretta had performed well under adverse conditions before, but there was no reason to take unnecessary risks. Yet.

The electronic control for the C-4 charges hung from a clip on the harness at his chest beside an assortment of four grenades. Bolan began the climb up the length of nylon, hand over hand. At the top, he pulled himself in close to the ship, on the opposite side from the *Lady's Desire*. Directly in front of him was the wheelhouse, illuminated only by a low-wattage bulb that spilled weak yellow light through dirty windowpanes. Two dark-skinned men were inside, going over a chart. Both were dressed in light gray uniforms. Neither was Marino or a member of the crew Bolan had identified from the yacht.

Freeing the silenced Beretta, Bolan climbed over the railing and onto the deck. He threw the grappling hook into the ocean, then dropped to the brine-soaked deck, rolling the distance between the railing and the wheelhouse.

Bolan pressed himself into the wall of the cabin and made his way to the short ladder that led topside. Although he hadn't seen anyone during the swim in, the warrior was certain someone had to be stationed there. It afforded a clear view of both vessels. A solid sniper's position.

He climbed silently, keeping the Beretta fisted in his right hand. At the top of the ladder, Bolan peered over the edge. The guy he was searching for was hunkered down behind the radio antenna, an AK-47 with an infrared scope cradled in his arms. A walkie-talkie hung from its strap on a wall of the cabin.

As Bolan watched, the guard took the walkie-talkie down and spoke into it.

"You see anything more of that helicopter?" the guard asked in Spanish.

"No. I don't think it was anything to be concerned about. We're too far out yet for any trouble from the Americans."

The language put the guard's point of origin almost anywhere between Key West and South America. But the fact that this man carried an AK-47 would help narrow the possibilities. If he could get his hands on the ship's manifests, Bolan knew most of the mystery would be cleared up.

The first guard said, "I hope you're right. But I saw omens before we began this sailing. Evil omens that I feel I shouldn't have ignored."

The other man laughed. "You are too superstitious, Paolo."

The walkie-talkie crackled through the guards' chatter, sounding angry and menacing. "You two yo-yos had better clear this frequency now." There was no mistaking the nasal twang in the new speaker's voice, and Bolan guessed it was one of Marino's men.

The guard, Paolo, made a face and hung up the walkie-talkie, tightening his grip on the assault rifle as he muttered imprecations against Americans in general.

"Hey, Paolo," Bolan whispered.

The guard's head swung around, searching the darkness for the unseen speaker.

Caressing the trigger of the Beretta, the Executioner inflicted the guard with an evil eye above and between the other two that wouldn't close. The body slumped back quietly.

Aware that the opening move in his assault had been made and that the seconds were ticking away until his discovery, Bolan slid back down the ladder. Once more on deck, he moved for the wheelhouse, wanting to close off as many possible avenues of attack as quickly as he could.

A glance through one of the dirty panes showed him the two men inside were still occupied with the chart. Making sure the door opened outward, Bolan positioned himself on the other side, hooking his fingers inside and flipping it open suddenly.

The fat man wearing the captain's insignia clawed for the holstered revolver at his waist while the other man dived for an AK-47 leaning against the wall.

The initial 3-round burst from the Beretta shattered the captain's face, splattering blood and bone splinters over the other man's back. Then Bolan was in the small room, dropping to a combat crouch as he positioned himself to take out the remaining man.

The barrel of the assault rifle started to come around as the man struggled to get his finger inside the guard. Bolan squeezed the trigger again and watched the man's left ear dissolve into a violently gushing red flower. The unfired rifle clattered to the floor.

After checking the bodies for any signs of life, Bolan examined the chart they'd been going over. But it contained no information about the freighter, just the nautical details of the Caribbean Sea from South America to Florida. Which didn't narrow the Executioner's field of reference.

The warrior popped the single overhead light bulb and took out a penlight from an inside pocket. Holstering the Beretta, he began opening drawers and cabinets, looking for the ship's manifests. It didn't matter if they were phony, as long as they could give him an angle to work on. This ship had cleared a harbor in Atlanta, near the source of the cocaine Brognola's friend had died trying to dam up. Bolan wanted the location.

Piles of paperwork and charts dropped to the floor as he searched. He moved quietly, scrutinizing everything before deeming it useless. A marine radio in the corner crackled from time to time as different ships' captains and duty officers hailed one another in light banter.

Bolan knew he was pushing his own time limit as he continued his search. Marino was undoubtedly on board somewhere, checking out the merchandise and making the buy. At any moment the deal could be concluded, and whatever guards they had below to watch one another would come topside.

Without warning, the door to the wheelhouse opened and a man peered in. Bolan cursed silently as he pushed himself backward toward the wall, realizing the constant static and conversation from the radio had masked the guard's approach.

"Capitán," the guard said as he blinked and tried to accustom his eyes to the darkness. "Your light is out. Do you want me—" The guy's voice froze abruptly as he gazed at the bodies.

Bolan had the Beretta up and was firing, but the bullets penetrated only empty air. The guard had vanished around the corner of the cabin.

The man yelled a mixture of Spanish and English as he alerted the rest of the crew. Bullets from the automatic weapon he carried chewed into the wooden frame of the cabin, showering the interior with splinters.

As the shouts of other men joined those of the first, Bolan realized the small wheelhouse had become a cage.

9

"What the hell is going on here?" a harsh voice demanded in Spanish.

"The *capitán* has been killed. His murderer is still in the cabin," the guard answered. "Both he and Melendez are lying on the floor. I saw them myself. Mother of God, I swear to you it looks like their heads have exploded."

Bolan moved, keeping to the meager security of the shadows lining the small cabin. The Beretta was snugged deep in its leathers again as the Executioner unlimbered the MAC-10 and charged it, the dry snap of the slide echoing around him.

The firing had died down for the moment as the shooters made an attempt to find out what was going on.

"One man?" the harsh voice asked.

"Yes, Franco. But a man like I've never seen before. He's dressed all in black, like he was carved from the night around us. And he moves quickly. I was almost too slow in getting away or he would have murdered me as well."

"Federal?"

"I don't know, Franco. He didn't identify himself to me."

"He's still in the cabin?"

"There's no other way out."

"You men there, move around to the front of the ship. This man must not escape. I want to know who he is and who sent him."

Tugging a smoke grenade from the webbing, Bolan tossed it through the door, hearing the startled yells of the men who recognized its baseball shape. A soft crump let him know the grenade had started to spew its contents across the deck. He lifted the MAC-10 and pointed it toward the windows in front of him. Hopefully the men around him would think the smoke bomb was a diversion that would enable him to get through the door.

Bolan squeezed the trigger and felt the machine pistol start in his hands like a wild thing. The handful of carefully controlled bursts quickly emptied the clip, but they also removed the glass barrier.

After ramming another clip home, Bolan forced his way through the shattered window, coming up out of the shoulder roll with the Ingram tracking. Stuttering automatic fire searched the dark pall that filled the doorway of the cabin, lancing into the old wood of its walls and the deck. The warrior wheeled and lunged around the other side of the cabin away from the small force clustered near the doorway.

Two men raced around the corner, facing Bolan. Both brandished automatic weapons. "Roberto, there," one man shouted as he brought his Kalashnikov to bear on the Executioner.

Without breaking stride, Bolan raked a bloody figure eight across the chest of both men. The sudden hail of bullets pummeled the gunners backward, blowing the life from them as their rifles clattered to the deck.

Bolan paused at the end of the cabin, holding the Ingram in one hand while he checked for the detonator with the other. After assuring himself the control was still in place, he left the shelter of the cabin and sprinted across the open deck, following the steel cable railing at the edge of the deck as he maneuvered for position.

The startled yells behind the Executioner let him know the bodies had been discovered.

Hawsers as thick as a man's arm lay in coils along Bolan's path. More than once he found himself searching for his balance as the hemp spun free underfoot. He grabbed the steel cable in one hand to keep himself upright as the mob pursuing him came into view. Bullets flew through the air, searching for him.

From an unexpected direction, the 5.56 mm tumblers of an M-16 smacked into the cable railing with shrill screams, whining away into the gloom. A shower of yellow sparks darted along its length beside Bolan as he raced across the deck.

The Executioner dived forward, worming through the thick ropes. He brought the MAC-10 into target acquisition, ignoring the bullets from his pursuers that splintered the deck around him. The sniper on the yacht had gotten too confident, too sure of his own skills, thinking Bolan had been hit, and the warrior watched the guy lean forward, straining to look up onto the deck of the freighter with the M-16 still at the ready.

The MAC-10's sudden stutter hammered the man backward from Bolan's view.

Still prone, Bolan wheeled on his elbows and directed his fire against the handful of men advancing cautiously toward his position. Even as he laid down his chosen field of hell, the warrior saw that Marino wasn't among the men.

The MAC-10 clicked dry while Bolan's attackers were searching for cover. He gathered his feet under him and ran for the temporary safety of the boom arm assembly housing.

Bolan changed magazines on the run, then slung the weapon and started climbing into the welcomed embrace of the steel cables that were the sinews of the massive arm. The smell of hydraulic fluids and diesel closed around him as he climbed for a new vantage point. He paused on top of the housing, feeling the motion of the sea and the unsteadiness of the flimsy metal beneath him, knowing it hadn't been fashioned for holding his weight, yet hoping it would all the same.

Careful to keep his profile averted, Bolan examined the deck. Parts of it were still hidden from him, but there were enough places available for him to complete the picture.

The freighter was in a state of mass confusion. The men who had tried to rush him were staying behind cover, ignoring the repeated commands from the man called Franco, who was standing by the blasted remains of the wheelhouse.

Retrieving a small pair of night glasses from a slit pocket of the blacksuit, Bolan focused on the man. He had the massive build of a heavyweight, his hair falling in a long braid halfway down his back, and a thick mustache covered his upper lip. He kept his back to the cabin; a big-bore pistol was clutched in his fist.

Where was Marino? And where had all the Soviet weapons come from? Even the size of the crew on this operation seemed suspect. There were too many men involved, even considering the amount of cocaine they were transporting. Counting the four men he'd killed, Bolan put the figure somewhere over twenty. Almost twice as many as would have been needed to safely operate the ship.

So there was more to it than met the eye, Bolan thought as he continued his search for Marino. He found the *Lady's Desire*'s lieutenant a handful of seconds later, hunkered down by the shelter of the hold in the center of the ship. The H&K jutted out from Marino's hands, a thick briefcase sat in his lap. As Bolan watched, Marino ripped the sporty sunglasses from his face and threw them away, seizing the pistol tightly again.

"Do you know where he is?" Franco demanded.

One of the men near the boom arm answered. "No, Franco. He was here one second, then, poof, he was gone."

"Nice security system you guys got here," Marino sneered from his place by the hold. "I fucking love it, Franco. How in the hell could you guys have let one man get away with this kind of shit?"

Franco ignored the sarcasm, stepping out onto the deck. "Get him," he ordered his men. "I want this man found *now*."

"You keep standing out there like that," Marino said, "and you're going to get your ass shot off. This guy isn't dicking around."

"He's just one man," Franco yelled back, frustrated. "One cop against all of us. You think he's a threat we should let concern us? I say he's a dead man waiting for the moment of his death."

Bolan replaced the night glasses in the slit pocket and drew the Beretta. His motions were slow and steady, even though violent death lay in wait all around him. He knew the silencer and flash suppressor of the weapon would maintain the integrity of his position. He took the roll of the freighter into consideration, adjusted for the height difference, estimated the distance between himself and Franco at almost thirty feet. He closed his left eye as he entered the lonely world of the sniper, feeling the oneness between himself and the pistol, the neutrality, the no-man's-land between good and evil, barren of any feelings of success or failure.

The gray material of Franco's shirt under a dark jacket was marred by the sudden appearance of a dark blotch over his heart that was quickly followed by two more.

When Franco sank to his knees, clutching at his chest, shouted curses filled the air as the men onboard the freighter broke under the quickness of their leader's death. Automatic fire speared through the night as panic seized the crew. Men scattered, running for whatever imagined safety their minds conjured.

Bolan used the Beretta on the nearest targets, shifting subtly in the cables so the night still cloaked him under a shield of invisibility. Three more of the freighter's crew joined Franco in quick succession. Choosing to mask the area of death so that the crew wouldn't be able to pinpoint his position, the Executioner tugged the pin from a grenade and lobbed it toward the knot of men gathered near the wheelhouse.

"What the hell was that?"

"He's inside again."

"He can't be."

One of them thrust the muzzle of his AK-47 into the doorway just as the grenade exploded. For a moment the light created garish shadows that became new targets for the fear-ridden men.

Marino threw himself over the side of the hold, maintaining a grip abovedeck only long enough to plant his feet on the ladder that led into the bowels of the freighter. One of the men Bolan recognized from the yacht followed on his heels.

Abandoning his position, Bolan dropped soundlessly to the deck, moving in a crouch toward the hold, the MAC-10 clearing the way with short bursts. Then his feet were on the ladder as he stalked Marino.

The hallway leading through the hold was lighted by pale yellow bulbs. The air inside the hold reeked of fish, age and cramped quarters, generating a sourness that had permeated the wood and metal over the years.

Bolan catfooted across the empty floor of the hold, moving in on the hallway leading to the crew's quarters. Someone poked his head down from topside and the Executioner triggered a quick burst of 9 mm mindbombs. The body hit the wooden floor of the hold with a hollow thump of deadweight.

Movement farther down the short hallway sent Bolan spinning for cover only a heartbeat ahead of the chatter of an M-16. Chunks of wood flew from the wall near Bolan's head. When the initial firing abated, the Executioner dropped to one knee as he whirled around to face the hallway. The MAC-10 locked into target acquisition and Bolan caressed the trigger, the burst beginning at the exposed man's crotch and tracking all the way up to the guy's throat. The corpse jerked against the bulkhead, dropping to the floor in a wet heap.

Protected by the wall once more, Bolan switched magazines. How long would it be before someone discovered the man they were looking for had trapped himself in the hold of the ship? Grimly the warrior checked the remote control again, knowing he still held the trump card that would stalemate all of their efforts.

But the Executioner had never fought for a stalemate.

Bolan flicked a glance down the hallway. Where was Marino? Taking careful aim, he shot out the row of lights between the bunkroom and galley.

"McKay?"

Bolan recognized Marino's voice.

"McKay?"

"Yeah." Bolan tried to triangulate the man's position, but the sound distortion caused by the small hallway threw his hearing off.

"I knew it was you," Marino called. "I knew you were trouble when I saw you up close this afternoon. I should've killed you when I had the chance."

"It wouldn't have been any easier then, Marino."

"Who the hell are you working for?"

"Me."

The answer silenced the man for a moment.

Bolan studied the closed doors of the bunkroom and the galley. Which one? The lady or the tiger?

"I got a lot of money in this case, McKay."

"The way I figure it, that money's not going to stay in your possession anyway."

"You're a stupid son of a bitch if you think you can get away with this."

"I seem to be doing a hell of a job so far."

"You aren't off this ship yet, asshole."

"Are you always this charming when you're trying to cut a deal?"

Only silence responded to the question.

The Executioner stepped quietly into the hallway, head turned so that he could keep track of anyone who entered the hold. Trusting his other senses to protect him, Bolan concentrated on his hearing. Where was Marino? Which room would he choose to hide in? Behind the swing door of the galley or the latching one of the bunkroom?

Switching the MAC-10 to his left hand, Bolan pushed at the galley's door gently, watching it glide inward soundlessly. When no bullets shattered the door, he twisted inside, holding the machine pistol chest-high before him. Only the darkened bulk of cooking equipment, freezers and the hanging silhouettes of pots and pans greeted him. Nothing moved. There was no other way out.

The crew's quarters then, Bolan decided as he stepped over the dead man in the hallway.

The door was locked. For a moment Bolan wondered if Marino had left his man out to die in the hallway. It fit the image he'd generated of the man. Tight control and no personal relationships. No matter what the hired help thought.

Training the MAC-10 on the lock, he triggered two bursts to either side of the lock, splintering it from the door. He lifted a foot and kicked the door in. He was surprised when no muzzle-flashes lit the cabin. The smell of burnt cordite flushed the fish odor from Bolan's nose.

Edging around the door frame, expecting to see a muzzle-flash spray at him at any moment, Bolan peered into the cabin. The cramped crew's quarters held at least ten bunks, confirming Bolan's guess that the freighter was running top-heavy on deckhands. Sheets and blankets hung in disarray from the beds, creating a multitude of hiding places for someone calm enough to take advantage of the cover.

Letting the ugly little snout of the MAC-10 follow his scan of the room, Bolan moved forward, nerves hardwired to react instantly to any threat.

Something was wrong.

The warrior eased around the closest bunk, left hand sliding a hanging sheet away so that he could take in the entire cabin. The small area left between the bunk beds was empty. Marino was gone. He'd found another way out.

The guy had known about it when he went into the hold, and the spiel he'd given Bolan about the money had only been a delay. But a delay for what?

Bolan ripped a mattress from one of the bunks and removed a wooden slat, then jammed it against the door so it would at least serve to warn him if anyone else tried to enter the cabin. Only then did he turn the majority of his attention to discovering Marino's means of escape.

Evidently the smuggler had been in a big hurry to leave the bunkroom. Bolan found a small gap left by the sliding panel on the opposite wall. On the other side of the panel was a small passageway, leftover space between the inner and outer hulls.

Hollow thumping sounded on the door that led into the bunkroom, and Bolan knew he had been followed, leaving him no choice but to go on. After tugging the panel back into place, the Executioner marched forward into the darkness.

The lap of the ocean's waves was magnified inside the passageway. Bolan slung the MAC-10, pushing it behind him while he freed the more maneuverable Beretta. He knew that if he used a penlight he'd be an easy target for whatever forces must surely be waiting. Instead he staggered through the struts, his left arm feeling the way ahead of him, his right folded protectively across his chest.

The passageway ended abruptly.

The numbers had been falling on this play for too long now, and the Executioner could feel the last of them trickling through his fingers.

Mentally summoning the image of the freighter's skeleton, Bolan tried to figure out his location. He couldn't be sure how far he'd traveled through the passageway, but he had to be near the bow of the big ship, far enough away from the huge diesel engines that idled at a steady throb of raw horsepower. Far enough away, maybe, from the C-4 he'd planted outside on the ship's outer skin.

Bolan holstered the Beretta and secured his other weapons. He pressed the button on the remote detonator as more men poured anxiously into the cramped passageway.

A triple explosion rattled the insides of the freighter, and the ensuing shudder that passed through it shook Bolan as he held on to a metal strut for support. One of the diesels died, the silence that took its place weighing as heavily on the senses as the engine's constant chugging. A Klaxon started to blare, screaming a warning as shrilly as a banshee in heat. Another shudder passed through the freighter and the second diesel died.

Bolan felt the big ship listing to one side and realized the freighter would take only minutes to slip into the merciless sea. Already a few inches of water had gathered around Bolan's ankles, reminding him that if he didn't move he'd go down with the ship.

His hands found the short ladder leading to the overhead hatch, and the Executioner forced himself upward. With one hand ready to push against the hatch, Bolan was unprepared for the sudden reeling the freighter made as the sea reached for its wounded prize with a million greedy talons.

Bolan fell, slamming backward onto a strut with stunning force. The impact numbed his left shoulder, and his arm went limp. Gasping for breath, he fought against the rushing water that had already risen to his waist.

10

Chase Murphy forced his hand to unclench from the control stick and worked circulation back into his fingers. How long had it been? Long enough for McKay to have been killed, that was for sure.

He kept the small craft in a wide circle around the drop site, far enough away so the backwash of the rotors wouldn't be heard. Too far away to allow even binoculars to be of use.

His eyes moved mechanically as he read the information that the dials and gauges in front of him had to offer. It was just habit, though. Murphy knew the small helicopter inside and out. He'd rebuilt it three times himself. He and his father. The only gauge he ever really needed to be apprehensive about was the fuel gauge, but he'd topped the tanks off himself only a couple of hours before the flight.

The automatic was a clammy weight at his waist, a blunt reminder of what McKay had to be encountering at this very moment.

What would happen to him if McKay failed? Murphy asked himself as he pulled back slightly on the stick and gained more elevation. Marino already knew he was involved. If the drug runner survived, Chase Murphy would become an endangered species.

Could he live a life where he had to constantly look over his shoulder? Like McKay?

You're getting antsy, Murphy told himself. A few more minutes and you're going to start sounding like somebody's maiden aunt.

McKay would come through. The pilot had backed underdogs before, had gotten involved in problems that didn't belong to him. Hell, that was just Murphy's Flaw. Nothing new. This game was just for a few more marbles.

He reached overhead without looking for the cassette player, flipped the cassette over and hit the Play button. The familiar strains of Creedence Clearwater Revival pushed away some of the loneliness that seemed trapped in the cockpit with him.

Letting his left hand take the pull of the control stick, Murphy reached over to the passenger seat and stroked the heavy butt of the M-16 nestled there. It had been his father's rifle in Vietnam, the only companion the elder Murphy had had for almost two weeks when the Huey he'd been piloting was shot out from under him behind enemy lines. His father had always taken good care of the rifle, and Murphy had too. Until tonight he'd only thought of it as one of his father's prized possessions. Now it seemed more like a necessary piece of equipment.

Lost in memories of his father, Murphy didn't hear the complete broadcast over the radio the first time. He just caught enough of it to know that it was directed to him. Creedence Clearwater Revival was jamming through "Bad Moon Rising" when Murphy turned the volume up on the maritime radio.

"Identify yourself," an authoritative voice crackled over the speaker. "This is the Coast Guard."

Glancing overhead, Murphy found the lights of the large Coast Guard helicopter hovering against the star-filled sky. It was still too far away to make out the markings, but Murphy was willing to take them at their word. What the hell was the Coast Guard doing this far out tonight? he asked himself as he tipped the helicopter forward and shot out of the orbit he'd been maintaining.

After a moment's hesitation, the big helicopter nosed after him. The silence over the radio let Murphy know the men aboard the Coast Guard chopper weren't just cruising. Was it somebody Marino had bought off, he wondered, or the real McCoy? Either way it was going to be bad news.

And how the hell was he going to warn McKay?

Murphy moved the stick and felt the g-force push him back against the pilot's seat. His helicopter was smaller than the big monster that trailed him, more maneuverable in tight corners, slower in the long-distance hauls. And over the open Caribbean, there were no fancy tricks to pull that would hide him.

Dammit. Murphy pulled the stick again, tilting the helicopter over as he worked the pedals, heeling toward the yacht and the freighter anchored below.

"Put that helicopter down, mister," the Coast Guard officer ordered. "Otherwise we will shoot it down. This area is being contained by U.S. Drug Enforcement agents. You're being shut down."

Reaching overhead, Murphy snapped the radio off.

Where the hell was McKay?

Murphy was closing in on the freighter, and figures started becoming visible to him. Brief flickerings of light illuminated the deck of the ship, and it took the pilot's mind a moment to make the connection between them and gunfire.

"Shit," he breathed as he considered his position. If he kept on, he'd be within range of the small arms weapons on the freighter. If he tried to change directions now, the Coast Guard crew would probably try to shove a heat-seeking missile up his ass. It was a hell of a choice.

And another perfect example of Murphy's Flaw. He promised himself if he got out of this alive, he'd never involve himself in something that wasn't his business again. Knew at the same time, though, that he would renege at the first opportunity.

McKay, he told the night, you're a real son of a bitch.

Murphy swung the chopper into a course that would take him over the stern of the freighter. Son of a bitch or not, the young pilot knew he wasn't going to leave the big man alone. Not if he was still alive, and judging from the amount of gunfire aboard the ship, that was questionable.

He'd almost reached the freighter when he heard the bass booming of muffled explosions. Seawater roiled on both sides of the big ship and the yacht, spewing white cascades that pelted the Plexiglas bubble of the helicopter. As he passed over the freighter he saw tongues of flame lick from the stern, reaching for the sky with a vigor that let the pilot know the ship would burn in minutes.

If it didn't sink first, he amended as he watched it list violently.

THE WATER in the passageway had risen to Bolan's shoulders before he was able to secure a hold on the ladder again. The sea's solid strength batted him around in the enclosed area like a child's toy.

Gritting his teeth against the shooting fire in his shoulder, Bolan forced himself up the pipe-formed steps. His feet felt treacherous under his weight and slipped repeatedly, causing him to scrape his shin against the rough metal. But it was a lesser pain, easier to ignore than the shoulder.

At the top of the ladder he hooked his injured arm around a strut, willing it to hold the position as his right hand searched for the closed hatch. He pushed against it but nothing happened.

Had Marino locked it? Bolan asked himself as he felt for a locking mechanism. Or had the explosions wedged it? Already the water had risen to his chin, leaving only precious inches of breathing space.

From the angle of the water, Bolan judged that the freighter was going down stern first. It was too far to try to swim back to the hold; too far and too hard to navigate between the struts with his injured shoulder.

The freighter shook again, resettled into the depths as it rolled once more. Without warning the hatch over Bolan's head popped open.

Unhooking the injured arm, Bolan pushed himself onto deck. He had to scrabble for his balance, operating more or less one-handedly against the thirty-plus degree tilt of the freighter.

The exit opened up near the bow of the freighter, near the railing and partially hidden by coils of rope. At one time Bolan was sure it had been designed to fit precisely in the planking of the deck, rendered so it couldn't be noticed even under close inspection. Now the force of the explosion had warped the frame.

When some of the feeling had returned to his fingers he brought around the MAC-10, leaving it on its sling as he looked around the deck for survivors. Occasional yells cut through the groaning of the freighter as it continued to sink.

Bolan looked for Marino, marching aft through the rising waters that now swirled at his ankles, submerging the wooden deck. By the time he reached the exploded wheelhouse, the water reached his thighs. A body floated into him, the sightless eyes peering up at a night they would never see again.

The beams of bright searchlights lanced the deck just as Bolan was about to push the body away. The sound of a helicopter's blades beat the air above the dying ship.

Murphy? Bolan wondered as he fitted himself into the darkness of the wheelhouse. Then he remembered Murphy's helicopter hadn't been set up for searchlights as powerful as these. Who then? He raised the MAC-10 as the pain from his arm created cotton in his brain, making it hard to think.

The helicopter floated sedately into view, too big to belong to Murphy. Twin searchlights, mounted fore and aft, played over the deck of the freighter.

"This is the Coast Guard, working in conjunction with local U.S. Drug Enforcement agents," a loudspeaker announced. "You will throw down your weapons now and give yourself up to our custody."

Bolan tightened his grip on the Ingram. A figure broke from the boom arm, running through the water toward the wheelhouse. Someone on the helicopter moved the searchlight over him, washing the color from the guy until he looked like a gray phantom.

The man held an AK-47, pointed straight out beneath the thick handlebar mustache that covered his upper lip. When he saw Bolan, his eyes widened and he loosed a burst.

The bullets drummed into the wood near the Executioner's head only heartbeats before the MAC-10 sent the guy spinning over backward to disappear under the rising water.

Shouts came from the bow of the deck, on the other side of the cabin. Bolan glanced through the shattered windows and saw a handful of men standing waist-deep in the water with their hands on their heads. None of them was Marino.

The searchlight pulled away and spotlighted the men waiting to give themselves up, giving Bolan the chance to leave the freighter unnoticed. Shooting pains ripped through his injured shoulder as the Executioner dived into the water.

He swam unhurriedly, striving for distance and not speed, knowing the Coast Guard helicopter would be occupied for some time with rescuing their prisoners. The sea was chill about him but it was a welcome relief, as it helped to abate the discordant throb in his shoulder.

He felt the postbattle fatigue soak into him as he watched the orange-and-yellow flames that devoured the freighter. Some of the fire had spread across the water as the fuel from the ruptured engines flowed into the sea and ignited. The Coast Guard helicopter hung like a great white shark over the inferno. The yacht was a burning skeleton next to the transport ship, flaming down to its own ashes.

The warrior moved his legs mechanically, trying to get away from the burning wrecks. He realized the Coast Guard would have called in a backup by now and would be doing a systematic search for any survivors. Then a different throb echoed overhead, a smaller rendition of the whirling rotors of the Coast Guard gunship.

Bolan searched the night sky for the helicopter. He didn't doubt that he could survive at sea for hours if he had to, but escaping detection was a different problem. Then, outlined by the faint moonlight behind it, Bolan saw Murphy's helicopter. He reached for the flare clipped at his belt, then broke it open and threw it back toward the freighter. It would be a race, he knew, between the young pilot and the men of the Coast Guard and DEA. Bolan was betting on Murphy's skills. Betting his life.

A green glow shot up from the flare as something bumped into Bolan's legs under the water. Before he had a chance to react, he was dragged under, seeing the stars overhead as dulled pinpoints as more and more water separated him from the surface.

Bolan twisted, cleaving through the water to reach for his adversary. Already his lungs felt constricted, and he had to fight to keep from drawing a breath.

A man's hands, Bolan realized as his fingers clenched around a powerful wrist. The guy had to have been hiding under the deck section, waiting quietly for this moment after he recognized Bolan.

The warrior yanked on the fingers, prying one hand loose. Suddenly another man swam down from the surface to circle his arm around the Executioner's neck. Realizing he didn't have much time before the lack of oxygen caused him to black out, Bolan pulled one of the knives sheathed on his legs and raked the blade across the knuckles of the hand still holding his feet.

The man let go, still invisible in the dark. Bolan felt sure his opponent would head for the surface to find out how badly he was hurt. Wrenching his body around despite the sharp incisors of pain in his shoulder, Bolan grabbed a handful of his second attacker's pants, pulling the guy into a more accessible position.

The razor-sharp combat knife sank easily in the man's abdomen. Bolan felt the hands release his neck but maintained his hold, forcing the knife up through the abdomen and sternum. Something warm and soft touched Bolan's face then squirmed away as the man jerked out his life in the Executioner's grasp. Bubbles erupted from the man's mouth, a scream that would never be heard.

He released the body to float upward, but forced himself to stay under longer. Black spots appeared in the limited vision he had. Where was the other man? The cut had been enough to discourage but not to incapacitate. The guy was waiting somewhere. Bolan knew it. He tightened his grip on the knife.

Murphy wold be landing within seconds. The Coast Guard people were probably approaching the flare, wondering who had set it off. The men aboard the gunship had seen enough to shoot first and ask questions later.

As he surfaced, Bolan heard the steady throb of a helicopter's rotors. A series of concentric circles fanned out from the dark bulk of the pontoons and from the wind of the whirling blades.

The warrior shook the water from his eyes and sucked in deep breaths as he got his bearings. Murphy had landed only a few yards away and was leaning out of the chopper; the flames were still burning on the freighter; the yacht was nowhere to be seen; the Coast Guard helicopter was moving in their direction.

When Bolan looked back at the young pilot he saw his underwater attacker throw an arm over one of the pontoons then pull a pistol from a shoulder rig.

Before Bolan could yell a warning, the man pulled himself farther onto the pontoon, leveling his arm out as he pulled the trigger on the pistol.

The report sounded harsh, flat and final. Murphy flipped back inside the cockpit as Bolan reached for the Desert Eagle.

11

The .44 bucked in Bolan's fist. A 240-grain boattail skated inches above the surface of the Caribbean as the warrior felt misty saltwater sear his eyes. The recoil pushed him back in the water and the muzzle-flash left his vision spotted. He brought the barrel of the powerful Magnum back in line, searching for his target as he tried to stay afloat.

His enemy floundered near the pontoon, holding on to it with one hand. The second round from the Desert Eagle ripped him from the pontoon.

Bolan swam toward the helicopter, breaking through the small waves generated by the turning rotors. As he laid a free hand on the pontoon Marino's man had been using for support, a square object floated toward him, which he recognized as the briefcase Marino had been carrying.

The bright beam of a searchlight covered the water and helicopter in front of Bolan, urging him into motion.

"Murphy!" Bolan called as he grabbed the briefcase and stroked to the cockpit. He pulled himself aboard after shoving the briefcase inside.

The spinning rotors overhead drowned out sound, but the searchlight bounced over the interior of the chopper, reminding Bolan how close the Coast Guard craft was.

"Get your butt in here." Murphy's voice sounded disjointed, faraway.

Bolan scrambled to his feet and went forward, listening to the scream of the engines increase. The helicopter shook and shimmied around him.

Chase Murphy sat in the pilot's seat, his hand clutched his side, just below the ribs.

"How bad is it?" Bolan asked as he took the other seat.

"I'll live. Did you get the bastard who shot me?"

"Yeah."

Murphy nodded as he closed his free hand around the stick. "Figured you would. That's why I came in here. The goddamn G-men aren't going to give us much breathing space tonight."

"I noticed." Bolan looked over his shoulder. The Coast Guard chopper was only a few yards away now, bearing down on them like a giant dragonfly. "Can you fly?"

"Damn right I can." A sheen of perspiration covered the pilot's upper lip and the green eyes looked wild.

"I've piloted choppers before," Bolan offered.

Murphy looked at him and grinned. "Somehow that doesn't surprise me, McKay. But you hired me for the round-trip, and I always hold up my end of the contract. Besides, those guys back there aren't going to let us just waltz out of here, and you don't know this area the way I do."

The small helicopter leaped into the air at Murphy's touch, snarling under the bigger Coast Guard craft by only a few feet, banking back the other way.

Bolan noted the blood soaking into the material of Murphy's shirt, oozing between the young pilot's fingers. He kept his mouth shut. Murphy would raise the same objections Bolan had voiced earlier when the younger man had tried to dissuade the Executioner from attempting the strike on the freighter.

The Coast Guard pilot was good, but Murphy was better. The young pilot made the helicopter dance, climbing through the night skies or skimming the waves of the Caribbean. The chopper became a living thing in Murphy's hand, a grasshopper that winged its way unerringly toward the shoreline of Key West.

Murphy held the edge when it came to maneuverability. Every time the Coast Guard flyer tried to close the distance between them, Murphy branched off on a tangent.

The searchlight licked over them again, splashing off the interior of the helicopter briefly before bouncing away. Bolan craned his neck and saw the big-bodied Coast Guard craft barrel behind them as the pilot tried to force them down.

"You ever play 'chicken' before?" Murphy yelled over the roar of the straining engines.

"Yeah." Bolan noticed the small, tight smile the younger man wore.

Without warning, Murphy powered the chopper into a straight line, heading for a hill, skimming the tops of the trees. Bolan looked behind them and found the Coast Guard gunship closing the distance. Brief flickerings from the portside of the pursuing chopper told him someone on board had opened fire. The blacksuit felt cold around him as he waited for the tracers to zero in on Murphy's craft.

The helicopter waggled slightly under Murphy's control, still screaming straight for the approaching hill. Bolan scanned their target as it rushed at them, noting for the first time how much it towered above their present altitude. The gunner on the Coast Guard helicopter stopped firing, as if he'd just realized they were on a collision course with the land mass in front of them.

"This is where it gets hairy," Murphy said grimly.

The pilot of the pursuit chopper had already started nosing up for more airspace, as though assuming Murphy's craft wouldn't make it.

At the last moment, Murphy worked the stick, throwing his helicopter into an altitude-eating climb that took them up and back from the mountain.

Bolan felt the press of the suddenly increased g-force, then an almost sickening weightlessness as Murphy maneuvered his chopper behind the Coast Guard craft. Before the pilot had the chance to react, Murphy had reversed direction and shot back the way they'd come.

"Thermals," Murphy said as he slotted the helicopter only yards above a two-lane highway and followed the road. "You get more lift if you're in a plane, none at all if you're in a helicopter that size. And just enough if you're in this baby."

Bolan nodded, grinning to himself in the darkness of the cockpit. He'd flown with Grimaldi countless times into other missions, and Jack's abilities with anything that flew never ceased to amaze him. Yet he figured Grimaldi would have been proud of the maneuver Murphy had just pulled off. "Now what?"

"Now we hide. There are a lot of roads through here. By the time that pilot gets his bird turned around, we should be lost."

"I need a place to chill out for a few hours," Bolan said. "I have a friend who can process what little information I got tonight and maybe turn it into something worthwhile."

"Marino wasn't the end of it?"

"No. I can't even confirm he's out of it."

"Where does it end for you?"

"It doesn't. But for this operation maybe with the next name I turn up. If he's the guy who's supplying the cocaine."

"How the hell did you get a job like yours, McKay."

"I'm an all-volunteer army, kid."

Murphy was silent as he moved the helicopter onto a side road. A convertible screeched below them as the driver locked the brakes.

"You're really not backed by anyone?"

"That's a long story, Murphy. Let's just say that sometimes I'm not and sometimes I am. Sometimes I even stay backed."

"And if you go down?"

"I go down alone," Bolan said simply. He looked the young pilot in the eye. "But I knew that when I got into this."

Murphy nodded. "I got a friend who'll put us up for a couple of days and run interference for us with the local cops."

"The DEA's going to be involved in this too."

"You don't know Drake. He thrives on shit like this. If somebody even mentions unfailing bureaucracy around him, they're in for a fight. He's got enough lawyers on retainer that by the time all the introductions are made, you'll be safely on your way."

"What about you?"

"They got to prove I was there tonight. And I sure as hell am not going to confess. As far as anyone knows, this helicopter doesn't even exist. It's not listed anywhere, and the warehouse we'll be leaving it in tonight was abandoned a long time ago. If the cops find it, I lose some elbow grease and some sweat, but they can't tie me to it. I use it to do a few favors for friends who don't always have recourse to legal help. When I want to go incognito. Like you, I've seen times when the system didn't work."

Bolan didn't pursue the line of inquiry, thinking there was more to the young pilot than he'd first guessed. He studied the crimson-drenched shirt and Murphy's fingers, noticing how the pilot kept the blood absorbed by the material so it wouldn't drop into the seat. Professional, he thought, and wondered to what extent Murphy's "favors" had gone. He was no stranger to violence and knew what to expect of himself and his equipment.

"How's the side?"

"It gave up hurting a few miles back. Drake will get a doctor, and I've already got a story in mind that will help a guy get what's coming to him. That son of a bitch ruined me for low-cut bathing suits though."

"DO YOU THINK Mike's okay, Mom?"

Abby Nichols looked at her son and tousled his dark hair. He'd come to sit by her on the bed in their hotel room while she'd been lost in thought, thinking of Bill. God, it had been two days now, and she still couldn't believe it.

Not Bill. He'd been the youngest of them. The one whose life had always seemed touched by sunshine and happiness. Twenty-six years old.

"The police said he wasn't in his room," she told him. "I'm sure he's all right."

"Why would somebody try to kill him?" Jase asked as he looked up at her.

It hurt her to see the innocence in his eyes. The same innocence that would gradually be erased by all the questions he asked. "The policeman I talked to seemed to think he was a bad man, Jase."

"Mike wouldn't have done anything bad," the boy replied. "He was a war hero in Vietnam."

"Did he tell you that?"

"No. I mean, he told me he was in Vietnam. But he didn't talk about the war. I kind of figured that out on my own. You know, the way you sometimes look at people and try to guess things about them for your stories."

"That's just a writer's trick," Abby said, smiling. "I'm not always right about those people. I just try to fit what I'm thinking into the story."

"I know, Mom," Jase said patiently. "But Mike is real. If you'd had the time to meet him, you'd understand. He's a good guy. These cops just don't know that."

Abby just nodded and kept her arguments to herself. Hero worship was the last bastion of childhood. From cartoons and comics to wrestlers and sports figures, then graduating to close friends over the years. Even to marriages, she reminded herself. It had taken her divorce and the evidence of her husband's infidelity to shatter that for her. She'd placed so much trust in him. Even then she had been willing to forgive him, willing to take him back if he would give up his new mistress. And she didn't really hate Greg Nichols until he stopped seeing their son. Sure, the support checks kept coming regularly, but Jase didn't understand his father's loss of feelings about him and it took a long time for her son to reach a place where he could deal with them. Then, eighteen months ago, she finally sold her first novel and was contracted for two more through the help of a very aggressive agent.

Everything seemed so idyllic. Until she had received the news about her brother on Tuesday.

Someone knocked on the hotel room door and Abby felt a chill scratch down her spine, knowing Jase had felt her involuntarily tighten up.

Leaving Jase on the bed, Abby made sure her nightgown covered her and went to answer the door. "Who is it?"

"Police, ma'am. We've got a few questions we'd like to ask you and your son."

Abby peeked through the peephole and saw three men standing in the hallway. Richardson was one of them. She looked at her watch and found that it was a little after eleven. The police had already spent hours investigating the room down the hall, what could they want now?

"Couldn't this wait until morning? My son and I were just going to bed."

"I'd really appreciate it if you could talk to us now, Ms Nichols. There have been some other developments since this evening's shooting. We need whatever information you and your son can give us."

Abby opened the door reluctantly and let them enter.

Richardson was the youngest of the three. Abby had earlier estimated his age to be almost thirty. His dirty-blond hair looked even more unruly than it had before.

"I'm Harry Preston, Ms Nichols." He held out his hand and Abby took it. He was a big man, with the square shoulders of a former athlete. Probably football, Abby told herself, then became frustrated at her irritating habit of trying to see through people.

"This is Peter Vincent," Preston introduced the third man.

Vincent inclined his head but didn't offer his hand. Abby thought he held himself aloof and couldn't help noticing the way the man swept through the room with his eyes, as if she'd been trying to hide something. Or someone.

Richardson shut the door.

"What can I do for you gentlemen?" Abby asked as she resumed her seat on the bed. Jase snuggled close to her, as if to remind her she wasn't alone.

Richardson leaned against the door, content to let the two new men handle the questioning. Vincent walked to the window and peered out. His stare as he passed told Abby he was stripping her naked in his mind, and it made her feel dirty.

Preston took a chair from the desk against the wall and seated himself. He gave Jase an easy grin, then reached inside his jacket and pulled a wallet out. The quick glimpse Abby had of the massive handgun tucked under the man's arm was more than enough to increase her fears. Preston opened the wallet and showed her his ID.

"I'm with the Drug Enforcement Administration, ma'am," Preston said, "as is Mr. Vincent. We think McKay, the man down the hall, might have been involved in an incident at sea tonight. A lot of people were killed."

"What makes you think McKay was involved?" Abby asked.

"The men we found in his room earlier were working for a man named Ruffino Marino, a local in Key West. Marino was also skipper of the *Lady's Desire*, a yacht that was blown up less than an hour ago. We believe McKay was behind that attack as well."

Abby felt her son's arms slide around her waist. "You're saying McKay attacked those men inside his own room?" She couldn't name the urge that made her counterquestion the DEA man's statement. Maybe it was because Jase believed in McKay's innocence so much. Or maybe it was her own rebellious feelings toward authority. Bill had been murdered two days ago and the whole process of getting him home, or finding out who had murdered him and why seemed to be lost behind miles of red tape.

"Look, lady," Vincent said from the window, "we're here to ask the questions, not you."

Abby gazed coolly over her shoulder, kept the anger from her voice as she spoke. "Maybe you'd like to take your questions up with my lawyer."

Vincent spun around and took a step forward. "The man you're protecting is a killer. Tonight alone he's racked up over twenty guys, and no telling how many over the past few days. You'll answer any goddamn question we ask you, or I'll see to it that you're booked on withholding information."

"Vincent." Preston's firm voice cut through the room like a scythe.

Vincent turned his attack on the other DEA man. "Look, Preston, this is my turf. You're just a visitor here. You can handle your investigations in Georgia any goddamned way you want to, but you're not going to fuck me over. You got that?"

Preston moved without warning. One moment he was sitting relaxed in the chair, the next he had Vincent pinned up against the wall—one hand on Vincent's neck, the other to stop him from reaching under his jacket.

"Go wait in the hall, Peter," Preston said in a voice filled with quiet control, "and you won't say another word to me or Ms Nichols."

Vincent sent Abby a withering glance and started to say something, but Preston closed one broad hand on his neck.

"Not one word."

Vincent started to struggle again, but he was helpless in the bigger man's grip.

Preston held his captive against the wall, seemingly without effort. His features were composed, serene, Abby thought, as if he did this kind of thing every day. And considering Preston's job, maybe he did.

"I've only been here one day," Preston told Vincent in a whisper that barely betrayed a Southern accent, "and I already have a lot of questions I want to ask you about the way you handle DEA business around here. If I don't get the chance to ask them, I'm going to see to it that someone does.''

Vincent relaxed and nodded.

Without turning, Preston said, ''Don, escort Agent Vincent to the hallway for me and make sure he doesn't reenter this room.'' Then he released the man and stepped away as Richardson moved into position.

Abby could feel the tension between the trio. Vincent left without another word. Richardson followed and shut the door behind them.

Preston loosened his tie, looked at Abby and asked, ''Do you mind if I open the window?''

Abby shook her head.

He raised the window and let the wind rolling over the nighttime panorama of Key West blow gently into the room. The DEA man leaned against the wall next to the open window, sticking his hands in his pockets. A sheepish grin crossed his face. ''That wasn't quite professional.''

''I meant what I said about the lawyer,'' Abby said with an edge to her voice. ''I'm not going to have my privacy invaded or subject my son to this kind of violence.''

Preston nodded. His voice was soft, the accent more pronounced when he spoke, and he sounded tired. ''Believe me, Ms Nichols, I don't think any of us thought it would reach that point.''

''Especially that guy Vincent,'' Jase said as he pushed himself away from Abby. ''He was going to try to shoot you. I saw him reaching for his gun.''

A more somber look filled Preston's broad face. ''I don't think so, Jase. I think he was just reacting without thinking. The way you sometimes do when you get mad.''

''Yeah,'' Jase went on, ''but I don't like him. I don't think Mike liked him either.''

''You've seen Vincent before tonight?'' Preston asked quickly.

Jase nodded. "Mike saw him too. This Vincent guy was spying on Mike when we were down in the restaurant, and Mike knew it."

"Jase, that's enough," Abby said when she noticed the interest that gleamed in Preston's eyes. She didn't want to be detained in Key West any longer than she had to be. Richardson had helped push things along this far, even to arranging a flight for her tomorrow. But it was the first of several hops because there were no seats on a direct flight.

"Ms Nichols, I really appreciate your position in all of this. I believe you were just caught up in a series of circumstances you had no control over. But, on another hand, I have a job to do. I started following McKay, or whatever his name is, as part of an investigation in Atlanta, Georgia. He's left a highly visible trail behind him that leads here. I don't know for sure who he is or what he's doing, but he's tracking a large drug operation that extends up and down the Eastern Seaboard to somewhere in the Caribbean. Maybe as far away as Colombia."

"Is this Ruffino Marino a part of this drug operation?" Abby asked.

"We think so," Preston replied. "We were on board a Coast Guard helicopter tonight searching for Marino's yacht, when it blew up in our faces." The DEA man flicked a glance in Jase's direction. "Sorry."

"It sounds like McKay is doing your job for you," Abby said. "If he was involved."

"I don't believe in vigilantes. I've given almost half my life to law enforcement. I'm not going to believe we've achieved nothing."

"Yet the wheels of justice turn slowly."

Preston nodded grudgingly. "Sometimes, but largely because of the safeguards built into the system that protect the innocent."

"Except for the innocent who are dead." She thought of Bill, lying cold and still in a morgue a thousand miles away.

"Your brother?" Preston asked.

"Yes."

"Richardson told me about that. I'm sorry."

They were interrupted by a knock on the door.

Abby was aware of the small movement Preston made toward the gun under his arm. "Who is it?" she asked.

"Richardson."

"Come in."

Richardson opened the door enough to stick his head inside. He nodded to Abby then moved his attention to Preston. "Vincent split."

"Did he say anything?"

"No."

"Get somebody on him. The boy just told me Vincent was watching him and McKay only a few minutes before the hotel room was hit."

"Terrific."

"Yeah."

"You already had it figured that way, though, didn't you?"

"Yeah. I'll cover him myself."

"Only until you can get someone else to take over. If he *is* tied into this thing, Vincent is going to start burning bridges anytime."

Abby watched Preston rub his eyes wearily. She could almost sense the big man's thoughts as he closed the window and shut the draperies. She had heard that a sniper had tried to shoot McKay, as well as the two men who broke into the room.

"Could we start over, Ms Nichols?" Preston asked. "I don't know if you or your son have any information I can use on this thing, but I'd like to ask both of you a few questions just the same. Jase has already helped nail down one theory I was working on."

Jase tugged at Abby's hand. She looked down into her son's eyes. "Let him ask, Mom. Maybe he can help Mike. After this guy figures out him and Mike are on the same sides."

"All right." Abby relented, hoping she was making the right decision.

Preston started with Jase first, and she had to admire how he did his job. The DEA man asked one question after another, spinning from one tangent to the next, dropping back occasionally to ask the same question in different words, gradually building a net of information that had been thoroughly cross-referenced. But there was little information Jase had to offer. That the boy had liked McKay was readily apparent.

Abby had even less information to add to the small hoard Preston gathered. The most salient fact was Vincent's involvement.

When he finished, Preston folded his small notebook and slipped it into a jacket pocket.

"Those men attacked McKay in his room. Isn't that true?"

"That's what we think happened," Preston admitted.

"Then it was self-defense."

"Not necessarily. As I said, I've been following this case from Atlanta. If McKay is the same man, his presence here wasn't innocent. He would have expected an attack. Did expect to be attacked," Preston amended. "He didn't kill those two men with a nail file. He used a gun, a very big gun."

"And it doesn't matter if those men were criminals?"

"To paraphrase an old worker in your profession, Ms Nichols—a vigilante by any other name is still a vigilante."

Abby remembered the small wave McKay had given her in the restaurant when Richardson left the table to go upstairs. Remembered, too, the sad, inquisitive smile that had been on the big man's face.

"Tell me," Abby said as Preston walked toward the door to let himself out. "If McKay is the one you have been following, and if he's the one who's been wreaking havoc with the drug operation you've been investigating, why is he finding it so easy to track these men down? If your investigation is so thorough and so involved, why hasn't the Drug Enforcement Administration been able to arrest them?''

"Laws were made by the larger whole, Ms Nichols. I follow them because they do work, even if they do so slowly. Until the larger whole decides these laws don't work and something else needs to be done, I'll continue to operate in the prescribed manner. It's what separates us from the beasts. I'm sure a writer came up with that as well.''

"What will you do with McKay if you find him?''

"It depends a lot on what he's willing to let us do. You never know with these types. Whatever has set him off on this violent roller coaster of revenge could make him snap at anytime.''

"Yet he seems to have made big strides.''

"Yes. Which makes me think this guy has given a lot of thought to what he's doing now. Richardson told me you're leaving tomorrow.''

"To identify my brother's body so it can be shipped back to the States.''

"Chances are you won't see McKay again, but you need to keep one thing in mind if you do. The man is dangerous, not really in his right mind. He could do anything. You're very lucky the men who tried the hit on McKay didn't move in on him while you were still in the hallway with your boy.''

A chill chased itself down Abby's spine at the thought of that. It had only been scant minutes after they'd gone to meet with Richardson in the downstairs restaurant that the violence in McKay's room had erupted.

She gazed at Jase, lying so peacefully in her lap. God, she couldn't lose him. Not now. Not ever.

"If you see him again,'' Preston advised, "stay away from him. Keep Jase away from him.''

Abby ran her fingers through her son's hair and nodded as the agent let himself out.

BOLAN PRESSED the receiver tightly to his right ear and covered his left with his palm. Even back in Bobby Drake's bedroom, the noise from the party made talking impossible.

He had reached Brognola at home, and the big Fed had put him on hold until he could take the call in the den and not disturb his wife.

"Where the hell are you, Striker?" Brognola asked gruffly when he picked up the extension. His voice was low and sleep-filled, making it even harder for Bolan to understand him.

"You wouldn't believe it if I told you, Hal."

"Still in your previous vicinity?"

"Yeah."

"So how goes the war?" Brognola meant the question as light banter, but Bolan knew the real emotion behind the big Fed's words was worry.

"Hot and heavy. Picked up a few more players since we last talked. I retired a few of them tonight, but I'm still trying to find home plate and the ball is in the air."

"I've been picking up some hot flashes on this end too. It's been hard, since I'm supposed to be out of it now. A hard-nosed DEA cop named Harry Preston tried to get to me to find out what happened to the Justice agent I authorized down there a few days ago. I never talked to him directly, but I let it be known that a certain Michael Blanski had been pulled for duty in another spot and that they would have to continue on their own. The way I get it, Preston seems to think I let the fox into the henhouse with the way certain facets of the drug operation have been talking about a nightfighter dressed all in black."

A girl's raucous scream of primitive glee echoed the length of the boat.

"That," Brognola said, "tells my keen, deductive brain that you've got to be at a party."

"You know me Hal, a regular party animal."

The scream sounded again and Bolan shifted, trying to turn away from the noise. He sat down on the floor beside the massive water bed.

"Must be some party," Brognola growled.

"You'd have to see it. How much heat are you getting?"

"I can handle my end, Striker. Justice has been scoring some pretty big cases lately. With the help of a certain, unnameable person. And the President is backing you fully. There's not a department around that's not busy with housecleaning of its own. Preston has already gone his merry way. If you get access to a computer port, I'll have Kurtzman fax you some intel on the guy so you won't be tripping over each other."

"I can receive it here." Bolan read off Drake's phone number. The ex-reporter had given Bolan the go-ahead when he got back with Murphy. The young pilot had passed out shortly after landing the helicopter, and Bolan had had to carry him to the houseboat from the car.

"How secure is that line?" Hal asked.

"Tight. Tell Bear we even got a satellite hookup on this one. This guy buys satellite time on a shares program." Bolan gave him the coordinates.

"Who are you with, Striker?"

Bolan told him Drake's name.

"I thought he was dead."

A bass guitar boomed loudly through the frame of the houseboat.

"The dead couldn't sleep around here. I need some intel on a freighter I hit tonight. I want to find out where it came from. Following it home is definitely out."

The warrior pictured the freighter in his mind, made a spatial hologram and turned it until he had the ship's numbers in memoryview. He dictated them precisely to Brognola.

"It's going to take some time," the big Fed told him when he finished. "Even the Bear can't pull freighters out of a hat."

"I have a feeling that finding a home for this one is going to be like looking for a needle in a haystack," Bolan admitted. "I'd also be willing to bet that a drug operation isn't all these people are involved with." He told Brognola about the large crew and the overabundance of AK-47s he'd seen.

"I'll have Kurtzman on it as soon as I get off the phone."

"I'm going to sack out here for a few hours, Hal, so you can reach me anytime. Drake has an impressive network here, and I need a safe port for a little while. Too many people seem to know I'm here. Good guys and bad. Once I'm out of Key West, see if you can send the word out that Marino hasn't shown up yet. He didn't turn up on a positive body count tonight. I don't like leaving loose ends, but I've got to move on this one before all the traces are pulled in."

Brognola grunted an affirmative and broke the connection.

After cradling the receiver, Bolan massaged his shoulder. Drake's physician had looked at it and said there'd been some bruising and muscle damage, but nothing that a few days' rest wouldn't take care of. He also suggested the warrior wear a sling. Bolan wished he had the few days.

He sat in the darkness, cross-legged and barefooted, still clothed in the blacksuit because Drake didn't have any clothing his size. Already the operation had taken turns he hadn't expected, reached a lot farther than he had guessed. The Key West connection, yeah, that hadn't really been much of a surprise. But how far did the pipeline really travel? Maybe Kurtzman's computers could tell him that. Bolan was fresh out of leads in Key West.

Bolan pushed himself to his feet and walked back down the hall to the cabin where Murphy lay. The pilot was awake when he walked in.

"How are you doing?" Bolan asked.

"I've been better. Isn't there some water around here?"

Bolan lifted Murphy's head so he could get a drink from the Styrofoam cup that the warrior held to his lips.

"I noticed I got bandages now. I guess the doc's been here."

Bolan nodded. "About an hour ago. Drake wanted to wean some of the guests away before you stage your big scene. Less hassle that way when the police start interviewing."

"Makes sense."

"You're also in charge of a briefcase I recovered from Marino's man. I didn't do a count on it, but it looks like there's over a million dollars in there. I figured you'd know what to do with it."

"Yeah. There's a few people near here who've been caught in the budget crunch a few times. And I know a couple other places where donations would be welcome."

"Your cut comes out of there too, for your charter services. And don't forget you're going to have medical expenses."

"What did the doc have to say?"

"The bullet went through without any major organ damage. Your system just went into shock with the blood loss."

Drake opened the door. "The local heat is on the way, and I have our prisoner ready to enter stage right. You guys can talk later." He pointed at Bolan. "You need to get the hell out of sight. From what I've been able to put together from my police contacts, there's a DEA agent with them who's real interested in you."

"Did you happen to get a name on this DEA guy?"

Drake slid his sunglasses farther up the bridge of his nose. "You know a guy named Harry Preston?"

Bolan nodded. "I've heard of him," he said, wondering if the man had any solid evidence that had led him here, or if he was just feeling out the situation. Cop work or coincidence? Either way, the running room the Executioner had figured for himself had grown noticeably smaller, turning him from the hunter to the hunted.

12

"Yuri?"

The quiet unease in Natasha's voice drew Yuri's attention immediately. He saw the uncertainty etched in her face when he looked at her reflection in the mirror above the bathroom sink. "What is it, Tasha?" he asked as he rinsed his razor.

"A man is here to see you. A very old man."

Kirov, Yuri thought as he patted his face dry on a towel. What the hell was the man doing, coming to his home? He tried to mask his feelings, knowing Natasha would probably sense them anyway.

He turned to find her standing in the doorway, arms wrapped around her chest as if she were cold. She still wore the black nightgown but had thrown her robe over it.

"Is there anyone with him?" Yuri asked as he stepped into his pants.

She shook her head. "He's alone."

"Why didn't you come to me before you let him in?"

"Because he looked so old, so harmless. I thought at first he only wanted directions, but he told me he was here to wait for you, and I couldn't just shut the door in his face. It was only after he was inside that I felt the coldness that hides behind his smile. Who is he, Yuri?"

"We're working together for a while, love. There's nothing to be concerned about. In a few days he'll go back to enjoying his retirement." Yuri wished he felt as confident as he tried to sound. But after last night's dreams and restlessness, and the computer tap, he felt more and more like he was standing on the edge of an abyss. He wished he knew whether Kirov was going to push him over.

Little Tanya's screams of delight came from the other room, and Yuri heard Kirov's voice, too low to be understood.

"Tanya seems to find him entertaining," Yuri observed as he put his shoes on. He debated putting on the shoulder holster, wanting to for the security it offered. But Kirov would notice he was sitting at his own breakfast table armed, and would perhaps construe that as a threat. Never before had his work come so close to his home life.

A longing filled him as he looked at his wife, and he reached out for her without conscious thought. Pulling her close, he held her for a moment, feeling the soft roundness of her body, breathing in her perfume.

Natasha pushed out of his embrace. "Yuri, please. We have company. And Tanya is awake."

Yuri grinned at her, pleased that he had made her forget the grim foreboding Kirov's unexpected presence had brought. He followed her to the small kitchen where breakfast was already in the midst of being prepared. Kirov had ensconced himself in a chair near the living-room window where, Yuri noted quickly, he had a clear view of the front of the small house. Little Tanya sat on Kirov's foot, waiting impatiently to be bounced. Natasha had fixed the little girl's hair in dog ears this morning, and the twin strands stood out from her head like small horns. And she wore a simple dress that was hiked up over her diaper.

"You're a very lucky man, young Mikhailin," Kirov said as he took Tanya's small hands in his own. "You have a very beautiful wife and a happy child. I only hope you realize how lucky you truly are."

Tanya jumped up and down and squealed for attention. She clapped her hands and gave Kirov the angry look that always drew laughter from Yuri, drawing her fiery eyebrows together until they almost touched.

Yuri felt the coldness Natasha had spoken of as he watched Kirov play with his daughter. It was an innate thing. Yuri was unsure if the old man knew it existed, tightly coiled inside the aged body like a poisonous viper.

Will it be like that for me as well? Yuri wondered as he helped Natasha set the table for breakfast. Was Kirov the end result of a life of service in the KGB? Had the seeds already been sown inside him? Would there be any room inside left over for his daughter and his wife if that happened? Yuri asked himself. For the other unborn child?

As he studied Kirov, Yuri wanted to ask the old man what had happened to his family, to the son Petrovsky had mentioned. Then he wondered what made him so sure Kirov lived alone now. But asking wasn't part of being a Russian, he had to remind himself. Those questions, those feelings, were part of the Scott Josephs identity he had assumed while living in Berkeley.

"Have you eaten, Comrade?" Yuri asked. It surprised him that he didn't know how to address the old man. To call him Boris felt too daring. Yet addressing him by his surname seemed to put too much distance between them. And the man was a guest in his house, invited or not.

At the sound of Yuri's voice, Tanya shoved herself away from Kirov and ran to him, yelling, "Daddy, Daddy."

Yuri scooped her up in his arms in midstride and pulled her close. She laughed and squealed in protest. Holding her before him, he made his monster face then gave her a big kiss.

"What do you think of your young Russian spy now?" Natasha asked Kirov.

Kirov smiled as he pushed himself from the chair. Not without taking one last visual sweep out the window, Yuri noticed. "I think he's an excellent father and husband."

Even as Yuri placed a bib around his daughter's neck, he was conscious of the small stretching movements Kirov made and the way the old man kept his jacket from gaping open to reveal the pistol.

"To repeat my husband's earlier question," Natasha said, "have you eaten?"

"I didn't mean to interrupt your breakfast, young Mikhailin," Kirov said. "Nor create an imposition on your beautiful wife."

Natasha smiled and Yuri was aware of the embarrassed flush that colored her cheeks. "It will be no imposition. I have made plenty, even taking into account little Tanya's large appetite." She offered him a chair with the wave of her hand.

As they ate, Kirov talked with Natasha and paid attention to Tanya. Yuri sat mostly in silence. The old man was a social chameleon. Today, watching him share the breakfast table with his family, it was hard to believe Kirov was the same man who had so impassionately killed another man's son only two days ago. It was as if two very different spirits shared the same body, guided the same hands.

The conversation Kirov offered was high-spirited, often very humorous, but none of it was personal. Even when breakfast was finished and Natasha was clearing away the dishes, Kirov still remained an enigma to Yuri. It was hard to dislike the old man, yet hard to know him.

"I hate to rush you," Kirov whispered as he smoked his pipe afterward, "but we have a plane to catch."

His words, spoken too lowly for Natasha to hear, brought Yuri back to the realities that were larger than his small house. "You have found a lead to Ivanovitch?"

Kirov nodded. "But time is slipping away from us, young Mikhailin."

"I'll go pack."

"Don't bother. I have taken care of that."

Yuri looked at Tanya as she stared out the window at the gray day. How many times, he wondered, had she stood just so, waiting for him to come home? He felt tired and empty and traitorous to his family for staying away so much. He hadn't been there when his daughter was born and hoped it wouldn't be the same with the new baby.

"Where are we going?"

"New York City."

"You think Ivanovitch has gone to America?"

"Yes."

"Does Kulik know?"

"I talked to him this morning."

"And he's sending us?"

"Yes."

Yuri shook his head. "It doesn't make sense for Ivanovitch to go to America. He has no allies there. What can he possibly hope to do?"

"Perhaps we'll ask him when we find him." Kirov emptied his pipe into the ashtray Natasha had given him. "I will say my goodbyes."

Natasha followed Yuri into the bedroom to get his coat. "How long will you be gone, Yuri?" she asked.

"I'm not sure, Tasha. Not long, I think. This investigation Kirov and I are on is nearing completion rapidly."

She stepped into his arms and they held each other tightly. "I worry about you when you are gone, Yuri."

"I know."

Her eyes glistened with unshed tears when she looked up at him and kissed him. "I love you," she breathed into his mouth.

"I love you too." Yuri had to force himself to release her and slip the shoulder rig into place. The coat felt heavy across his shoulders, but he knew it was only a reflection of the burden he bore every time he left his family.

When they walked back to the living room, Kirov stood at the window looking out. Tanya lay quietly against the old man's shoulder, almost asleep in her contentment.

Yuri kissed his daughter goodbye as he took her from Kirov and placed her on the couch. He held Natasha a final time, told her a final I-love-you and stepped into the chill of the day.

"STRIKER?"

"Yeah."

"The Bear found a home for your freighter. Want to take a guess where the owner turned up?" Brognola asked.

Bolan sat on the water bed and wondered how long he'd been asleep. His shoulder twinged with the movement and brought consciousness to a knife-edged reality.

"Striker? You awake?"

"Getting there, Hal." Bolan took the receiver from the headboard and slid across the sheets until he could reach his personal effects. His watch lay nestled under the combat harness. It was 7:37 a.m. "Have you been up all night?"

"Off and on. I keep dozing here in the chair in between phone calls. The Bear's been at it all night, though."

Bolan flexed the shoulder, finding the joint stiffer, yet not as painful. Pushing the hurt away, he stretched the arm, striving for the suppleness he might need to keep himself alive. The strained muscles gave grudgingly, surrendering to a more natural movement but not without cost. If he worked at it, maybe it wouldn't prove to be much of a hindrance. He flipped on a small light over the bed and moved to Drake's computer terminal. The computer hummed gently as the system came up. "Tell Aaron I'm ready when he is."

Brognola set the receiver down and Bolan listened to dead air for a few seconds.

Overhead the party still continued, though it seemed like things had died down somewhat. The arrival of the local police had dampened the enthusiasm of the guests. Long enough for Murphy to explain that the man Drake had been keeping guard over had shot him. The guy had denied it, but Drake's testimony and the fact that many of the party goers swore they'd never seen Murphy leave and had, in fact, heard the shot that struck the pilot, convinced the investigating officers.

The printer came to life and started chattering. The laser enhancement allowed it to transmit pictures as well as script. Bolan cradled the phone in his uninjured shoulder and started inspecting the connected pages as they came out.

"Striker?"

"Yeah, Hal."

"I don't know what order Kurtzman is sending this stuff to you, so we'll have to kind of piece it together."

"That's fine."

The first sheet contained a list of ports, company names and cargo. Bolan shifted so the light from the small lamp fell onto the page. The names were so meaningless to him, consisting of corporations between Key West and Venezuela.

"Find the sheets pertaining to the freighter," Brognola said.

"Got them."

"This is what took the longest. The Bear said the actual owner was hidden by dummy corporations, over a span of several years, which lets us know this guy has been in business for at least that long. On a grand scale. The Eastern Seaboard connections through Atlanta might be new, but it told us this guy is a pro. Aaron had to sift through a lot of documentation to find the owner's name. You should have a couple of pictures there."

Bolan flipped through the growing printout and looked at the first one. "I see a middle-aged guy with a broken nose."

"That's Preston. I'll get to him later."

The other picture was of a more slimly built man, at least ten years Preston's senior. The dark hair was combed backward. The features were effeminate, thin, almost fragile. Someone had taken the time to carefully manicure the pencil-thin mustache.

"Meet Ramon Diaz," Brognola said. "The picture is almost ten years old, so we have to assume the guy still looks about the same."

Bolan studied the narrow eyes, knowing the man was a killer without Brognola saying so. "What have we got on him?"

"Nothing. Not a goddamned thing. Oh, there are a few rumors in various departments concerning drug trafficking, white slavery, among other things. But nothing concrete. Until the past few years, it seems Diaz has been content with servicing the Caribbean and South America. For a while he was on very friendly terms with Castro's boys in Cuba. The only thing we do have on him as far as the United States is concerned is his involvement in the crisis in Grenada in 1983."

Bolan studied the first sheet again, running down the list until he reached Spice Island Shipping, whose home base was Grenada. "Diaz lives in Grenada?"

"No. He lives in a fortress on Carriacou, one of the lesser Grenadines. It's a thirteen-square-mile island about sixteen miles north of Grenada proper. I'm not joking about the fortress. Give me a couple of days and I can get some aerial footage of it."

"We don't have the time, Hal. Any letup now might cost me weeks or months on this operation."

Bolan heard Brognola sigh. "Dammit, Striker, how did I know you were going to say that?"

"When I started on this, I didn't know it was this big. I can't back off now."

"I wish I could do more for you. I'm the one that got you onto this thing. I didn't intend for a personal vendetta to get you in this deep.

"Diaz was on the wrong side of the U.S. invasion," Brognola went on. "He supported the Marxist regime and even helped transport Cuban troops onto the island. Charges were filed, but Diaz covered himself with subordinates, saying the captains of various vessels he owned made the decision to ship troops on their own. These captains were all either executed before our guys tried to sort things out, or they conveniently disappeared."

"Sounds like a man who covers all his bases."

"To say the least. Military investigators didn't want to rock the boat any more than they had to, so they left Diaz in place. His family is old money, but twenty years ago the family fortune was dwindling. A few years later everything began to suddenly look up. Diaz put on more bodyguards and started entertaining more. His guests have included a number of debutantes, political figures, as well as names who have been connected, but never proved with international crime.''

Bolan felt the beginning of hunger pangs gnaw at his stomach.

"Diaz keeps house at Gun Point," Brognola said. "It's the family home, but he's added a number of surprises over the past few years. Getting to him there won't be easy."

"It won't be expected, either."

"There are area maps and street maps in the package Kurtzman is sending you."

"What about Preston?" Bolan asked.

"He's a good cop. I've never heard one bad word about him from the Atlanta end. A stand-up guy."

"I'll try to stay out of his way."

"Do that."

Bolan laid the papers to one side after the last one finished. "Can you get me any official clearance into Grenada, something I can use to infiltrate the local authorities?"

"I got some stuff prepped, ready for you to acknowledge. The U.S. liaison in Grenada is getting a presidential letter hand-delivered first thing this morning, asking that a government official be allowed to coordinate activities through the local law-enforcement teams. The feeling throughout the country is still pro-U.S., so I don't envision any glitches."

"Does it say what I am investigating?"

"We decided to leave that at your discretion. You'll be limited to personal side arms going in, but I'm sure you'll be able to come up with any extras you might need. You can pick up your ID at Frederiksted on St. Croix. It will be ready for you by the time you can arrange a flight there. What name do you want me to register the documents under?"

"Michael Jamison," Bolan answered.

"Be careful while you're down there, buddy," Brognola warned. "I haven't been able to track the information down yet, but there's been some Soviet activity in the area. A couple of CIA types I hobnob with occasionally have been acting stranger than usual lately. Conversations lull suddenly when I enter the room. That sort of thing. There might be a lot more traffic down that way than either one of us expects."

"I read you, Hal. As soon as I get a handle on something I'll get back to you."

"Just make sure you damn well watch your ass."

Bolan broke the connection and brought his knees up to his chin, flexing the kinks out of his back and working on the shoulder again. He sorted through the stack of computer printouts until he came to the picture of Ramon Diaz. Carnage ahead and behind. He could deal with that. Hell, he'd been living it for years. Hal had known he wouldn't be able to talk the Executioner out of confirming shutdown on the operation after coming this far. Not now. Not when he had a name. And a face.

KNOCKING ON THE FRONT DOOR woke Natasha Mikhailin from the light drowse she'd been enjoying with her daughter, who lay sprawled beside her, tiny fists pressed tightly into Natasha's breasts.

She sat up when the knocking was repeated, at first thinking it had only been a fragment of a dream that followed her into wakefulness. Her sleep hadn't been restful, but she had succumbed to it anyway. Often, after Yuri had first left each time, she had terrible nightmares about the things that could happen to him. She didn't think there were any new scenarios, but the terror that filled her at each dreaming was just as chilling.

This time was different though. She'd seen part of Yuri's world that took him away from her and Tanya. This time it had invaded her house in the form of the old man.

Careful not to disturb her sleeping daughter as she got out of bed, Natasha put her robe on and walked into the living room. She felt lazy with this pregnancy and was glad in a way that Yuri wasn't home today. She hadn't even fully dressed herself, content to remain in her nightgown even after her morning bath.

A chill raced through her when she peeked out the window beside the door and saw the man standing on the porch. He was big and broad-shouldered, and had a face with sharp features. It was difficult to guess the man's age, somewhere between Yuri's and the old man's, she guessed. But it was the official air about the man that scared her, an authority that passed through the heavy woolen coat the man wore against the cold afternoon. As she watched him the man raised his hand and rapped again.

Hesitantly she opened the door, making sure the chain lock was in place.

"May I help you?" Natasha asked through the narrow space.

"Mrs. Mikhailin?" The man's eyes were hard and bright, his voice low and hoarse, his manner secretive.

"Yes. Who are you?"

"A friend, Mrs. Mikhailin. Please. You have to get your daughter and come with me now. Your lives are in danger at this very moment."

"Where is Yuri? I need to talk to him."

"I don't know. Mrs. Mikhailin, please, we haven't got much time."

"Who sent you here?"

"He said you didn't know his name. The old man who stayed for breakfast. He sent for me after he left with your husband this morning. He told me the KGB was watching your house, that the man didn't follow them when they left. He thinks you are going to be used against your husband."

Natasha stood frozen. Never, not once, had she prepared herself for this set of circumstances. Yuri's death, yes. His captivity in foreign prisons. But never had she thought his business would ever touch her or her daughter's life so directly.

"Mama?" Tanya called from the bedroom, her voice thick with sleep.

Frantically she tried to shut the door and lock it, remembering the cold fear the old man had instilled in her despite his genteel manners. Her fingers clawed for the bolt and she felt a nail break. The bolt touched for a second and she almost had it locked. Then the chain snapped, and she was falling backward. Her head hit something hard and everything went black as the man towered above her.

13

Fyodor Ivanovitch sat easily in the stern of the yacht, watching the man who watched him.

The fellow had evidently grown up in the United States, the ex-KGB agent thought as he covertly studied his guard. He wore the grimly sardonic expression American movie goers seemed to prefer in their spy heroes. The man was thin, almost anemic-looking, with only the barest hint of a tan. Already the sallow skin was beginning to redden in the noonday sun. The solid black sunglasses wrapped around the guard's head seemed to divide his face, making the angularity of the features more apparent. His suit was of a dark material that wasn't quite black, reminding Ivanovitch of an undertaker. Young, and already intimate with death.

"When do I speak with Diaz?" Ivanovitch asked.

"When he is ready to speak with you," the guard replied, his lips barely moving with the effort.

"I didn't come halfway around the world to have my time wasted." Ivanovitch shifted on the vinyl seat, feeling the heat that was already building up in the plastic despite the rapid breeze. He twisted his left wrist and felt the pressure of the concealed throwing knife flex until only a small additional movement would drop it into his palm. It would have been an unsure attack at best, but Ivanovitch had killed men with the weapon at greater distances. Why was Diaz taking so many precautions? Even when he was a close contact for Ivanovitch and the Cubans, it was a known fact that Diaz trafficked in drugs and white slavery. Perhaps, thought Ivanovitch, the caution was simply a result of that other business and had nothing to do with his coming to Grenada. Or maybe Kulik or one of his representatives had already worked something out with Diaz. The possibility was a sobering one.

"You will wait."

It had been foolish to agree to meet Diaz on the yacht, Ivanovitch told himself as he gazed out at the colorful sails filling the horizon. Foolishness and desperation. He should have waited and made Diaz play the game his way. The afternoon could have been better spent trying to recover the camera that had belonged to the man he'd killed the previous night. Whose hands had those pictures fallen into? There weren't many who would remember his involvement in the crisis those years ago, but it would only take one.

Today was Friday. Saturday would be the best time to set his plan into motion, and the weather conditions in the forecast would allow him the greatest number of casualties. The grin that spread across his face felt tight, as if someone had screwed it into place.

Two of the leggy blondes who had been sunbathing at the front of the yacht strolled to the back where Ivanovitch sat. He stared at them as they laughed and carried on their conversation, oblivious to anyone around them. They paused at a massive ice chest long enough to get diet soft drinks, then made the return trip. Ivanovitch was sure neither girl had reached twenty-one yet.

Decadence, the ex-KGB agent thought as he watched the smooth sway of the tanned hips. It was one of the reasons the KGB had not wanted to use Diaz in the invasion. But at the same time, it was the greatest lever they had had on the man.

"Ivanovitch."

He looked up at the sound of his name and saw Miguel standing at the ladder leading to the helm of the yacht.

"Señor Diaz will speak with you now." Miguel motioned him up the ladder.

Ivanovitch moved forward without speaking, aware that the guard followed him like a dark shadow. The powerful engines of the yacht, combined with the crashing waves of the sea around them, created a sound barrier that made him deaf to the guard's movements.

Ramon Diaz held the wheel of the yacht, peering out to sea. He didn't deign to acknowledge Ivanovitch's presence.

The years had been kind to Diaz, the Russian thought as he walked to the empty place beside the man. Silver now tinged the once dark hair, but it had brought dignity with it as well. The flesh hung more slackly on the gaunt frame than it had before. Diaz's tailors had taken care of whatever discrepancies that had caused, though, just as a skilled plastic surgeon had eradicated some of the tattoos of age around Diaz's eyes. He was dressed as jauntily as ever, enjoying the playboy image he had maintained before the American invasion of Grenada took away some of the flash the Diaz name had built up over past generations. His blazer was royal purple with gold trim. The buttons shone bright gold, matching the trim on his captain's hat. His pants were white silk.

Ivanovitch came to a stop at the helm, well out of reach of Diaz, so that no motion on his part could be misconstrued by Miguel or the bodyguard.

"*Señor,*" Ivanovitch said.

Diaz nodded. "It has been many years since I've been approached by your country, Ivanovitch. I was most surprised when Miguel told me you were in St. George's trying to set up a meet with me."

"Times have changed since the last time I saw you, *señor.*" Ivanovitch chafed at having to be so formal. But even last time, when setting things up with the Cubans, he had played this game with the man's pettiness. Before, he'd been ordered to. Now, it was a necessity if he was to achieve his goal.

"I thought the KGB had forgotten about this part of the Caribbean after the fiasco last time."

"Not forgotten. Merely waited until a more opportune moment."

Diaz made a slight adjustment with the wheel. "And that moment is now?"

"Yes."

Diaz turned from the controls and looked at Ivanovitch with watery, brown eyes.

Looking down at the smaller man, the former KGB agent found it hard to remember how much power Diaz controlled. All it would take, he was sure, was one hard slap and the man would be dead at his feet. Except then the guard behind him, or perhaps Miguel, would kill him. That was real power. Not just the strength that lay in a man's two hands.

"Miguel tells me you're the only representative your country chose to send this time," Diaz said as he turned back to the steering. "The last time there were many others. Some, even, from Castro himself."

"There will be others after me."

"We'll see if there's any truth to that. But how much will it cost me to find out?"

"I don't know what you mean."

"You people always want something first," Diaz explained. "A token of my sincerity or of my allegiance. The last time it almost cost me a major portion of my wealth and much of the small empire I had built up over the years. The Americans came into these islands in armies. First the soldiers, then the politicians, the reformers, the reporters. Many of my distribution points were disrupted. Shipments were lost. I had to go into a hibernation of sorts for months before world view shifted focus again. It was a most trying time for me."

"And for us as well, *señor*."

"Bullshit. The KGB didn't lose one damn thing in that skirmish other than a few soldiers who thought they were dying for a cause."

Ivanovitch remained silent, knowing that whatever he said would be turned against him at this point.

"I surprised myself by even agreeing to this meet," Diaz said. "After your government backed out and left us and the Cubans to take the brunt of the Americans' involvement, I had even toyed with the idea of having you killed and sent back to your masters. But you made me curious."

Ivanovitch took off his sunglasses and placed them in his jacket pocket. If they happened to get shattered the polarized shards might cause a lasting blindness. He popped his wrist and let the small throwing knife slide down into his waiting palm. It would at least prove a distraction to the guard behind him after he used it to open Diaz's throat. Even then it would place him miles from shore on an enemy vessel.

"You have always been more careful than curious, *señor*," Ivanovitch said softly.

Diaz inclined his head. He flexed his fingers on the wheel as he took a fresh hold. "True, but then before this I could have said the same thing of you. It's not like you to risk your life in an unsure situation. Remember, I worked with you for many months before the invasion. Contacting me is a job you would have reserved for one of your subordinates. Instead, you come to me yourself. Why?"

"To give more weight to my proposal, and to let you know I have a personal interest in this affair."

Diaz grinned. Under the hooded lids, the man's eyes were hard and dull. "Maybe you have a personal interest in what you offer, Ivanovitch, but what could you possibly hope to entice me with?" He waved toward the prow of the yacht where the blond-haired women lounged.

Ivanovitch noticed some of them were entirely nude.

"I have everything a man could want—money, women, power. Can you name one thing I don't have?"

Ivanovitch let the seconds stretch out between them before making his answer. "A country, *señor*. At least the island you occupy." He stared silently into Diaz's eyes. "Would a country be enough to interest you?"

SIPPING ORANGE JUICE through a straw, Chase Murphy tried to ignore the man at the foot of his hospital bed. He'd tried to feign sleep when the DEA man entered the room, but that hadn't stopped the guy from waking Murphy.

"How many times are we going to go over this?" Murphy asked. He leaned across the bed to set the orange juice container on the small table, feeling the stitches pull in his side.

Harry Preston stopped his pacing and gripped the railing of the bed in both hands. "I don't know, kid. You're the one with all the answers. You tell me."

"I've covered everything so many times between you and the local law that I could probably tell this story in my sleep."

"Believe me, Murphy, the experience shows. You've got this little pattern you fall into every time you open your mouth. It's beginning to sound like one of those thumbnail sketches you get in the *TV Guide*."

"You sound like you don't believe me."

"Look, kid, I got a hotel room shot all to shit, complete with dead guys. I got a sunken yacht, a freighter that nobody owns and the Coast Guard is still pulling bodies out of the goddamned water. All of which are connected to Ruffino Marino who runs drugs here in Key West. His seems to be the only body we haven't turned up. Of course, it could come washing up on the beach most any day now. It would make a hell of a tourist attraction, don't you think?"

Murphy flipped the bed controls to raise himself up. "What does that have to do with me?"

Preston counted points off on his fingers, reminding Murphy of a history teacher he'd had in high school. "A helicopter was involved in the destruction of the yacht and the freighter. You're a helicopter pilot." Preston moved on to another finger. "The hotel room that got shot up belonged to a guy named McKay. The same guy that was seen going into your office yesterday afternoon."

"There are a lot of helicopter pilots in the Keys."

"Yeah, but not many of them have bullet wounds."

"It's a new thing, Preston. Hell, after a few days it'll probably catch on." Murphy felt his irritation with the DEA agent grow. Neither McKay nor Drake had told him Marino was still alive. Some of the security he'd felt with the cop standing outside his door had disappeared. He wished he'd had more time to talk to McKay.

"Don't be a smartass, kid. I don't have time for smartasses today."

Murphy gave him a sarcastic grin. "Sorry, Chief, it's an unconscious reaction. Happens every time a cop calls me a liar."

Preston pulled out a small notebook. "Speaking of you and the law, Murphy, you seem to have had a few close calls over the past couple of years. Somebody told me you have trouble keeping your nose where it belongs."

Murphy reached for the buzzer. "I'm going to have some more orange juice. You want some?"

"I want you to tell me the truth, goddammit."

Murphy sighed tiredly. The local police had left him alone after he told his story and Drake verified it. "You think I was lying?"

"Let's just say I think there are a few inconsistencies."

"Oh, and where would you like me to start? How about when my statement was completely error-free?"

"How about when you got up yesterday?"

"How about you talking to my lawyers?"

Preston leaned back against a wall. "You mean Drake's lawyers, don't you? The local guys have already been notified that if they have any more questions they can set up an appointment with one of their representatives."

"Which you ignored."

"Murphy, do you understand how much shit you're in? We're talking about the lives of several men here."

"Who, from what I understand, were entirely guiltless. Ask anybody on the Key and they'll tell you what kind of operation Marino was running. The only people who seemed ignorant of it were the cops. Including your partner, Vincent.''

''McKay is a killer.''

''Maybe. You haven't established that yet. For all you know the guy was the first casualty in this whole thing.''

Preston shook his head. ''No way. I've been following McKay for almost a week. He's an easy guy to trail. Every time you get the least little bit uncertain, you can count on tripping over a dead body or three.''

''And you figure it's the same guy?''

''Either that or everybody involved in this thing is sporting a .44. We've found spent cartridges from the same gun at every scene.''

Murphy closed his eyes. He felt drained. It seemed like someone had taped sandpaper to the inside of his eyelids. Christ, why did Marino have to still be alive? The drug-runner wouldn't be hampered by the laws or lawyers. Once Marino even got a hint Murphy had been involved, the pilot knew he'd be a target. A sitting duck in the hospital.

''McKay is dangerous,'' Preston went on. ''I don't know what gave him such a hard-on for Marino and his merry band of murderers, but in my book he's no better.''

''Maybe you're reading from the wrong book. The only people you're accusing him of killing were all known dope dealers. People who have been responsible for murders and overdoses all over Key West. In my neighborhood that would almost ensure him a sainthood.''

''He's a goddamned vigilante.''

''Evidently a goddamned successful vigilante.'' Murphy lay back on the bed. He hoped McKay had told Drake where he was headed before he left.

Preston fell silent, his eyes boring into Murphy's.

Murphy returned the stare. ''Look, any other time I'd really enjoy the chance to stare you down. I work on that. I live for it some days. Hell, I've got a reputation all over the Key. Go into any bar and ask anybody there who can go the longest without blinking. They'll tell you Chase

Murphy. But I'd like to get some rest today. Got a big date tonight.''

Preston buried his hands in his pants pockets. "I'm going to keep digging, kid, because you're the only lead I've got to McKay. I can't touch Drake because I don't know how deeply involved he is. For all I know, you lied to him too. But I'll warn you now—if I find one piece of evidence to work on, I'm going to be more trouble for you than you ever thought possible.''

"Don't forget your rubber hose.''

Preston didn't say another word as he passed through the doorway.

A nurse entered the room and stuck a thermometer under his tongue. Murphy ignored the pleasant chatter she made, giving her monosyllabic replies until she left. He shifted the thermometer around as his jaws got tired of maintaining the position.

When the door opened again Murphy thought it was the nurse returning to read the temperature. Instead it was Peter Vincent, Marino's pet DEA agent. The smile on the man's face was unctuous as he walked closer to the bed.

Murphy removed the thermometer and powered the bed into an upright position.

"I only got a few moments," Vincent said, "so I'll try to make this as interesting as I can." He reached under his jacket and took out an automatic pistol. Taking a silencer from his pocket, he started threading it onto the barrel. "You can go ahead and yell if you want to, Murphy. It doesn't matter anymore if I'm seen. I've got a chartered plane waiting for me as soon as I finish here, and enough money accumulated over the years to keep me living comfortably in South America indefinitely.''

Murphy kept still, knowing any sudden movement on his part might be his last. His breath seemed suspended in the back of his throat. He could still hear the flat report of the pistol when he'd been shot last night, could still feel the impact that had knocked him backward. He squeezed his hand tightly. The thermometer was a flexible bar in his right hand. He moved his fingers, got more leverage, then broke off the end of the thermometer, leaving a jagged edge.

"No snappy patter?" Vincent taunted. "You planning on dying quietly, Murphy?" He pushed the pistol toward the pilot's face.

Murphy fisted the broken thermometer, leaving a good three inches protruding from the bottom of his hand. He stared at Vincent's trigger finger, watching as the nail started to whiten with the increasing pressure.

"No regrets?" Vincent asked.

The muzzle of the pistol was mere inches from Murphy's face.

"Only one," Murphy said, then he was moving, pulling his body to the right as his left arm swept up, knocking the pistol to the left. He heard a sharp hiss, the tug of the bullet passing through his hair, the hollow thump it made as it burrowed into the pillow and bed. His hand shot forward and buried the jagged end of the thermometer in one of Vincent's eyes. He twisted, shoved again as a thick, liquid warmth spilled down his arm.

Vincent fought for a moment but Murphy held on tight, twisting the thermometer violently.

Then the DEA man slumped forward onto the bed, blood staining the sheets. Murphy released the body as pain from his own wound flooded his consciousness. "Only one," he repeated as he looked at Vincent. "But you'll never see it."

Moving as swiftly as his wounded side permitted, Murphy muscled Vincent's body into the small bathroom and locked the door from the inside. Then he took his clothes from the closet and got dressed.

The cop was gone from his door when he walked out. Murphy figured Vincent had supposedly relieved the man. At any rate, it served his purpose as well as it had Vincent's. He was sure not even Preston could order him held without some kind of charges, but Vincent's death would change all of that. And he didn't intend to remain in the hospital thinking Marino had no one else in the police department on his payroll.

The nurse at the desk stopped him as he stood waiting for the elevator. She was pleasant and busty, and about forty pounds over her best weight. "And where do you think you're going?" she challenged, her professional smile in place.

"I'm checking myself out."

"You can't do that. The doctor won't release you." Her face seemed to be fighting to decide what emotion to show.

The elevator doors pinged open and Murphy stepped inside. "Sure I can," he said as he punched the button for the bottom floor. "I've had plenty of experience. I've seen every Dirty Harry movie." Then the doors closed.

14

Mack Bolan pulled the rented Cherokee to one of the scenic stops and got out after retrieving a pair of Bausch & Lomb binoculars from between the seats.

On the other side of the metal railing, down the gentle slope of hills that ran from north to south across the whole island of Carriacou, the Caribbean lay as quiet and still as a sheet of blue glass. A thick shelter of tropical rain forest grew between Bolan and the white sands of the beach, broken only occasionally by dwellings.

Turning his back to the sea, Bolan fitted the glasses to his eyes and directed his vision inland. The particulars of Gun Point, the northern area of Carriacou, were not readily revealed. Still, after reading the material Kurtzman had transmitted to him, he was able to get the lay of the land.

Ramon Diaz's estate sat perched on top of one of the many hills that bisected the island, surrounded by a seemingly impenetrable wall of green that was the rain forest, and high stone fences. According to the Bear's notes, there were only two roads leading to the French-built mansion. Both of them were kept under constant surveillance by Diaz's private army.

After finding the estate, Bolan upped the power on the binoculars, zeroing in on the whitewashed walls. The main house stood three stories tall, dwarfing the stone fence that traced the outer perimeter of the yards. Inside the fence the lawn was well kept, resembling a dark green carpet dotted here and there with small fruit trees.

A swimming pool, looking no larger than a postage stamp to the naked eye, shimmered at the rear of the mansion. Figures moved restlessly around the area, but Bolan was unable to improve the magnification enough to bring any of them into focus.

Impenetrable, Bolan thought as he scanned the estate again, placing everything in his memory. It would look different at night, but a recon was a recon. You used natural markers to set your directions. They didn't change with night and day. Kurtzman had used that word—impenetrable—when finishing the brief he had sent Bolan, advising Bolan it might be wiser to forget a frontal assault on the estate and consider taking Diaz out while he was away from the mansion.

From the figures Kurtzman had been able to get his hands on, the head count in the mansion usually ran between thirty and forty. Not counting the women and whatever guests Diaz happened to have.

As the warrior watched, a yellow Mercedes 450SL glided from the four-car garage and passed through the electronically controlled gates. Only one man was in the car. Bolan caught a glimpse of brown hair before the polarized window on the driver's side slid up and erased the driver.

Tracking the Mercedes with the glasses, Bolan followed the vehicle as it wound down the road leading to Hillsborough, Carriacou's main town. He returned to the Jeep, slipped behind the wheel and put the vehicle into first gear, taking off at an easy pace that would put him a comfortable distance behind the Mercedes.

He had no idea who was driving the sedan. The quick glimpse he'd been afforded matched none of the descriptions of Diaz's known associates. But it was a chance to gather information that might relate to his mission.

As he drove down the busy streets of Hillsborough, Bolan could hear strains of wild calypso music as musicians gathered on corners. He felt sweat gather under the lightweight sport jacket he wore, and the shoulder harness stuck to his skin.

When the Mercedes pulled to a stop in the parking lot of the Inter-Island Air Transports, Bolan guided the Jeep past and found an empty space.

The driver of the Mercedes was big, well over six feet tall, with close-clipped brown hair and a square face that almost glowed with the red of a recent sunburn. The Executioner could tell from the way the guy walked that he was armed. And he was hunting.

Sunburn walked to the ticket window and made his purchase. Bolan watched him move over to the waiting area for island hops to Grenada. Maybe it would be a wasted trip, the Executioner thought as he bought his ticket, but he'd learned to trust his instincts a long time ago. And right now they were telling him the man he followed was more important than first glance would suggest.

Was it Diaz's business? Bolan wondered as he stood on the fringe of the group of people waiting for the next flight. Or something else? Something more personal? Whatever it was seemed to be occupying the man's full attention.

The fact that it was one man alone drew attention to the guy. From the reports Bolan had gotten concerning Ramon Diaz, Diaz would have sent a crew to take care of a matter. Not one man. Diaz's empire hadn't been built on trust. So, whoever the guy was, the Executioner figured he rated highly in Diaz's organization.

The rumble of a small plane cut through the myriad conversations that surrounded the warrior. A trio of children near the front pointed excitedly at the approaching aircraft while their parents hovered tiredly nearby. A man, dressed casually in jeans and knit shirt, stopped beside the children and ran his fingers through his blond hair. Another man standing by the ticket window gave him a minute nod and dropped his cigarette to the ground, then crushed it beneath his foot.

The new arrival hung back from Bolan's target, but the Executioner could tell he was tailing his quarry, too.

Okay, Bolan thought as he moved forward to file onto the plane with the rest of the waiting crowd, Diaz's man was drawing a lot of attention. But from who? Neither of the newcomers fit any of the descriptions Bolan had been given, so they belonged to someone else. But what made the man so special? If the new guys were cops or DEA, they'd be focused on Ramon Diaz. There wouldn't be enough manpower to follow everyone who came and went.

Unless Sunburn was their intended target.

Bolan figured they had at least one other man watching the mansion who kept the rest of the team advised by radio contact. That explained why Bolan hadn't spotted the tail earlier. They'd come in from another direction and linked up here.

Which meant they knew Bolan was following their man.

The blonde turned around as if giving the crowd a curious glance before boarding the plane, but Bolan knew when he was being given the once-over.

GET A GRIP on yourself, Abby Nichols ordered as she clutched the sides of the watercooler in the hallway.

She closed her eyes and drank, hoping to shut out the visual impressions of the long corridor that ran just outside the morgue. The water felt cool to her lips, but she couldn't drink. Her stomach rolled every time the image of Bill's body rose in her mind.

It was her own fault, though. She had insisted on seeing her brother's body despite the policeman's warning. God, she hadn't known it would be so bad.

The skin had been drawn so tightly across Bill's features that the freckles she had once teased him unmercifully about had been almost invisible. His shock of red hair had never been more prominent. Yet those were superfluous details. The thing that had drawn her attention the most was the blue-black hole in the center of her brother's forehead where the bullet had entered. Powder burns had scorched the skin around the wound, leaving black stains.

Someone touched her elbow and she drew away instinctively. Her eyes snapped open and she saw the young policeman standing before her.

"Are you all right, Mrs. Nichols?" he asked.

"Yes," she replied and was surprised to find that her voice didn't crack.

"It's always hard. I couldn't tell you how many times I've been through this with somebody, but there never seems to be anything I can say."

"I know. Thank you." Abby released her hold on the watercooler and stood with her back to the wall, letting it take some of her weight.

The policeman was dark skinned and dark haired, handsome and lean in his uniform. Too young, Abby thought, to have to live this close to death.

"He was your brother?"

"Yes."

"Do you feel up to a few questions?"

Abby wanted nothing more than to curl up somewhere and pretend the events of the past few days were nothing more than a bad dream. She didn't even want to be around her son. She felt like screaming and shouting. Nobody had told her Bill had been shot.

BOLAN HAD RENTED a car on Grenada earlier that afternoon when, as Detective Sergeant Michael Jamison of an ambiguously named presidential task force, he had checked in with the local law in St. George's. He stood by the Subaru compact for a moment until he was sure Sunburn was heading for the car rental agency at the airfield. The blonde joined another man waiting in a car near the main entrance. The vehicle was a small brown Toyota with rental markings. Bolan wrote down the plate number, thinking it was probably wasted effort but knowing it was at least one avenue of investigation.

The blonde and his associate were evidently nervous about the man they followed. When the guy pulled onto the main highway leading to St. George's, they quickly fell into place behind him.

Bolan eased the Subaru into traffic. As he drove, he slid the 93-R free of its leathers and placed the weapon under his thigh.

Brognola had mentioned Soviet activity. Was this some type of Soviet operation, or were the two men following Diaz's man CIA? Either option could be the case. And in either case they were dangerous to Bolan. The Jamison identity would hold up under scrutiny but provided him with no reason to be involved. His only defense lay in maintaining a low profile.

Diaz's man parked across the street from the hospital and remained in the car. The Toyota took a space four car lengths down.

With the English style of driving on the left, Bolan had to go down to the first intersection to turn around. He left the Subaru in a nearby alley and walked inside the building through the emergency entrance. He felt confident that Sunburn wasn't going anywhere. The guy was hunting, and the game was here. The man had positioned himself just opposite the main entrance of the hospital.

The warrior quickly moved through the building until he was near the main entrance. There was no one in the waiting area where Bolan stood watch. A small glassed-in corridor formed a double wall that separated him from the reception area. Children's toys and magazines were spread out on the chairs around him. He took up position behind the large plate-glass window facing the street, confident its polarization would conceal him.

Sunburn and the men in the Toyota sat unmoving.

What was the guy waiting for? Bolan wondered. Sunburn hadn't taken his eyes off the people coming through the front entrance since he'd parked. And how far were the other two men willing to let him go before they took an active hand in the situation?

Minutes passed while Bolan tried to make sense of what was going on, knowing he didn't have enough information to piece it together. Movement attracted the warrior's attention to the corridor leading to the main entrance.

The man who walked outside and took up position to the left of the entrance was someone Bolan could place—Miguel Chavez, one of Diaz's top players.

As Bolan watched, Chavez signaled Sunburn. He also saw sunlight flash on something metal inside the car. The men in the Toyota still hadn't moved.

Bolan left the window, maneuvering for a better position nearer the entrance. It was a trap for someone, but who? With the Beretta already in his hand, held close to his leg so it wouldn't easily be seen, the warrior pushed his way out onto the sidewalk. He looked over Chavez's shoulder as Sunburn abruptly pulled into traffic, cutting across both lanes in an illegal U-turn that caused drivers headed in both directions to lock their brakes.

The target was a woman who had just left the hospital. She'd turned at the sound on the street, instinctively tightening her grip on the package she carried in her left hand, while grabbing her son with her other. Bolan recognized Abby and Jase Nichols at the same time Chavez ripped a pistol from under his jacket.

Too close to risk a shot, he told himself as he broke into a run. He saw the snout of an automatic weapon poke through the side window of the car as Diaz's man paralleled the sidewalk.

Bolan pumped his legs as hard as he could, throwing his body into a desperate bid for all the forward momentum he could build. The Executioner launched himself into the air. Abby Nichols's scream was drowned out by the sudden snarl of autofire.

THE SMALL BAR at La Guardia International Airport suited Yuri Mikhailin's purposes perfectly. It was dark and filled with passengers waiting for their next flights. Kirov was at the TWA desk arranging for their tickets. So far every flight through Europe had come off without problems. Yuri and Kirov had changed planes and identities at almost every stop.

He burned with anger as he lifted the receiver of the pay telephone near the end of the stand-up bar. This was supposed to be his operation, entrusted to him by Kulik. Instead he'd spent every moment since leaving his home, following Kirov's orders, never knowing exactly where they were going or why. All of the airports had been too busy to discuss the matter with Kirov, and Yuri had held his temper in check because he didn't trust himself to speak quietly.

But now they were in New York City.

Yuri dropped a quarter in the slot and dialed a number in the United Nations. A tiredness he had never known seemed to descend on him, intensifying the loneliness he had felt the whole trip. He hadn't been able to get his family out of his mind. It was as if some subconscious sense was trying to tell him something was wrong.

Once the connection was made, Yuri gave his code name and asked to speak to his contact.

"Where are you?" the man demanded once he was on the phone.

Yuri told him.

"What are you doing there, Comrade? Your commanding officer never gave me instructions that you were supposed to be in this country. He knows I'm to be informed anytime one of you is operating here."

"I don't think he knows," Yuri said.

"What do you mean?"

Briefly Yuri explained about Boris Kirov, after making sure the United Nations man knew about Ivanovitch.

"Give me the phone number there and I will contact your superior."

Yuri did. "I don't know how much time I have, Comrade. Kirov will come looking for me in only a few minutes."

"Wait," the man ordered, then broke the connection.

Yuri looked at the dead receiver in his hand and experienced another cold chill that skated across the back of his neck. His clothes were stiff, new, and just his size. It told him Kirov had planned this excursion at least a day or two in advance? But why? Why did Kirov feel he had to violate protocol while looking for Ivanovitch? Was it for the glory of catching the man himself? To prove that he wasn't an old man after all?

The phone rang and startled Yuri. His voice was an embarrassing croak when he answered.

"Comrade?"

Yuri instantly recognized the voice of the man he'd spoken to. "Yes."

"I have some bad news from your superior. Boris Kirov has broken all contact with your department. He's out of control. You are advised to terminate him as soon as possible and return home."

Yuri's head spun with the implications. A kill-on-sight order had gone out through the KGB with Kirov's name on it. And undoubtedly his as well. How many men were hunting him now?

"What about me, Comrade?"

"Turn yourself in. I have men working undercover at La Guardia and have had for several years. They will accept your surrender without question, and things can be sorted out upon your return."

"I didn't know about this."

There was a small hesitation. "Your superior has vouched for you. You have nothing to fear. He said you were young and impressionable and were probably being blackmailed into helping Kirov. He told me that your wife and daughter had been kidnapped only a little while after you left Russia."

Natasha and Tanya kidnapped? Yuri's heart seemed to explode in his chest then come to a sudden stop. He closed his eyes and could see Tanya's smiling face in front of him. He wanted to be able to reach out and touch her. Had Natasha been hurt? What about the baby?

"Have you any word of my family?" Yuri asked.

"No, but your superior has a team working on it now."

Why would Kirov kidnap his wife and daughter? To ensure getting his help in whatever mad scheme he pursued? It didn't make sense. There must have been plenty of people Kirov could trust without having to rely on him.

"Comrade," the UN contact said.

"Yes?"

"My operatives are already en route to your position. Please cooperate. It will make things easier for all of us."

"I'm going after Kirov."

"Leave the man alone." The order was terse and sharp, leaving no room for debate.

"I can't."

"You are disobeying a direct order if you confront Kirov."

"No, Comrade, I'm going to save my family." Yuri hung up the phone without waiting for a reply.

He walked out of the bar, heading back for the TWA desk. What if Kirov was gone? The old man had surely expected him back before now. What if he sensed that Yuri had established contact with someone in the KGB? Someone who knew Kirov had turned traitor?

Anxiety narrowed his concentration, blotting out the rest of the world that surrounded him as he pushed his way through the crowded halls of the airport.

Kirov wasn't at the TWA desk when Yuri arrived.

Cold fear flooded Yuri as he scanned the faces around him. Where was the old man? Why hadn't Kirov come in search of him?

When he'd almost given up, Yuri spotted Kirov sitting in a seat near a men's room down the other hallway. The old man appeared relaxed and unconcerned. Yuri hated him for that and found that his hands had become fists he couldn't unlock. He would beat the answer out of the old man if he had to, but his family would be found.

Yuri changed directions, cutting through the lines of passersby as he closed in on Kirov. Without any sign that he'd seen the younger man, Kirov got up and entered the men's room.

For a moment Yuri thought he'd heard someone tell him to stop, then he was shoving his way inside the men's room, searching for Kirov. The door slammed and the old man stepped from behind it. The pistol in Kirov's hand was unwavering as he leveled it at Yuri's face.

Yuri wanted to move, but he guessed the old man would shoot him if he attempted it. The long white urinals against the wall seemed to assume the cold impunity of tombstones.

15

Bolan vaulted over Miguel Chavez's shoulder, forcing the smaller man down, then succeeded in knocking both Abby and Jase to the ground.

A discordant blast from Sunburn's automatic weapon scattered chips from the brick wall of the hospital, leaving an unsteady trail of pockmarks behind.

"Stay down," Bolan yelled before the rolling echo of the shots had a chance to die away. He threw himself toward the street and the attack car, flipping over on his back to bring the Beretta into play. Miguel Chavez had gotten to his feet and started bringing his pistol up. The man was bracketed between Bolan's knees until a 3-round burst from the 93-R knocked him backward.

The Executioner finished his roll with the Beretta two-fisted in front of him, tracking the attack car. He triggered a burst as the car accelerated away. The rear window starred as the bullets hit, then shattered completely as the car swerved around a corner.

Glancing over his shoulder, Bolan saw the Toyota already on the move in the other direction. The driver took a left at the next intersection, leaving the Executioner no doubt that they were planning to link up with the Diaz car as it sped back to the airfield.

The empty clip hit the sidewalk with a tinny clink as Bolan recharged the Beretta. Without holstering the weapon, he knelt by Abby Nichols and her son.

"Are you okay?" he asked her.

"What the hell is going on?" Abby asked.

After visually verifying that neither mother nor son had been wounded, Bolan hoisted Jase to his feet and began herding the boy toward the alley and the parked Subaru.

"Where are you taking my son?" Abby demanded as she followed. She clutched the package to her chest, almost having to run to maintain Bolan's pace.

"Out of here," Bolan replied. "Somewhere safe until I can figure out how you're involved."

"I'm not involved, goddammit. I wasn't the one who left a handful of dead men in his motel room in Key West."

Bolan opened the door of the Subaru and told Jase to get in back.

"Get my son out of that car."

Bolan looked up at her, still alert that the chase might not be over. "They were trying to kill you, Mrs. Nichols," he said softly, "not me. I can't leave you here and take the chance they won't come back. If I have to, I'll put you in the car myself."

The hard set of the woman's jaw told Bolan she wasn't going to go easily. He'd just holstered the Beretta and started to walk around the car when Jase called out to his mother.

"Mom, please. I saw them. They weren't trying to shoot Mike. They were after us."

The keening whine of a police siren filled the air, drawing nearer. "We don't have time to argue," Bolan told her as he slid behind the wheel.

Without another word, Abby got in.

Bolan started the car and shoved the stick into first. He made a three-point turn in the alley and shot out across the street, narrowly avoiding a collision. He heard Abby tell Jase to fasten his seat belt. As he made the corner of the same intersection the Toyota had taken, he caught a glimpse of flashing lights in his rearview mirror. Even with papers and a presidential invitation, a firefight like this would get Sergeant Michael Jamison bounced from Grenada—if anyone connected him with it.

Bolan weaved in and out of traffic, making himself a mental map of the area, trying to find a route that would bring him back to the main road leading to the airfield. He fought the wheel as he made a tire-eating skid around another corner, just ahead of an ancient Cadillac.

He glanced at Abby. She was braced against the seat, her lips set in a thin, hard line.

Another turn and Bolan had gained the highway he'd been searching for. He checked the road ahead and behind, looking for the attack car. When he caught Jase's eyes in the rearview mirror he gave the boy a brief smile.

"What are you doing?" Abby asked as Bolan skipped lanes to pass two cars in front of him.

"Looking for the guy who tried to murder you and Jase."

"Why? That's what the police are for."

Bolan cut back into his lane just ahead of an oncoming truck. The driver blew his horn loudly. "Did you recognize the man who tried to shoot you?"

"No."

"Could you identify him if you had to?"

"No."

"Then what are you planning to tell the police?"

"You saw him."

Bolan nodded. "I followed him to the hospital, but I don't know his name."

"Why the hell didn't you stop him before he shot at us?" Abby's voice was unbelieving.

"I didn't know he was after you," Bolan said. "The last time I saw you, you were in Key West. What do you know about a guy named Ramon Diaz?"

"I've never heard of him."

Bolan glanced at her, trying to judge if she was telling the truth. The woman's eyes were locked on the road ahead. If she didn't know Diaz, Bolan asked himself, then how was it Diaz seemed to know her? Why risk killing her in broad daylight?

The Subaru crested a hill and Bolan saw Sunburn's car less than a quarter of a mile ahead. On the downgrade he floored the accelerator, plunging the car around the pickup ahead of them, nipping back just in time to keep from hitting traffic coming the other way.

Bolan wound down his window then fisted the .44 in his right hand. He heard a small, choked gasp from Abby, but she didn't say anything. The gap between the Subaru and the attack car narrowed as they rounded a turn. Bolan's quarry was trapped behind a slower moving flatbed, and the traffic going the other way was too regular to permit a pass. There were no other roads, no exits, only the rain forest and the hills on one side and the Caribbean on the other.

"Get down," Bolan ordered as he lowered the Desert Eagle in line with the other car, aiming for the tires. The .44 bucked in his fist twice but both shots missed.

The car moved from behind the flatbed and lunged forward. Bolan swerved to follow, aware that Jase and Abby were hunkered down well below the seats. He tracked the Desert Eagle back on target and squeezed the trigger just as the rear window of the Subaru imploded. One glance in the rearview mirror told the warrior the men in the Toyota had caught up with him as well.

Bolan wished he had more firepower. The .44 was a hell of a weapon, but it was damned hard to handle accurately and drive at the same time.

"Hang on," he yelled as he threw the car in a sideways slide. With the .44 in his lap, he fought the wheel as he worked the clutch and stick to force the car to a sudden stop halfway off the road. Before the Subaru had a chance to finish rocking, the Executioner had popped the driver's side door open and moved into a firing stance near the center of the road.

The blonde leaned out of the passenger window of his vehicle, holding an Uzi in both hands. Ignoring him, Bolan focused on the driver, then put the remainder of the Desert Eagle's clip through the windshield on the driver's side. The 9 mm slugs from the machine pistol stuttered down the highway, chipping their way toward the Executioner.

Then the Toyota was out of control, careering toward the beach. It left the road and flipped, landing upside down as it skidded through the white sand.

Bolan rammed another clip into the .44 as he ran to the small sedan. With luck the blond man had survived and would have some of the answers the Executioner needed. As he made his way down the embankment the Toyota blew, the concussion of the blast knocking Bolan off his feet. Then the world went dark.

THE DOOR behind Yuri Mikhailin splintered, and Kirov's first silenced shot whispered by his ear. He stood frozen, not believing the old man had missed him at that range.

An angry look filled Kirov's bearded face. "Move, Mikhailin. Move if you value your life."

Yuri threw himself forward onto the polished tiles, sliding helplessly out of control until he reached the stalls. When he looked over his shoulder, Kirov was standing above the bodies of two men dressed in security guard uniforms. The small pistol he held in his hand still smoked.

Another glance at the dead men told Yuri both of them had been shot more than once in the face. Kirov hadn't missed, he told himself, which meant *he* hadn't been the old man's target. He got to his feet, trying to sort things out.

"Were there only two?" Kirov asked as he went through the men's clothing.

Yuri forced his voice to work, wondering as he spoke where Natasha and Tanya were. "I don't know. I didn't see these men."

"Help me put them somewhere before anyone comes." Kirov grabbed a double handful of the first dead man's uniform and hauled him toward one of the stalls.

Yuri automatically obeyed, taking hold of the remaining corpse. His mind was numb, and he found it difficult to think. Following Kirov's example, Yuri left the body in one of the stalls. When he turned around, Kirov was already walking out the door. He had to trot to catch up to the old man.

Kirov stopped in a vacant part of the hallway where he could survey everyone around them. His voice was low as he spoke. "Who did you call, Yuri?"

The young man halted three feet from Kirov, trying to decide how to answer, knowing his wife's and child's lives certainly hung in the balance. He told Kirov the UN contact's name.

Kirov nodded, as if that somehow fitted what he had already assumed.

"My wife and child," Yuri said as he looked into Kirov's eyes. "I was told you had them kidnapped."

"I did, but not for the reasons you think."

An image of the young Israeli woman who had been Yuri's last kill flashed into his mind. Everything was the same—the blood, the smell of death, the loneliness as he had stood over her. Everything. Except for the face. The face was Natasha's, and it was her blood on his hands.

"Where are my wife and child, Kirov?" Yuri almost didn't recognize his own voice. Harsh and raspy. He didn't care that Kirov was armed and he wasn't, or that they had left the bodies of two men who were armed but not fast enough to save themselves.

"In a safe place," Kirov replied. "With friends I have trusted my life to at one time or another. These are good men, young Mikhailin, not like Kulik or the trash he has operating for him."

"I want to talk to them."

"You will, but first we have to talk. I have a lot to say, and you must listen carefully. Do you understand?"

"Why didn't you tell me if you thought they were in any danger?"

"First, because you simply wouldn't have believed me. And second, because there was no privacy in your home. When I had breakfast with you I found three listening devices in your living room. Kulik keeps everyone not devoted to him under surveillance."

"But why would he feel the need to threaten me? I'm doing nothing that he didn't order."

"You are succeeding in your mission because the politburo placed you with me. They knew I would find Ivanovitch because I trained him. I know how the man thinks. I know where he is now. Kulik didn't want him found."

Yuri leaned against the wall for support. He struggled to make sense of it all, remembering the computer tap that had been traced. Remembering Natasha and Tanya as he had left them. Let them be alive, Yuri prayed, let them be alive.

"Some members of the politburo realized Kulik had placed Ivanovitch in a position to escape," Kirov went on. "The quest Ivanovitch is on now was nurtured by Kulik while Ivanovitch was still in prison. Sadly it didn't come to anyone's attention until after Ivanovitch was already running."

"But why didn't the politburo remove Kulik from power?"

"Because it was decided it would be better if the Comrade Major General passed away in his sleep a few months from now. The Americans have an uneasy truce with us now through the efforts of Gorbachev. If we can stop Ivanovitch in time, Kulik's fangs will have been pulled. Then, one night, he won't wake up. Sometimes the politburo moves slowly, but it never forgives. This way maybe the peace that lies between the United States and the Soviet Union won't be so restless. Knowing what Kulik had planned through Ivanovitch would simply start CIA heads thinking up new ways to respond in kind. And careers would have been made by the media people."

"Those men in the washroom . . ."

"Were KGB agents sent by your contact in the United Nations. There are still many who believe as Kulik and Ivanovitch do. Your contact is one, but already his replacement is being groomed. He, also, will pass quietly away in time. Until then, his power base will be negated so he can prove to be no embarrassment." Kirov looked into Yuri's eyes. There was more compassion in the old man's voice than Yuri had ever heard. "It was too late to keep you out of this thing, Yuri. You are a good agent. You have an open mind when there is need for one. You think twice before you kill. Our future, Tanya's future, will be built upon agents like you. On both sides of the iron curtain. Men like me, we are like dinosaurs, slowly dying out if madmen like Kulik will leave things alone." He took the pistol from his pocket and handed it to Yuri, holding it so that it wasn't visible to passersby. "When I was younger, I wouldn't have tried to prove myself the way I have tried to convince you of my innocence. I would have gone on the mission alone if I had to. But I'm older now, slower. I want you to be there in case I'm unable to complete the termination of Ivanovitch. I have held your daughter, young Mikhailin, and envied you your life because I have never known the complete happiness you enjoy with your family. If you think I could have brought about the deaths of your wife and child, kill me now and walk away."

"I want to talk to Natasha." Yuri kept the gun hidden, pointed toward Kirov's chest.

Kirov led the way to a pay telephone and gave Yuri an exchange and number to call. "Speak briefly," the old man said. "Our time is short. Already more of Kulik's men may be falling into place around us."

Yuri's vision blurred as he talked to Natasha, painfully aware of how much he wanted to tell her he loved her, yet wanting to sound unworried at the same time. Kirov pulled out a pack of American cigarettes and lit one, constantly on the alert but apparently unaware of Yuri.

After promising to explain everything when he returned home, Yuri gave his wife a final goodbye and looked at Kirov. "Where is Fyodor Ivanovitch?"

The old man dropped ashes onto the floor. Down the hall a uniformed New York City Police Squad arrived wearing bulletproof vests and riot gear. They spread out around the men's room containing the dead guards.

"You've heard of Grenada, of course?"

THE MUFFLED EXPLOSION caused Abby Nichols to peer cautiously over the door frame of the Subaru. Two cars approaching from the south end of the island were slowing down. Across the highway, a thick column of black smoke had formed, pouring skyward. Where was McKay? She brushed away a wisp of hair that fell across her eyes.

"Mom?"

She looked over the seat and saw her son lying prone, still secured by the safety belt. "Are you okay, Jase?"

The boy nodded. "Where's Mike? Did those guys hurt him?"

"I don't know," she said as she looked back at the smoke. "I don't see him."

Jase sat up and pressed his nose against the window. "If he's hurt, we've got to help him. He doesn't have anybody else."

He's got to be dead, Abby thought, and we might be too if we don't get out of here. She glanced around the car anxiously, feeling stupid when she saw the keys were still in the ignition. She slipped into the driver's seat, keeping an eye on the highway. Three cars had stopped now and two of the drivers had gotten out to see what had happened. What if the men who had attacked them had a backup? she asked herself.

The Subaru's engine turned over sluggishly, and for a moment Abby wondered if the rough treatment it had received had broken anything vital.

"Mom, you can't leave Mike here," Jase protested. She could hear the frenzy in her son's voice. "Even if he's not hurt, we can't let the police get to him. You heard what that Preston guy said—they want to lock Mike up."

"I'm sorry, Jase, but we're getting out of here. Your friend is a big guy, and from the sound of things, he's used to playing these kind of games. We're not. It's just you and me, and I'm not taking a chance on either one of us getting hurt.'' The Subaru lurched forward and drew the attention of the people standing by the roadside.

''He's a friend, Mom.'' Jase had released the seat belt and was clinging to the back of her seat as she made a U-turn that would take them back to St. George's. ''If it hadn't been for Mike, those guys would have killed us.''

Instead of seeing the grim mask McKay had worn when behind the wheel, Abby kept seeing him as he had been yesterday when he'd taken care of Jase. Fatherly. Not the rabid animal the DEA agent, Preston, had tried to make him out to be. The encouraging smile he'd given her when she had been in the restaurant last night with Richardson. There wasn't, couldn't, be a mad killer hiding behind those blue-gray eyes. And on the sidewalk, the man McKay had shot had been after her and Jase. But why would someone try to kill them? Why had someone killed Bill?

Cursing herself for being a fool, Abby brought the Subaru to a sudden stop at the side of the highway. ''Stay in the car,'' she told Jase as she started down the hill.

The Toyota was lying on its top, spilling black smoke. Two of the tires were on fire. For a moment Abby stood frozen as she surveyed the scene. Then she lost her footing in the grass and slid the rest of the way to the bottom. Some of the onlookers called down to her, but she ignored them.

McKay was getting to his feet only a few yards away, still holding the big silver gun in his hand. For a moment she was stunned by the physical threat of him. With his jacket torn and his face smudged with black, he looked like a dark angel.

''You okay?'' he asked.

She nodded and moved toward him in case he needed help.

''Is Jase all right?''

''He's fine. How are you?''

''Getting it together. We don't have a lot of time, though.''

"I know." Abby started up the hill and slipped. When she looked up, McKay was beside her, holding out a hand to help her to her feet. He kept hold of her hand as he forced his way to the highway.

Some of the bystanders rushed toward them until they spotted the gun in Bolan's hand, then they stepped back.

"No sign of the other guy?" Bolan asked.

"No."

Bolan slid behind the steering wheel as Abby got in on the passenger side. He turned the car around, heading south.

"You're not trying to catch up to that car again, are you?" Abby asked as she belted herself in.

The warrior shook his head. "He's gone by now, and we need to get rid of this car before the local authorities start looking for it." He wiped away a small trickle of blood from his forehead.

Abby found a handkerchief in her purse and handed it to him.

"Thanks."

"What are you going to do now?" Abby asked.

"With you and Jase?"

"Yes," Abby said, aware that at least part of her wanted to know that he was going to be safe as well.

"That depends."

"On what?" She couldn't mute the anger in her words. Dammit, she didn't have to stop for this man. She could have kept going. Surely he realized that. How the hell could he sit there thinking he had their lives in his hands?

Evidently Bolan picked up on the emotion because he turned to look at her when he spoke. "On what you want to do. The man who tried to shoot you, as well as the one I stopped on the sidewalk, work for Ramon Diaz."

"The man you asked me about earlier?"

"Yes. He's a dangerous man in these islands. He's built an empire on drugs and other criminal activities that reaches from South America to Florida."

"But why would he send anyone after me?"

Bolan shrugged. "I was hoping you could tell me." He checked the rearview mirror and Abby found herself involuntarily looking over her shoulder. "What are you doing in Grenada?"

"My brother was killed here two days ago. I was coming to make arrangements for his body and to talk to the police."

The warrior's voice softened, as if he knew how hard everything was for her. "Killed how?"

"Somebody shot him." Abby felt the tears she couldn't cry in the cold bleakness of the morgue vault suddenly break loose. She looked away from McKay, angry with herself for losing control in front of the man and her son. Jase needed her to be strong.

"I'm sorry, Abby, but there are a lot of questions I have to ask. Your life and Jase's might depend on the answers."

"I know."

"But first we need to find a safehouse."

"What about the police? Won't they be able to help us?"

"Do you know anybody here who you can trust?"

"No."

"There's no way to tell how many people Diaz has in his pocket until it's too late. And you can bet there are some. For now, can you trust me? I can't protect you or Jase unless you cooperate with me."

Abby studied her companion's profile, trying to see past the side of him that carried the gun and took men's lives without hesitation, remembering the way he'd talked to her when she'd been scared out of her mind when she woke up in the hotel room and Jase was gone. That man she knew she could trust, but the other, the vigilante side of him that the DEA man had warned her was on the verge of snapping, that man scared her. But that violent side of him, that was the side that had saved her and her son. Twice.

"Okay," Abby sighed as she wondered if McKay knew how much of a commitment she was making. Wondering, too, if there was such a thing as a safehouse for any of them now.

16

Bolan carried the bag of groceries they'd picked up after catching a flight back to Carriacou. Abby followed with her brother's personal effects, which had been given to her at the morgue. The warrior hadn't spotted anyone at the airfield at either end of the trip, and he felt more secure. Either Diaz was sure the warrior hadn't escaped from the second team or he was confident no one could touch him in his mansion. Of course that was assuming the second team was working for Ramon Diaz. A niggling bit of apprehension still lay uneasily at the back of his mind. Why send two teams? Why did the second team remain pacifist until it looked like Bolan was going to bring the first man down?

Pieces of the puzzle were missing, and what he had to do was find the missing pieces, or at least enough of them to guess the overall picture. And do it in a manner that would leave Abby Nichols and her son in the clear.

Abby pitched in wordlessly to help put the groceries away, but the kitchen was small and it was hard to keep their bodies from touching. Bolan felt her cringe each time it happened. He wished there was someone he could leave them with, someone she could trust who could protect them from Diaz's influence. Being there with him after what she'd seen was more hardship than she deserved. The silence that had developed between them in the Subaru had become a palpable thing.

"How long are you planning on us staying here?" Abby asked without looking at him.

"I have a contact in Washington. When I call him tonight, we'll work out a way to get you off the island safely tomorrow."

She stopped what she was doing and turned to him. "You're connected with the government?"

"Somewhat," Bolan replied, not wanting to explain the loose arm's-length relationship he'd developed with the Feds.

"Why didn't you tell the police back in Key West? Some people there are looking for you."

"For the same reason we aren't going to the police here." Bolan took out the steaks and started gathering seasonings. "This is a big operation, Abby. A lot of people have gotten killed trying to get as far as I have. I learned a long time ago not to trust anybody I didn't have to."

She put her hands on her hips and gave him a cold stare. "That's a hell of a philosophy, considering you asked me to put my life and my son's life in your care."

Bolan leaned back against the counter, the steaks forgotten. "You were in over your head. You still are. I didn't make your choices for you. Neither did you. I'm good at what I do, and when I say I can protect you and Jase, it's because I can."

"What do you do, McKay? Kill people? You seem to have left quite a string of bodies behind you. And now, thanks to you and your goddamned zeal for doing such a good job, Jase and I have both seen examples of your work up close. Do you think he's going to forget the things he saw today?"

"At least he's going to get the chance to try," Bolan said softly.

Without warning, Abby brought her right hand up and slapped Bolan across the face. The sound of flesh striking flesh drew Jase's attention immediately. The boy started to get to his feet, but Bolan checked the movement with a wave of his hand. Just as quickly as it flared, her anger was gone.

"I can't live like this," Abby cried in a broken voice. "Maybe you get used to it, but I can't. My brother was killed here just two days ago, for God's sake, now I find out someone wants my son and me dead too."

"Nothing is going to happen. I promise. You and Jase are going to be kept out of harm's way."

Her arms wrapped around him, holding tightly. She felt secure and child-small against his chest.

AFTER THE DISHES had been cleared away, Bolan brought the box of personal effects Abby Nichols had been given to the dinner table. The woman had gone to the bathroom for a shower, and Jase was still occupied by the television. Bolan kept an eye on the boy, surprised at how well he was holding up considering the events he'd been subjected to.

Bolan spread the contents of the box on the table, aware that Jase would know he was going through his dead uncle's things. But it couldn't be helped because he needed the information now. Why had Diaz been interested in Abby Nichols? Bolan asked himself as he took a mental inventory of the contents. She'd never been to Grenada before, had no reason to come in contact with any of Diaz's contacts. Her brother had been murdered, but why? Because of something he knew? He discarded that immediately. Such knowledge would have to have been written down. The only papers in the box had been William March's driver's license, passport, credit cards and a small daybook he kept a log of expenses in. No journal. No notes.

Maybe someone had thought March had a written document, Bolan thought. But of what? Only her brother's camera, five rolls of undeveloped film, a watch and a ring, set with a turquoise stone, remained. The other items had been clothing, and Abby hadn't had room to pack them in her bags. They would be traveling to Miami with the body.

"Did you find anything?"

Bolan looked up as Abby Nichols took a seat across the table from him. She was wearing a terry-cloth bathrobe, and her wet hair stuck to her head. She smelled of shampoo and soap, reminding Bolan he still had traces of smoke in his clothes from the explosion. He shook his head. "What was your brother doing in Grenada?"

"I don't know. Bill was a free-lance photographer. He took assignments all over the world, provided he could find a magazine editor willing to finance whatever project he was currently working on."

"You don't know who he was working for this last time?"

"No. He was free-lance. I could give you the names of a handful of editors he did a lot of work for, but it would take time to check them all. Even then you might not get the right one."

"What kind of subjects did your brother usually work on?"

"Anything that involved a camera. Billy loved taking pictures. I have several at my home that he took of Jase and me, of places I'll probably never see, of people he found interesting. He usually sent a small note with each picture, detailing how he happened to take the shot or how he met the people in the picture. Little stories that made me laugh when I read them. We were really close when we were kids and kind of drifted apart when I got married. Bill and my ex-husband didn't get along very well. We started talking more after the divorce, but we were each wrapped up in our own work. I free-lance too. I'm a novelist. It was kind of like a superstition between us, but we never talked about a work in progress."

Bolan picked up the rolls of film and tapped them thoughtfully. A record, he thought as he turned the small black cylinders around in his fingers. Maybe even more damning than the written word. He took the remaining rolls of film from the box and dropped them in his pockets.

"You think Bill saw something?" Abby asked.

"It's the only option I have left," Bolan said, picking up the camera and rewinding the film. "Chavez must have been waiting at the hospital to see who picked up your brother's things. They didn't know you until then. So something in this box is important to them. Your brother was a photographer. He might not have even known what he saw and just happened to be in the wrong place at the wrong time." He popped the camera open and removed the film. "Or he might have found what he was looking for and someone saw him. Hopefully these pictures will tell us more." He stood and took his jacket from the hall closet. "Will you and Jase be all right here until I get back?"

Abby nodded, but Bolan saw her hesitate.

"If Diaz does have someone patrolling the streets," Bolan said, "I'll be less noticeable by myself." The warrior took her hand in his, halfway expecting her to fight back against the contact, knowing she hadn't fully made up her mind about him. Instead she squeezed his hand.

"Hurry back," she whispered.

"I will. I noticed a little place only a few blocks from here that offers overnight developing. I'd rather have the prints tonight, but it's probably going to be the best I can find." Bolan let himself out after reminding her not to let anyone in while he was gone. He saw her watching him from the window as he got into the Jeep.

BOLAN FOUND a phone across the street from the photo place. The clerk was young and hungry, dark eyes centered between long black hair and a bushy beard. At first he'd been adamant about not being able to process the film until the morning, saying he closed at ten o'clock, which was only twenty minutes away. When he saw the two hundred-dollar bills Bolan laid on the scarred counter, he turned on a smile. He agreed to let Bolan back into the shop once he finished his telephone calls.

Standing inside the glass skin of the phone booth, Bolan stared through his intangible reflection at the slow moving traffic and considered his options. Brognola would be able to get someone down tomorrow—Bolan had no doubt about that—but whether he could get someone down quietly was another matter. Diaz was wired in tight to his sources of information. No one had ever penetrated his network as far as the Executioner had, but that had been because Bolan was a lone wolf. If a pack had been pursuing, Diaz would have known.

And if Brognola and the Feds were out of it, where did that leave Abby Nichols and her son?

Bolan dialed a long-distance operator and gave her a credit card number that couldn't be traced back to him, switching through areas until he found someone who could help him place a call to Key West.

The phone was answered by a man's voice that Bolan didn't recognize. Knowing Preston might have had the telephone lines tapped, Bolan identified himself as Bradley Kingston, a senator whose career Robert Drake had sent down in flames years before during the Vietnam War. Hard metal rock blasted through the receiver when the man laid the phone down and opened a door. Within two minutes Drake was speaking.

"How goes the war, Mike?" Drake asked.

"Hot and heavy so far," he replied, "but all the casualties belong to the right people."

"Anybody ever tell you that you move faster than an avalanche?" Drake asked. "The people up here haven't finished counting casualties at this end."

"Have they found anything to work with?"

"No. The few survivors of the freighter aren't talking, and from what I've been able to learn, none of the law-enforcement agencies have been able to trace it. Your friend must be an ace when it comes to computers."

"He's one of the best." Bolan watched as the young clerk switched out the lights in the photo store and put a closed sign on the door. "How's our young friend?"

"On his own again. The hospital wasn't exactly a safe place for him. One of the local *federales* Marino had in his pocket tried to take him out this afternoon. There's a pissed-off homicide captain downtown who wants him for questioning concerning the body they found in his bed, but doesn't blame him for not showing up. They still have some housecleaning to do in the division, and everybody knows it. Preston seems to have had more of a handle on things than anyone guessed.''

"The *federale* had friends."

"You got it."

"How is the patient doing?"

"He's sore as hell but he's getting around."

"Do you think he feels up to some flying?"

Drake chuckled dryly. "If it had been humanly possible, that boy would have been born with a stick in his hand."

"I've got a couple of friendlies at this end," Bolan said, "and I need a way to see them clear. I've got a few other options, but none of them are as quick as he would be. Or as untraceable."

"I'll tell him. He also had a message for you, in case you called. He said to make sure you knew Marino was still alive."

Bolan digested that. Sunburn hadn't had a real chance to see him. With a change of clothes, the Executioner would have been able to preserve his anonymity. If Marino chose to come to the source, that part of his defense would be stripped from him. But that was a chance he would have to take. This afternoon's assault on Abby Nichols convinced him something on the island was about to break loose. "How soon can you get a message to him?"

"Give me thirty minutes," Drake said. "Hell, Merlin Olsen couldn't promise anything better, and he isn't tripping all over cops during those FTD commercials."

Bolan chuckled. "Tell him I'll call him where we first met."

"You got it. Just make sure you take good care of the little son of a bitch. He's one of the few people I'd miss around this island."

Bolan hung up. He walked back across the street with his hands in his jacket pockets, mind whirling with stray thoughts as he tried to sort them out. Abby's and Jase's presence complicated things, sure, but they had also brought to light another angle that Bolan hadn't been aware of. What could Bill March have uncovered in a few days that would have made someone kill him? The locals on the island already knew Diaz and his crew for what they were, yet Diaz had sent at least one team, and maybe two, to make sure March's personal effects didn't fall into the wrong hands.

The police hadn't had the film developed because they didn't know what kind of work March did and had no reason to think his death was tied in with anything Diaz was doing.

But, Bolan thought as he rapped on the locked door of the film processing store, if Diaz had sent someone to recover March's camera and the film, it would have gone by now. If it hadn't been for the fact that Bolan had seen the hit man drive from Diaz's mansion, he would have been doubting his logic. Ramon Diaz wasn't the type of man to leave loose ends. If the drug lord had sent two teams, they wouldn't have been operating independently. It would have been a joint operation. So, if the brown-haired man and Chavez were one team and belonged to Diaz, where did the other team fit in? An opposing force? Bolan dismissed that conjecture immediately. No, they'd been protecting the brown-haired man even if he hadn't known it. But why?

The clerk opened the door and Bolan stepped in.

"You got some real scenic beauty in some of these shots," the clerk said as he led the way to the rear of the shop. "Did you take these pictures?"

"No."

"Well, whoever did was a real talented person. Got an eye for color and perspective, I got to admit. Usually pictures like these are taken by tourists who snap and run. It gets so you're sick of looking at them after a couple of dozen. But these are good."

Pausing at the table where he'd left the color prints, the clerk indicated them with a wave of his hand. "I don't know why you were in such a hurry for them, actually, but it's your money."

Bolan nodded and started going through the pictures. Maybe March had discovered something that wasn't readily noticeable. "How many rolls have you got here?"

"The first three."

"Are any of these from a roll that wasn't completely shot?"

"No. I got that one developing now. It's a thirty-six exposure roll but less than half of it has been used. I was going to ask you about that."

"Get that one for me next."

The clerk nodded and checked a clock on the wall over a closed door that said Darkroom. "It's got about another five minutes before it will be ready."

"Keep those separate for me."

"Okay." The clerk took a manila envelope from under the counter and disappeared into the darkroom.

Bolan pulled a chair from another table and sat down. He flipped through the pictures twice, but nothing caught his eye. It would have helped, he thought, if he'd known what he was looking for. He checked his watch and saw that he'd been gone from the cottage for over an hour, realizing that the time was probably wearing on Abby Nichols in her current frame of mind. He wished there had been a phone in the cottage so he could have called her.

The clerk wore a puzzled expression when he returned. "These pictures are different from the first," he said as he laid the stack of proofs on the table.

Bolan shoved the first group of pictures to one side and flipped through the small number of exposures. There were eight stills in all. The first five were of a café with wrought-iron furniture and of the beach that spilled down from it. The last three were of Miguel Chavez and Sunburn, the brown-haired man Bolan had tailed from Diaz's estate, sitting at one of the café's tables.

Holding up the one that had the clearest view of the brown-haired man, Bolan said, "I need an eight-by-ten of this guy." He tapped the picture.

"You want me to crop everything else out?"

Bolan nodded.

After making a quick trip to the soft drink machine in the customer lobby and getting a Coke, Bolan resumed his seat and started flipping through the pictures again, wondering if he'd missed something. Now that he had a perspective in his search, maybe something else would stand out. He sipped the Coke and wished he had coffee instead. He rubbed his eyes tiredly when the photographs started to blur as he studied them.

He placed all of the pictures but the remaining two of Chavez and the unknown man in the manila envelope. He laid the two side by side and tried to figure it out.

Chavez was a known accomplice of Diaz. Bolan had seen the man's name and face in the package Kurtzman had dug up for him. But not the brown-haired man. Why?

Diaz would have been especially leery of picking up anyone new at this time, Bolan reasoned, with all the pressure that was coming down from the Atlanta connection. Which implied the brown-haired man was someone out of Diaz's past, someone he could trust.

Yet, judging from the way the man and Chavez sat across the table from each other, their meeting had been awkward. Neither man looked as if he were enjoying the conversation. They weren't eating, so Bolan figured he could assume it was a business meeting of some sort. But why meet in a public place?

Unless the brown-haired man hadn't been sure of exactly where he stood with Ramon Diaz. Chavez could have acted as a liaison. But if that was the case, what did the man possess that would convince Diaz to risk his presence now?

Something impressive, that was for sure.

When the clerk returned from the darkroom, Bolan tucked the two pictures into his breast pocket.

"Here's your eight-by-ten," the clerk said.

After inspecting it, Bolan replaced the blowup in the protective jacket the clerk gave him. "What about the fifth film?"

The clerk handed the last batch of photos over. "More or less the same as the first three rolls. Like I said, the person who took these exposures knew what was what when it came to camera work."

Bolan took the time to go through them, scrutinizing each one before moving on to the next. He was fairly certain he had the pictures that had been responsible for Bill March's death, if not the reason for it. After placing the last pictures with the others in the manila envelope, he studied the eight-by-ten again.

Part of the man's face was hidden by dark sunglasses, but Bolan could feel the coldness locked inside the features, the arrogance that was evident from the way the guy held his head and shoulders, a military bearing, borne out by the short crop of his hair. The sunburn that covered the exposed skin on the man's face and hands showed a deep and ruddy mahogany against the paleness of his complexion, further evidence that the man was new to the island. Probably even new to this side of the world, he told himself as he remembered Hal Brognola's warning about the latest Russian involvement in the area.

Realizing that the clerk was waiting for him to leave and that Chase Murphy was probably at his office by now, Bolan put the photograph away and left, crossing the street to the phone booth. He had another piece of the puzzle, sure, but none of them seemed to be fitting together yet.

The center of the operation had skewed slightly, hinging largely on the identity of the man in the eight-by-ten. After checking his watch and finding it wasn't quite midnight, Bolan decided to see if the Jamison identity would still hold up after the encounter in St. George's. It was risky, but even riskier for a soldier to try to outline and define his hellground without a full recon of the opposition. And the Executioner had a gut feeling that the nameless man added up to more than what appeared on the surface. The man was running his own game through Diaz's machine. But what did he have that would convince Diaz to let him?

Bolan was sure either the brown-haired man or Chavez had killed Bill March and hadn't been able to remove the camera at the time. He was also certain Ramon Diaz didn't know about March or the pictures. Chavez and Sunburn had joined forces to remove the threat of exposure, both from law-enforcement agencies as well as the drug lord. And that left the backup team, which neither Chavez or his partner seemed to be aware of.

Bolan was just as certain a third party was involved in whatever operation the brown-haired man was heading, whether the man knew it or not. But, he wondered, how would Diaz react if he knew about the men keeping tabs on his latest associate?

There were too many variables, too many to correctly plot a plan of action. And Abby Nichols and Jase were trapped somewhere inside a constantly shifting center. Even his help was a threat to them, he realized sourly, because he didn't know how much the other group knew about him. If they were Russian, Mack Bolan had already carved a reputation in their ranks. They would be looking for him, would know him on sight perhaps. Even trying to get the woman and boy off the island might result in their deaths if someone recognized him.

But as he dialed Murphy's number he realized there weren't a lot of choices. Things were already heating up, and the island wasn't big enough for a lot of subterfuge.

Murphy answered on the fourth ring. "Yeah?"

"Carriacou," Bolan said.

"Anyplace special?"

"The airport. There's too much activity here for anything fancy. Deviations will be noticed."

"Run into a lot of players?"

"More than anticipated." Bolan smiled despite himself when he heard the professional edge slide into the younger man's voice. He was also aware Murphy was keeping questions to a minimum in case the line was bugged.

"You got a specific time in mind?"

"Can you make it by midmorning with a sweep in from Grenada? I want it to look like local traffic."

"No problem. I'll throw a couple of surprises in for free."

"There might not be a chance for a retake if things start going down at this end. I've got people I want clear of this thing."

"I'll see you then," Murphy promised.

Bolan broke the connection, moving toward the Cherokee. Night on the island had closed in around him, but it was the pressure of the unseen enemy camps that felt most restrictive. The Executioner had been in tight situations before, but usually there was more intel to push with. At the moment he felt as if he was in a deep dark tunnel with only a matchstick to use as a feeler as he made his way along. Two inches from having his arm bitten off.

He climbed into the Cherokee and put the pictures in the glove compartment. Abby Nichols would want them later. He placed the eight-by-ten between the seats as he started the vehicle and moved into the darkened streets. A pang of guilt stabbed through him when he realized it would be longer still before he returned to the cottage, leaving Abby and Jase feeling vulnerable, but it was time for Sergeant Michael Jamison to introduce himself to the Carriacou law division.

And hope they weren't looking for anyone that answered his description.

17

Major General Vladimir Kulik ignored the bitter and rancid taste of the hours-old coffee, drinking it more for the caffeine it contained than for its flavor. The events of the past few hours had left a lingering sourness that nothing short of success could erase.

Setting his cup to one side, he went over the papers before him again, studying the charted movements of Kirov and Mikhailin, of Ivanovitch, and of the team lying in wait on Grenada and Carriacou. The incident involving Kirov and Mikhailin in New York City had already been taken care of. The American forces investigating the killings were being directed away from useful information that might have revealed either Kirov or Mikhailin. The only problem there, Kulik told himself as he tapped the sheets with angry fingers, was that no one knew for sure where the two men were, although their destination wasn't really in question any longer.

Kulik pushed himself back in his seat and closed his eyes, trying to convince himself everything was still within his control.

He was sure Kirov knew that Ivanovitch had been manipulated, both in prison and since his escape. But how long had Kirov known? Kulik wondered. Their passage through New York City was one tip-off. Kirov had always loved working out of that city whenever he had the chance. It wasn't surprising to discover that the old man still had contacts there who could steal him away quietly. And he'd had the foresight to arrange the removal of Mikhailin's wife and daughter, taking away the leverage Kulik could have used to reach the younger agent.

But why stay with Mikhailin? There was no reason to be protective of the younger agent, Kulik told himself, unless Kirov hadn't been able to secure the blessings of whatever members of the politburo he had spoken with and needed Mikhailin to confirm his findings.

Or maybe retirement had eroded the confidence the old man once had in his own abilities. Maybe he felt he needed a backup when going against Fyodor Ivanovitch and whatever agents he felt would be placed in his way.

Kulik grinned despite his tiredness.

If that was the case, Boris Kirov had truly lost his ability to judge men. Mikhailin was worthless as a field operative. Very intuitive at times when planning strategies, good with public relations and with handling departmental flack, with an impressive track record, but the man simply wasn't a killer like Kirov. Mikhailin would hesitate before taking the life of another person. The experience with the female Israeli spy had ruined him for handing out death on a personal level.

It would be a weakness, Kulik knew, that the team commander on special assignment to Grenada would exploit without lengthy consideration. Anton Chernetzsky was the son Kulik would have had if he had made the time. That was why he'd put Chernetzsky in charge of the Ivanovitch situation, because of the loyalty the man held for him and for his view of world politics, which Kulik had carefully nurtured over the years. Just as he had nurtured them in Ivanovitch before Kirov had stepped away from the KGB. Only Ivanovitch had been a weapon, a tool to be discarded after use. Chernetzsky was a separate shade of Kulik's own shadow, a younger pair of hands to accomplish tasks with, a quick mind that followed channels Kulik was familiar with.

The major general stood up from the desk to stretch cramped leg muscles, surprised to find his left foot had gone to sleep. Sharp needles signaled the returning circulation in the foot and caused him to limp as he walked to the large map on the opposite wall. He stood before it, hands clasped behind his back, and surveyed the islands dotting the Caribbean Sea.

So many countries, Kulik thought as his gaze flicked from one island cluster to another, packed in so little space. Together they amounted to very little political clout, but seemed to be a focus for international affairs from time to time.

Kulik recalled the early 1960s, when Kennedy took a firm stand against Castro and Cuba, opposing the Soviet missiles that were being brought within such close striking range of the United States. Now the Americans considered the islands to be more nuisance than anything else, the major general knew. Drugs flowed freely through the island countries, and no matter how many agents American enforcement threw into the fray, it was doomed to be a losing battle.

But still, Kulik thought, the islands were a strategic place for military operations. So far the Americans ruled the area, but their control seemed to be slipping away as the attempts to stop the drug trade became stronger. For many of those countries, as well as countries in South America, the American demand for cocaine and marijuana supported a major part of the economy.

And the ruling power of those countries was usually in the hands of only a few men, men who marketed in the traffic of controlled substances and who covertly deflected the American agencies.

Panama had been such a country. The CIA had made deals with Noriega over the years, until the dictator tried to slip away from their control.

It wouldn't have been a large problem for the United States to stage a military coup and place many of the larger countries under a puppet leader. It had been done before. But now, Kulik thought in silent satisfaction, the Americans were losing favor in the eyes of the world. No longer were they in control of the Arab oil fields. No longer did their technology far outstrip anyone else. The third world countries were taking a bigger piece of the pie now.

And that was the thing that scared Kulik the most. Russia was by far the biggest country in the world, but she was also by far one of the lesser endowed with natural resources.

Under Gorbachev and his predecessors, Russia had become more dependent on the goodwill of other countries, had demanded less of herself and her people than at any other time in her history. Rather than try to produce the things they needed, the governing body was content to continue to import wheat. It was embarrassing to think that the country couldn't even feed itself.

The space race had deteriorated to a halfhearted joint effort over the past decade—one more factor joining the many that had been found out-of-date.

The world was moving closer together. Kulik knew that to be true. And Gorbachev seemed to be content to let it, and to let ties with the Americans grow to the point that the world leaders felt at ease traveling to each other's countries.

But Ivanovitch's effort in Grenada would end much of that, Kulik thought as he touched a forefinger to the island on the map. After tomorrow and the international mishap that would occur there, international affairs would be thrown into the winds again. Russia would be forced to draw back within herself, of course, but Kulik thought that was one of the best things that could happen. Russia would become hungry again instead of being so complacent, would take charge of her destiny once more.

The Americans would lose more in the end.

And that would happen tomorrow morning. If everything went as he thought it would.

Ivanovitch was in place, already deep within Ramon Diaz's protection, unaware of Chernetzsky's team waiting in the wings in case he failed. Chernetzsky was under orders to succeed where Ivanovitch failed, as long as he could keep his involvement unknown.

Kulik knew the Americans were aware of Russian activity in the area, but he had let the story leak of Ivanovitch's escape to give the CIA people pause while everything fell into place.

The only thing that troubled him was the loss of the two agents that had been following Ivanovitch earlier that day. Their cover papers had been in place once the car rental agency was contacted, and the local authorities hadn't pursued the issue further than notifying the "families" of the deceased. Things in the Caribbean moved slowly. Maybe there would be more of an investigation within the next few days, but Chernetzsky had made sure the trail they followed would end quickly.

At any rate, after tomorrow morning it would all be too late. Whatever investigation was planned into this matter would be easily forgotten as a new disaster took shape.

If, Kulik thought as he turned from the map, anyone remained alive who could remember the incident.

Still, the question nagged at him as to the identity of the man who had Ivanovitch under surveillance. From the reports Chernetzsky had gathered, the man had been working alone, something the CIA never did. So how did he fit into the present scheme of things? And what did he know of Ivanovitch's task?

It really didn't matter, Kulik told himself as he sipped at the cold coffee. The operation had gone past the point of cancellation.

And Chernetzsky had been given new orders just within the last hour. The nameless man was to be shot on sight the next time his path crossed Ivanovitch's. Just as Boris Kirov and Yuri Mikhailin were to be.

Those men were the only flaws Kulik had found in his design, and none of them would be fatal. Even if Chernetzsky and his men failed to get them, the death that Ivanovitch was going to unleash would. He permitted himself another small smile of satisfaction and rose to refill his cup.

MACK BOLAN STOOD outside the telex area, grimly aware that the Michael Jamison identity could peel away at any time and leave him at a disadvantage—to put it mildly—in the police station. So far the letters he'd been given had drawn little more than casual interest, and the young policeman who had been assigned to see to his needs seemed bored. The man was at the other end of the hall, gossiping with an officer who was pecking slowly on a typewriter.

He watched the telex operator through the glass window, finding the hum of the machine and the flashing lights across the panel to be hypnotic. Tiredness washed over him like a lazy ocean wave. It would have been so easy for him to retreat to the cottage and grab some sleep. But he needed a few more answers first.

After dancing his fingers across the keyboard in front of the telex machine for a few more minutes, the potbellied operator stood and walked over to the glass door separating the room from the hallway. The guy stuck his head out long enough to say, "Your man received the transmission just fine. I had him send me a copy back to make sure."

Bolan nodded. "Any messages?"

The telex operator shook his head.

"Can I have the still back?"

"Sure." The man retreated into the room long enough to recover the glossy as well as the copy.

Replacing them in the folder he had gotten at the film processing shop, Bolan said thanks and left, dropping by the front desk to return the visitor ID badge he'd received earlier.

The balmy night air closed in around him as he deserted the air-conditioned environment of the police station. It was cooler now, making the lightweight windbreaker he wore more useful than just masking the presence of the Desert Eagle and the Beretta.

The rear parking lot of the police station was dark, a flat slate of blackness where night melded into the unreflecting surface of the tarmac. The sounds of passing cars lisp-

ing through the wire fence that separated the area from the
street, pushed along by floating bits of conversations that
drifted in from passersby.

There was no warning when the first man reached for
Bolan, only the slight tug of the man's fingers on the warrior's jacket.

Bolan whirled toward the touch, dropping his right
shoulder as he brought his left leg up in a roundhouse kick
that connected with the man's head. Letting the reaction
of the impact start his backward movement, the Executioner fell away, going to the ground as he rolled backward in an effort to drop from sight.

He continued rolling as he sought the protection of the
line of parked cars to his left, knowing there would be
more than one man. An automatic weapon traced silent
fire after him, bullets splatting against the tarmac before
whining away into the night.

Bolan rose to his feet behind the battered hulk of an ancient pickup, raking the silenced Beretta from his holster
as he surveyed the sudden hellzone. The first man who had
attacked him had vanished.

Were they Diaz's men? Bolan asked himself as he
changed positions and moved to the front of the pickup
truck. A quick movement to his right, across the empty
lane that allowed access to the parking area, alerted the
warrior. He spun away from the pickup, sliding across the
hood of a nearby car as a halo of orange and yellow muzzle-flashes erupted in the hands of one of his attackers.
Silent death tumbled at him as 9 mm teeth bit into the
windshield of the pickup. The shooter traced his fire across
the hood of the car only a heartbeat after Bolan regained
the ground.

The Executioner kept low as he moved, knowing time
was working against him. Even if he succeeded in putting
down the attack unscathed, the police inside the adjacent
building wouldn't be willing to release him soon. He
flicked the Beretta to 3-shot mode.

Muffled curses reached him as shoes scraped across the rough surface of the parking area. It didn't surprise him to find that the words were Russian.

Three men at least, Bolan decided as he kept moving. One man was giving orders and had called out the names of two other men, directing them to close in around the last position Bolan had held. Then there was silence again as the hounds closed in for the kill. Which was fine, the Executioner told himself. They were going to find out soon enough that the rabbit they pursued had fangs and claws of its own.

He heard leather scrape behind him, at least three car lengths away, and angled off in that direction, maintaining his cover behind the parked cars as much as he could.

When the warrior found the man he was looking for, he took no chances. Before the Russian ever saw him, the Executioner triggered a burst from the Beretta that started at the hunter's throat and rode its bloody way up to the man's right eye, gagging his death scream in the crushed and broken larynx.

He stripped the silenced Skorpion machine pistol from the dead man and eased the body to the ground, then rolled it under the concealing bulk of the car. The Beretta was returned to its holster as Bolan gripped the Czech-made weapon. He found three more clips for the subgun inside the corpse's jacket and dropped them in the pockets of his windbreaker.

Leaving his position, Bolan angled wide, determined to reach the Cherokee as soon as possible. There would be a guard on the Jeep. Someone had staked out the police station in an attempt to cover all bases. That was why the attack hadn't occurred until Bolan left the building. Reinforcements had to have time to arrive. He remembered the man who had been standing by the ticket window at the airport earlier, realizing the guy had probably made him then.

Ten minutes later he halted three car lengths down from the Jeep, peering cautiously through the rolled up windows of a Japanese compact. Two men sat in a late-model sedan beside the four-wheel drive. Neither spoke as they watched over the parking area spread before them.

Not trusting the untried Skorpion for what he was about to do, Bolan slung it over his shoulder and drew the Beretta. Melding his profile in with the Japanese compact's low-slung windshield, the Executioner extended his right arm before him, accepting the weight the 93-R offered, making it a part of the overall man.

He sighted.

Squeezed.

Squeezed twice again as he shifted targets.

The man on the driver's side slumped forward as the center of his forehead was drilled by a 9 mm hornet. The remaining pair of 9 mm slugs took the second guy in the face and throat. One of the bullets entered through the man's cheek and spit blood, tissue and teeth out the open window on the other side. For a moment he tried to stem the rushing arterial flow that gushed from his throat, then he lost interest as his brain shut down.

Bolan gave the scene five long heartbeats before closing in, keeping the Beretta in front of him in a Weaver's grip. He held the silenced weapon in position until he touched the first man's neck with the heated barrel and got no reaction.

Conscious of the numbers falling, Bolan searched the man quickly but found no identification, although he did add another ten magazines to his cache for the Skorpion.

A quick check informed him the keys still dangled from the car's ignition. Dropping to the ground, he drew the Kabar he had sheathed on his left ankle and slid under the sedan. He found the gas line under the carriage by touch, satisfied when he felt the spongy rubber bend in his fingers. Using the combat knife, he sliced the hose just ahead of the gas tank, letting the gasoline pour out on the ground.

There would be enough fuel in the line running to the carburetor to do what he wanted to do, Bolan told himself. He knelt at the driver's side of the sedan, lifted one of the dead man's feet to place on the accelerator and snaked an arm inside to grasp the ignition key.

He scanned the parking area one more time as he dug out a pack of matches. The rest of the hit team wasn't visible, but he could feel the threat of them in the darkness. The strong aroma of the gasoline would draw their attention.

The warrior twisted the steering wheel as he keyed the ignition, aiming the vehicle for the fence that surrounded the parking lot. He used the dead driver's weight to hold the wheel in place as he dropped the column shift into drive. The car's rear tires spun and slipped in the pool of gasoline, finally gripping the rough surface in a rubber-shredding screech that Bolan was sure had heads turning.

Before he was inside the Jeep, bullets had already started turning the rented sedan into a metal Swiss cheese. The Cherokee's engine caught smoothly, and he powered into a tire-eating turn that would take him toward the open street. When the contents of the matchbook flared into hungry life, he dropped the book into the pool of gasoline as he drove by. He watched in his rearview mirror as the fire spread, refusing to be denied as it skated from the pool of gasoline down the narrow ribbon the sedan had dripped across the parking lot.

Bolan didn't know if the car reached the fence before the fire engulfed it. The explosion roared through the thick night air, creating a momentary lapse in hearing as the concussion buffeted everything in its path. With the lights off, the Executioner barely saw the man who suddenly rose before him with a Skorpion in both fists.

Without hesitation, the warrior shifted the Jeep into second gear and ran the guy down, riding out the bumps as the vehicle passed over the body. A final burst from somewhere behind him tracked across the back of the Cherokee, shattering the rear window and punching the passenger seat forward.

Then all four tires were straining against the street, pushing the Executioner away from his latest hellzone. Bolan checked the rearview mirror, partially satisfied when he found no signs of pursuit. Another enemy had found him, an enemy who had intimate knowledge of him and of what he was doing on the island. He felt like a rat trapped in a maze that seemed familiar, yet insisted on having new twists and turns that threw out logic and made planning almost impossible.

As he quit the firezone he hoped Brognola and Kurtzman would give him something to work with.

18

An unending wave of reggae music thundered into the thin walls of the bar. A steady flow of patrons kept the young waitresses busy, both serving drinks and trying to keep stray hands from wandering under the short skirts they wore. Bolan cupped the receiver of the telephone as he dialed Hal Brognola's home number, letting his gaze drift over the crowd in front of him. A waitress with too-red hair separated herself from the clutches of a tanned guy with a crew cut, shoving the man backward into his chair with practiced ease and adjusting her skirt so that a hint of black lace showed only briefly. She came to a stop in front of Bolan and gave him a once-over.

"Can I get you something to drink?" she asked. In the darkness it was hard to guess her age, but Bolan figured she was on the downside of forty. Old enough to still be sexy if the lighting wasn't too harsh, and skilled enough to be a survivor in a rough business.

"A beer," Bolan said as he heard the overseas operator make a connection.

"You got a favorite?" she asked as she held her serving tray in front of her in a move designed to take years off.

"A draw will be fine."

She nodded and moved away, casually avoiding the quick hands and lip service that followed her.

Brognola answered on the second ring. "Striker?"

The underlying excitement in the Fed's voice told Bolan that Kurtzman's computers had uncovered something. The Executioner checked the time. It was only a little after one, and already he felt as if things were closing in on him. "Yeah, it's me."

"What do you know about the man in the picture?"

"Not much," Bolan admitted. He relayed the day's events, ending with the Russian team that had tried to take him out at the police station.

"Well, you struck pay dirt on this one, big guy," Brognola said. "Does the name Fyodor Ivanovitch mean anything to you?"

"Maybe, maybe not. I got a feel for it, but nothing concrete comes to mind."

"It could be because you've never been directly involved with Ivanovitch. He's KGB. At least he was, according to the information Kurtzman has been able to access since you telexed the photograph. Hell, given the current state of political affairs, Ivanovitch might still be an agent and most of the Russian directorate is unaware of it."

The waitress returned with the beer balanced precariously on her wooden tray as she navigated through the forest of groping hands. Only a little of the foam trickled down the sides of the glass mug when she came to a stop. Bolan paid her and took the drink.

"Ivanovitch helped mastermind the Cuban involvement in Grenada back in '83," Brognola said. "The CIA caught wind of his activities, but he got away clean just before the invasion. The SEAL teams nearly nailed him on an early penetration effort, but he faded before they could close off his escape route. Ivanovitch stayed long enough to make sure there were no 'advisers' left behind who could be tied too tightly to the KGB. The man is good, Striker. Or at least he was back in '83. Kurtzman can't dig much up on him since then. It's likely that he's renegade."

Bolan sipped his beer. The music still hammered at him, vibrating the wall he leaned against. "What exactly do you mean by renegade?"

"This much of Aaron's report isn't too substantial," Brognola said, "but I'll give it to you for what it's worth.

According to what our guys have been able to ferret out, Ivanovitch hasn't been happy with Gorbachev's diplomacy or the way policy has been changing over the past few years. He was from the old school, bred to the hardline tactics of the cold war. He was one of Greb Strakhov's handpicked students."

The name spun into Bolan with the force of a runaway bulldozer, splintering his train of thought. Memories crept into his mind, mingling the suffocating grasp of a warm and rainy day, a death-dealing bullet from an unexpected enemy and the perfume of a lost love.

"Striker?"

Images formed and gathered in the smoky atmosphere above the tables, aloof from the quiet and loud conversations.

Greb Strakhov had been the indirect cause of the death of April Rose, the love of Bolan's life. The spymaster's own death at the Executioner's hands had been a hollow victory.

A harsh crackling that interrupted the phone conversation for a few seconds broke the tendrils of memory that had woven a tangled skein of emotion in Bolan's mind. He sipped the beer again and wiped the glass across his cheek to feel its coolness.

"Mack?" Brognola's worry was evident in his voice.

"Yeah, Hal."

"Are you okay?"

"Sure. So you think the Russian team I turned up is looking for Ivanovitch?"

"I can't say for sure. A contact I have in the Company told me only a minute ago that information concerning Ivanovitch's escape from a high-security facility in Dzerzhinsky Square was released this morning. Soviet liaisons say they have a team moving on him now and aren't expecting any trouble recapturing him. But if that's the case, why are these guys helping him stay free and running? Why are they attacking you and risking an international incident worse than what they already might have if Ivanovitch is planning something?''

"The guys I crossed paths with are running interference for Ivanovitch," Bolan agreed. "There's no mistake about that."

Brognola sighed heavily. "It scans. The guy I talked to wasn't ready to be pumped this close to midnight, but we've taken care of each other over the years when things have gotten tight. He says some of the brass in the CIA think the story is a smoke screen. Hell, according to what he told me, the CIA isn't sure where Ivanovitch is. Right now they're still trying to open up an investigation of the deaths of two Russian embassy aides in New York City. I don't have to tell you they're not exactly getting a gold-plated invitation."

Bolan played it through his mind, sorting through the pieces he had garnered from his efforts. "Ramon Diaz was Ivanovitch's contact in Grenada?"

"One of them. There were others, but Diaz was best set up to move the ordnance the Cubans and the Soviet-sympathetic faction needed for the takeover. If Ivanovitch is loose down there, it makes sense that he'd attempt to link up with Diaz again if he needed something."

Bolan recalled what he knew about the drug czar, melding the information Brognola had given him earlier about the man with the impression he'd gotten from his recon. Ivanovitch was operating more or less on his own, Bolan reasoned, otherwise Diaz would have exerted his muscle and influence to recover March's incriminating film earlier. Assuming Diaz didn't know about that angle, it made sense that the renewed relationship between the KGB man and the cocaine supplier wasn't what it had once been. Sure, Diaz had once listened to Ivanovitch, had taken orders from him and risks for him. But why now? Ivanovitch was in no position to offer Diaz anything. Before, the whole country had been up for grabs. Diaz would've been able to seize any piece of the pie left over by the Soviets and Cubans that he was big enough to hang on to. Ivanovitch had to have some kind of hook to even get Diaz's attention, much less any form of backing.

"We're missing something, Hal."

Brognola grunted assent.

"Ivanovitch baited Diaz with something to get him to come this far."

"And what can you get for the drug king who has everything?"

Bolan switched gears, dropping the question of what tied Ivanovitch and Diaz together. "How is the CIA handling the alert?"

"My friend was a little hesitant over that. I get the impression it's a very uptight matter with them."

"What are the chances of Kurtzman being able to break into their computer files?"

Brognola chuckled. "I've already got him working on it. Friendship will only take you so far these days. Hell, I still find taps in my office from time to time that trace directly back to the Company. They don't even try to be cute about it anymore."

Bolan smiled in spite of himself and the situation. The floor show in front of him continued as the crowd got louder.

"You're going to have some more company on that island paradise of yours tomorrow," Brognola continued. "I scanned news sources concerning that area this afternoon. I assume you've noticed you're heavily involved in the party season down there."

"It was kind of hard to miss."

"It's an annual celebration. You can expect almost anything at this time of year. The first weekend of August is always set aside for the Carriacou Regatta. The yacht races draw an international crowd as well as hundreds from the neighboring islands. Ivanovitch is going to have plenty of places to hide."

"I don't think hiding is what he has in mind. Sure, he seems like he's kept a low profile so far, but what choice has he had? Somebody like Diaz isn't going to welcome any extra attention. Especially considering the pressure I've been laying on. But Ivanovitch can't be hoping to outmaneuver his Russian tail forever. No, he's definitely got something planned. He wouldn't have tried relying on Diaz's good graces for his salvation. He struck a deal of some sort. The fact that the Russians have released the information of his escape to our side only emphasizes that he has something in his possession they're afraid of."

Brognola's voice was quiet and subdued when he agreed. A hollow click sounded, and the Fed put Bolan on hold while he answered the call-waiting beep.

"I think I've got your link," Brognola said when he resumed the conversation. He didn't try to mask his anger. "Three years ago, a top-priority defense shipment on board a Navy jet was jettisoned after an instrument failure and power shutdown. From the bits and pieces the Navy recovered, there were no doubts the jet was sabotaged. The Navy stayed strictly in-house with the seek-and-search mission and turned up a mole who connected directly back with Fyodor Ivanovitch's team, but it was too late to pin the guy down. The jet crashed south of Puerto Rico, en route to a naval base in the Virgin Islands. Like I said, it took the Navy a few hours to respond to the incident, and by the time they took control of the area, the cargo was gone."

"What was it carrying?"

"Three cannisters of an experimental nerve gas the Navy R&D boys had put together."

Bolan felt a chill slide down his spine. "There was no chance the payload was destroyed?"

"Maybe. The commander who put the Eyes Only report together tried to slant it that way. One of the cannisters was found burst. According to the report, the gas had still managed to spread through the water and kill thousands of fish. This is potent stuff, Striker."

"Did anyone do a follow-up on this?"

"Yeah. Bear turned up a stack of addendums. He said he hasn't had much time to go over them, but the last ones filed show that nothing substantial ever turned up."

"How sure were the investigators that Ivanovitch was involved?"

"There was never any question after their preliminary investigation."

"And the information was never released through public channels?"

"Strictly on a need-to-know basis," Brognola replied. "It's not exactly the sort of thing that the United States is supposed to be passing through that part of the globe. The repercussions would be international."

"They might still be," Bolan said in a flat voice. He forced the anger out of his mind, knowing it would only limit the scope of his thinking. It wasn't the first time a governmental department head had swept an incident under the carpet and hoped with blind faith that it would stay there.

"You think Ivanovitch has the missing nerve gas?"

"Can you think of anything else he would have to offer to Ramon Diaz?"

Brognola fell silent and the implications filled the void between them. Bolan tried to put himself in Diaz's place, tried to imagine what the drug king would do if he had access to the nerve gas. "What kind of damage could one cannister do?"

"A lot. Kurtzman didn't get into the specs on the gas. I can get the information if you need it." Brognola sounded pained. "This is high-tech stuff. Everything the research guys in the lab touch is to figure out how to kill the world and leave the buildings all intact.

"Nerve gas is traceable too," Brognola went on. "It wouldn't take anyone long to figure out that what's in those cannisters was made in the U.S.A. The decision to invade Grenada wasn't that popular with our allies when it happened in '83. If Ivanovitch is planning on releasing the gas in those islands, it's going to open up a lot of old wounds."

"If Ivanovitch sets the gas free somewhere off the coast, how much of a drift can we expect?"

"Kurtzman says if the wind is right and nothing happens to break the cloud mass up, it could drift for hours."

"Maybe into Grenada itself?"

"Yeah, maybe."

"With the resulting chaos and confusion, it wouldn't be too hard to imagine Ramon Diaz stepping into a political arena to rebuke American carelessness," Bolan said. "Diaz has money and power to burn. Ivanovitch doesn't have anything else to offer him. But what if these islands were up for grabs?"

The Fed sighed. "It would also serve to sate whatever thirst for vengeance Ivanovitch has against the KGB. They would be implicated, of course, but hell, everybody is so used to the Russians and Americans pointing fingers at each other that it wouldn't matter. The upshot would be that the U.S. was careless enough to lose something as dangerous as this nerve gas and not tell anyone. We would lose a lot of influence worldwide, not just in the Caribbean.

"I'm going to contact the Man about this," Brognola continued, "and I'm going to recommend a Special Forces team be sent down there immediately."

"You and I both know it'll take hours before the first plane leaves the ground."

"It's the best I can offer, Striker." Brognola sounded pained. "Able Team and Phoenix Force are heavily engaged right now, and I can't free up either of them. Regular channels are my only resource. Even then we're going to have to be careful about how we go in."

Bolan heard the Fed shoving papers and objects across his desk as the swivel chair squeaked in response to each movement the big man made. "I don't think Ivanovitch is going to wait that long. He's already been feeling the heat before I turned up. I figure he's waiting on Diaz's signal before letting all hell break loose."

"I'm going to try to establish your cover when I set this play into operation, Striker, to make sure you're recognized as one of the friendlies. I don't know how loud the CIA is going to squawk when they find out we raided their files or how the Navy brass is going to take it. Chances are they might want to shut down anyone on the island who doesn't belong to the family."

"Don't worry about it, Hal. I've been taking care of myself for a lot of years now."

Brognola sounded uncomfortable when he spoke, saying, "I got to get things kicked into gear from this end, guy. It's going to mean shaking a lot of people out of bed, and I'm going to have to start now."

"I've got to return to the war myself," Bolan said, thinking of Abby Nichols and Jase and wondering how the woman was coping with his extended absence.

"There's not a whole lot I can say, Mack," Brognola said in a quiet voice, "except to watch your ass."

Bolan broke the connection. He shook the smoky shadows of the bar from his mind and went outside to embrace the clear, black night. Halting by the parked Cherokee, he breathed deeply, smelling the spice that rode the night air. The wind felt cool on his face, gentle.

Looking out to sea as he drove from the parking lot, he imagined the breeze as it would be if Ivanovitch succeeded in releasing the contents of the nerve gas cannisters, knowing it would be tainted, deadly. A death wind rising to creep over the island on cat's paws, filled with invisible and slashing claws to rend and destroy.

ABBY NICHOLS WAS almost asleep when Bolan returned to the cottage. She sat in the easy chair in the corner of the living room while a muted test pattern filled the screen of the television. Jase was asleep on the floor in front of it, one hand tucked tightly under his chin. She'd felt guilty about leaving him there but hadn't wanted to disturb the escape he had found. Even though he seemed to have complete faith in McKay, Jase worried about her. He always had.

The lights of the Cherokee winked out, and Abby had to strain to hear McKay approach the door. Anger burned within her when she checked her watch. It was after 1:00 a.m. When he had left, McKay had told her he would be gone only for a little while. He had said nothing about leaving her and her son totally defenseless while he continued playing whatever game he was involved in.

Earlier she'd felt guilty about striking him, and guiltier still about the way she'd gone to pieces in front of him. Now there was only the anger. And the fear. What if someone had found them while he was gone? Her active imagination had proved to be a handicap while trying to remain sane in the cottage. Twisted shadows from the trees outside had belonged to every mass murderer she'd ever heard of.

The doorknob turned, and for a moment Abby's heart stopped as she convinced herself it wouldn't be McKay, that someone had killed him after forcing him to reveal where she and her son were. Only the uncertain flickering of the television lighted the room.

But it was McKay.

The big man looked down at her. "Sorry I wasn't back sooner," he said quietly as he relocked the door, "but things started breaking sooner than I thought they would."

"You've got one hell of a nerve, mister," Abby said sharply.

Ignoring her, Bolan stepped across the sleeping boy and headed for the bathroom.

Infuriated, Abby pulled her robe more tightly around her and pushed herself out of the chair. If McKay thought he could brush her off so easily, he had another think coming.

"Hold on just a goddamned minute," she grated, following, but before she could reach him, the warrior shut the door in her face. Breathing deeply in an effort to control the rage that consumed her, Abby faced the door and raised her voice, loud enough for the man to hear but not for it to wake her son. "McKay, can you hear me?"

The sound of running water came from the other side of the door.

Fired by an anger she hadn't felt in almost a dozen years, Abby reached for the doorknob, twisted and followed it in. She would be damned if she was going to let the man think he could embarrass her out of the confrontation.

"McKay."

The translucent shower curtain blurred the outlines of the big man standing under the spray. The air inside the small room felt muggy from the hot water. He'd put his clothing on the sink, leaving the butts of his pistols within easy reach.

"McKay, I want to talk to you now." Steeling herself, she grabbed the folds of the curtain and jerked them back, depending on the shock value of the move to impress on the man how determined she was.

The naked man looked at her calmly.

Her eyes unwillingly followed the past history of violence and pain that wound around Bolan's body. A memory of Ray Bradbury's *Illustrated Man* flashed through her mind, of how the tattooed man's tattoos came to life when a person stared at them, each with its own story to tell. How many stories lurked within the scars she saw before her?

Her gaze trailed down the muscular legs, wondering if this was a knife wound or that was from a bullet. Then she noted the pinkish tint of the water spooling down the drain.

"Are you hurt?" she asked in a much quieter voice. The guilt returned when she searched for a wound, studying the blue-black bruise that covered one shoulder.

He reached for a bar of soap. "No. It belonged to someone else."

Abby tasted sour bile at the back of her throat and fought to maintain control. "The men who were looking for Jase and me?"

"It's a long story and kind of complicated."

"Those are the best kind, McKay. Ask my editor."

He gave her a small grin. "We're getting the floor wet."

Abby felt a hot flush stain her cheeks as she reached out to close the shower curtain. "Do you mind if I stay?"

"No. You need to know what we're up against. I'm going to be depending on your eyes to help us get through this, and you have to know what to look for."

Abby made herself avert her eyes, tried to force the picture of the lithe and powerful body from her mind. She'd known only two lovers since her husband, and neither one had lasted long. Once the initial anger at McKay had evaporated she hadn't been able to stay unembarrassed. Yet it hadn't seemed to bother him when he stood naked before her.

She listened as he spoke, noticing the concise way he described their situation. And even though his words frightened her, she was grateful for the truth—as terrible as it was.

Abby handed him a towel when he stepped from the shower, and he wrapped it around his waist. She watched as he draped another towel around his neck and padded toward the door, snaring the holsters on his way.

Abby sat on the bed and looked away while he dressed. "So what happens now?" she asked. "Do we just wait until the Special Forces people your friend is sending arrive?"

"No. I can't afford to wait."

"Why do you insist on doing what you do?"

"Because it's what I do best, and because somebody has to do it."

"But you operate on your own?"

He nodded. "More or less."

Abby bit her lip to stall the words on the tip of her tongue, but they wouldn't go away. "Yet you don't see yourself as a vigilante."

"I didn't say that. I see myself as I am. I deal in death, Abby, because in the part of the world I live in, that's the only currency that will buy you a ticket to the next day."

"But you are answerable to no one for your actions?"

"I am answerable to me. There are a lot of people who don't think that's enough."

Like Preston, Abby thought.

He got up from the bed and walked back into the living room. Abby turned off the light and followed him. She watched as he gently picked Jase up from the floor and moved him to the couch, talking quietly with the boy until Jase drifted back to sleep.

"I need you to wake me up in a couple of hours," he said as he returned to the bedroom. "It'll almost be light by the time we get everyone ready to move. I don't think anything will happen before then. Later, maybe, when the media people are covering the yacht races and entertainment. Terrorism never works without an appreciative audience."

Abby nodded, not knowing what to say, trying to imagine the lonely world McKay had to inhabit. Yet, even with the clarity of vision she had when writing a book, she could not dredge up an image of a place that would be so bleak and hard and desolate. So dead. And there would be no home, she realized, nowhere to keep his trust and vulnerabilities. Except for his mind and whatever pleasant memories he had stored up.

Impulsively she joined him on the bed, stretching out beside him.

His eyes bored into hers.

"Don't worry," she said, "I won't go to sleep. I'm just afraid, Mike. I'm afraid and I want to be held and I want someone to tell me everything is going to be okay for Jase and me."

She felt his arm go around her easily, felt the heat of him through the thin gauze of her nightgown, wondering if he would mistake her need to be held for something sexual, the way so many men seemed to. Then she became aware of how his breathing slowed and grew gentle on her neck. She let her palm ride the slow rise and fall of his rib cage, wishing sleep could claim her as easily as it had him.

19

After fixing the scuba's mouthpiece securely between his teeth and slipping the mask into place, Fyodor Ivanovitch tumbled over backward from the anchored boat. He felt the water close in over him, slowing down his movements as he reacquainted himself with the sensations of diving.

He peered through the water, discolored by the rising dawn, and saw the two men Diaz had assigned to shadow him staring down into the ocean. Both of them were armed. Ivanovitch wore only bathing trunks, a single air tank, the mask, flippers and a double-edged combat knife that was strapped to his right thigh.

It was apparent from the way the men searched the water that he had disappeared from their sight, masked by the light that splayed across the blue Caribbean. Their presence was a blatant statement that Ramon Diaz didn't trust him.

Ivanovitch couldn't blame the man, though. When he was helping to organize the Grenada operation of '83, he hadn't trusted Diaz implicitly either.

Angling his body backward, Ivanovitch flipped over slowly, guiding his descent with his hands. He let his arms relax at his sides once he achieved the correct direction, letting his legs do the work of powering him forward.

It took longer than he expected to find the small cave where he had hidden the tanks of nerve gas years earlier. Two other agents had helped him stash the tanks. Both had since perished in the service of their country. Ivanovitch had seen to it personally. He'd been the only one unwilling to inform the KGB of the recovery of the cannisters, wanting to keep them as much a secret as the monies and identities he had hidden away to aid his escape from Russia. Greb Strakhov had always kept things to himself, things that often influenced the outcomes of situations that might otherwise go badly. It was why Strakhov had wielded the power he did in the KGB despite the softening of Russia's foreign policies. And Fyodor Ivanovitch had always considered himself a good student.

He felt anxious as he pushed his way into the small cave, wondering if the cannisters were still there. Anything might have happened to them, he realized as he pushed his face forward in an effort to see into the gloom. They could have leaked or been found. The deadly gas in them could have become inert.

Forcing the thoughts from his mind, Ivanovitch stuck his upper shoulders inside the opening. A wriggling body shot into the Russian's face, thudding soundlessly into his mask. He felt the rake of cold fins lacerate his forehead and cheek as the creature fought to escape. Ivanovitch brought his hands up to cover his face, feeling the fish slide over his shoulder with a harsh grating of rough scales.

When he took his hands away, the creature was gone. Doubtless it had already chosen another hiding place. Ivanovitch brushed his hands through the trailing wisps of blood that flowed into the water in front of him, entering the cave fully.

Three people would have been crowded inside the cave, would have been forced flush against the rough, uneven walls. The Russian experienced a moment of claustrophobia before turning his attention to the silt across the floor of the enclosure. The opening was framed by the cave's darkness and the light refused to penetrate enough to illuminate the interior.

Working by feel alone, Ivanovitch dug through the loose debris until he uncovered the first cannister. He gathered it in his arms, holding it protectively across his chest as he returned to the open sea.

The cannister was something less than a meter long, all polished steel despite the sea's corrosive nature, with a diameter only a little longer than the span of Ivanovitch's hand. The identifying numbers and warnings had almost been eaten away.

Floating over the cannister, using its weight to anchor him, Ivanovitch examined the seal and found it to be secure. How much death did it hold? He hoped enough to create the type of international crisis he wished for.

It would take a lot of death, a lot of innocent death, to rescue his country from the peacemongers who seemed to hold sway over the politburo. At least this way, he reasoned as he returned to the cave for the second cannister, the innocent deaths would not belong to the Soviet Union.

BOLAN SAT at a wooden table in the small, open-air café with a cup of coffee in his hand, trying to look inconspicuous. Abby and Jase sat across from him. Already the island had come to life, the muted throb of calypso music from a handful of nearby bands becoming an undercurrent that seemed to gain in intensity with each passing moment. Groups of off-key voices sung all over the beach in sporadic snatches that would quickly rise and quickly die. Newcomers seemed to arrive in increasing numbers in an effort to stake out an area near the sea.

The sky was bright, blue and warm, but Bolan could feel the heaviness of it, could almost sense the waiting death that would arrive in an unseen storm if Ivanovitch wasn't stopped.

He tried to make himself relax, but his mind constantly turned to Diaz. The drug czar wouldn't remain on the island while Ivanovitch released the nerve gas. Even if the man had an underground area to retreat to in the mansion, Bolan was sure Diaz would be unwilling to risk exposure to the death wind that would blanket the island. From the café, the warrior had a clear view of the small airport that controlled the flow of air traffic to the island. He had already checked to see if all of Diaz's personal craft were still hangared. One of the airport workers had parted with the information more cheaply than the Executioner had expected.

There was no other way off the island unless Diaz went by boat. The man didn't seem to be the type to risk sailing away, though. It was too unsure. The gas could possibly overtake his craft or change directions. And even Ivanovitch would be unable to guess at the nerve gas's full range.

No. Ramon Diaz would leave the island by helicopter because there was no other sure way.

"Mike?"

"Uh-huh?"

"Why don't you tell the authorities what you know and let them try to handle this situation?" She looked uncomfortable as she spoke.

Bolan kept his voice low and soft as he replied, leaning forward to keep his words between them only. "Look around you, Abby. If these people knew about Ivanovitch and the nerve gas, there wouldn't be time to evacuate the island. Even if they could do it safely. You're talking about a widespread panic that would kill just as surely as the gas itself. My only choice is to attempt to negate the threat before anyone can put it into action."

"But you don't even know where to look."

"Ramon Diaz does."

"Why couldn't the police take this up with him?"

"Because they're bound by strictures and protocol. I have a free hand here. The same way Diaz and Ivanovitch do."

"What if Diaz won't tell you?"

"He'll have to," Bolan said. "If I take away his escape route, he won't have a choice. He'll be trapped on this island too. I can't see someone like Ramon Diaz laying down his life for anything."

Bolan glanced at his watch, uncomfortable with the amount of time that had passed. If Diaz was going to evacuate, it was going to have to be soon.

A black limousine that Bolan recognized as belonging to Diaz rolled across the white sands of the beach, unmindful of the shouted curses that were hurled after it.

Bolan pushed himself away from the table, wishing Abby hadn't flinched so fearfully when he moved. She gave him a searching look, filled with confused emotions.

"Diaz," he told her as he watched the limousine continue toward the airport.

"Mike?"

He looked at her.

She said "Be careful," but her eyes spoke volumes.

Bolan nodded and tousled Jase's hair, then left. He angled behind the café, climbing into the Cherokee long enough to recover the Skorpion. He had hidden the machine pistol inside a canvas bag so that he could carry it with him unnoticed. The extra clips were already tucked into the pockets of his windbreaker.

Unzipping the bag for easier access to the Skorpion, the Executioner followed the limousine, feeling the sand give treacherously underfoot. The opening numbers on this one were going to start slowly, sure, but the ones that came after were going to go down hard.

A LITTLE BLOND-HAIRED GIRL sat making a sand castle only a few yards from Yuri Mikhailin's position against a palm tree. She was so intent on her work that she never felt his gaze on her.

Conscious of a sense of danger, he scanned the beach again, not really knowing what he was looking for but realizing it would be just as Boris Kirov had said: he'd know what he was looking for the instant he saw it.

Almost of its own volition, his hand had caressed the butt of the American 9 mm automatic that was tucked into the waistband of his pants under the light jacket. Would it be that easy? he asked himself as images of his two previous kills drifted through his mind. Given no choice, would he kill on command? Or would he hesitate?

He had no answers, though he'd searched his mind and soul most of the night while he and Kirov had flown to Carriacou. He wasn't like Kirov. He couldn't kill with impunity and resist the moral price. But with lives other than his own on either side of the balance, what choice did he have? He'd never been forced to take this kind of measure of himself. He was a brave man, he knew that, but was he brave enough to take on the kind of guilt this operation would call for?

The little girl he had been watching earlier ran in front of him, pursued by two older boys who looked enough like her to be her brothers. All three of them were laughing as they scampered between seated families.

Yuri felt the stares of the curious as he started walking among the people, knowing his light jacket set him off as an outsider. He took refuge in the dark sunglasses he wore, making his face impassive and his stride echo the feeling that he was just a man doing a boring job.

The earplug Yuri wore crackled, then Kirov's voice filled the left side of his head, treading over the conversations of the people around him. Yuri felt his throat tighten.

"To your left, young Mikhailin," Kirov's disembodied voice directed.

Swinging his gaze in that direction, Yuri saw the sapphire blue of the Caribbean Sea swell out before him, dotted with myriad rainbow colors of small souls. Kirov was a small stick figure in the distance, standing by a fresh-fruit stand near the docks. Behind him were the naked masts of dozens more yachts and sailing craft.

Yuri changed directions, wondering if he was as visible to the men they pursued as he was to Kirov. Before, he'd had his own information to guide him in whatever operation he was involved in. Now he was operating solely on what Kirov had released to him. There were no guarantees that Ivanovitch was in the area or that the nerve gas existed. Yet Kirov had to know something, or Kulik wouldn't have tried to have them killed in New York City.

"I've seen three of them," Kirov said in a low voice as Yuri joined him near the docks.

"Where?"

"They're roving," Kirov replied, "like vultures waiting for a catastrophe to happen."

"Have they seen you?"

Kirov gave him a bleak smile. "If they had, young Mikhailin, either they or I wouldn't be alive now."

Pushing away his chagrin, Yuri searched the beach again, grateful for the sunglasses. "Who do you think is running this end of things for Kulik?"

"Chernetzsky, though I haven't seen him. But two of the men I have seen are known to associate with him."

Yuri recalled the agent. He and Chernetzsky had never been introduced or come in contact during a KGB mission, but he had heard of the man. Chernetzsky was a man Kulik would use for something like this: the agent was quick thinking, totally loyal to Kulik and took enjoyment in his wet work.

"Has there been any sign of the American agent who killed two of Chernetzsky's operatives yesterday?" Yuri asked.

"No, but I think Chernetzsky's men are searching for him. They are too intent in their search, too willing to devote manpower to guarding the airport."

Yuri looked up the beach.

"You can't see them now," Kirov said, "but they are there."

"Aren't they afraid of the nerve gas?" Yuri asked.

"They are prepared for it. Another thing that sets Chernetzsky's men apart from most you will see on this island is the briefcase each carries. I'm sure you'd find gas masks and small oxygen tanks inside if you get the chance to open one."

"Do you think Chernetzsky knows where Ivanovitch is going to release the gas?"

"Yes."

"Then we need one of them to tell us what he knows."

Kirov nodded, searching the younger man's face with an unflinching stare. "They have a guard posted on a yacht near us, young Mikhailin. I figure it to be Chernetzsky's craft, awaiting their exodus from this island. The man will be alert and willing to kill first and ask questions later. Our problem is that we need him alive. I think what little time we have left is quickly running out."

Yuri looked down the dock, noting that the only approach was the narrow metal strip linking all the boats.

"The fourth one down," Kirov said.

Yuri saw one guard, seated in the stern of the small yacht. "There's only one way onto the boat," Yuri observed.

"Our only alternative would be to try for one of the men guarding the airport," Kirov pointed out. "We would be a lot more visible doing that."

"Do you think you can get behind him while I get his attention?" Yuri asked. It amazed him that he felt more comfortable trusting his life to Kirov's skills than he thought he would.

"We could trade places," Kirov said. "You are younger and quicker than I am."

"Maybe younger, Comrade, but I have seen you move. I might be unknown to these men because they might not have thought I would get this far. I feel that they would know you."

"Let me go first, young Mikhailin. I will pass by and double back after I'm sure he has taken no notice of me."

Yuri nodded, feeling as though he were standing on an unseen precipice. He'd never had to play bait before and he felt uncomfortable in the role.

Kirov clapped him on the shoulder. "Remember, there can be no hesitation in this. If it comes to a choice between his life or yours, it is your duty to your country to live. As well as to your wife and daughter."

Yuri wanted to speak but didn't know what to say. He watched as Kirov strode away from him, wondering if the old man felt as much pressure as he did. How did those thin shoulders bear the burden?

When Kirov had passed the yacht and faded into the lingering groups of youngsters hovering around the various boats, Yuri walked slowly down the tin dock and stopped within hailing distance of the guard. Assuming an officious tone in his voice, he called to the man, demanding him to approach.

The guard's head moved slightly as he changed fields of vision.

Yuri had no trouble making out the snout of an Israeli Galil protruding from under the seat. A black automatic filled the guard's hand as he pushed himself to his feet warily and walked close to the yacht.

"Who are you?" the man demanded in English.

Yuri extended his phony ID toward the guard, knowing the sunlight glancing from the plastic cover would prevent the man from reading it. "I want to see Chernetzsky immediately. There has been a change in plans. Kulik wants Ivanovitch stopped now."

Indecision rippled across the guard's face.

Yuri knew he'd given the man enough information to make him hesitate and rethink his position. The guard had been prepared to stop anyone actively trying to halt the operation, not someone who raised questions.

Then the matter was taken out of the guard's hands as the silent shadow that was Boris Kirov stepped from behind the yacht and pressed his automatic to the man's nape.

Yuri couldn't hear what Kirov said to their captive as he clambered aboard the yacht, but he saw the man's pistol drop to the deck. The old man pushed it away with his foot. Holding his own weapon close to his side, Yuri picked up the automatic and stuck it in his waistband.

"The engines," Kirov directed as he led the guard to the stern again. "Quickly. We haven't much time."

Still holding his pistol, Yuri tossed off the tow ropes then ran up the short companionway leading to the helm. The turbines caught smoothly, and he turned to ask Kirov what to do next. Sudden movement on the dock drew his attention. Two men were running toward the yacht.

Shoving the controls backward, Yuri shouted a warning to Kirov, watching in frozen horror as the old man spun around too slowly.

Bullets flared from two Uzis, chipping through the expensive trim on the yacht as they lanced toward Kirov. The yacht's props dug into the brine like a scalded wildcat, dropping the bottom of the boat into the sea and making balance impossible.

Yuri was flung to one side when the yacht hit the boat next to it. He managed to grab the steering wheel with his left hand to keep from going over the side. Kirov and the guard dropped to the deck immediately, Yuri not knowing if they'd been victims of the boat's violent motion or the 9 mm bullets.

WHITE SAND SPRAYED suddenly to Bolan's left, and he was in full stride before he heard the sound of the shot.

Ahead of him the limousine had come to a stop at the airport gates. No one in the vehicle had seemed to give him a second glance. Until now, when he was weaving through the sand, trying to avoid the unseen shooter.

He glanced over his right shoulder, scanning the people at the edge of the line of palm trees thirty feet away. A ripple of movement behind the crowd echoed his flight, and Bolan glimpsed a short, dark-haired man pushing his way forward. As people caught sight of the gun in the man's hand and realized what was happening, the human fence separating Bolan and the shooter thinned to nothing.

"Hey, photographer," Ruffino Marino yelled. He held the H&K 9 mm in both hands as he fired. "You should have killed me two days ago, man. You should have made sure that I'd never see you again."

Bolan dropped to his knees, sliding through the loose sand for a moment as he drew the Desert Eagle. He let his

forward momentum pull him into a prone position with
the big .44 spearing out before him. Sand kicked into his
face as Marino's next shot fell only inches short of its
mark.

Bolan squeezed the trigger twice, watching Marino's
body jerk like a child's puppet with each impact before
being blown backward with the force of the 240-grain
boattails. The H&K went spinning away from the drug
lord's hand, inscribing a silver arc as it caught the morning sun repeatedly before landing.

"I'm sure now," the Executioner said quietly.

Forcing himself to his feet with the .44 still fisted openly,
Bolan looked at the limousine, knowing the local authorities would be en route in moments, knowing he'd lost the
element of surprise.

At least most of it, he amended.

He ran toward the limousine in an all-or-nothing sprint,
ripping the Skorpion free of the bag and releasing the
safety. He held the machine pistol in one hand at waist-
level.

The driver responded to the threat immediately while the
men in back tried to open their doors to get into firing position. Twin spumes of dirt and sand rained over Bolan
from the spinning tires, the back end of the limousine
fishtailing as it searched frantically for traction.

Concentrating fully on his own efforts, realizing the men
weren't about to threaten him yet, Bolan kept running.
When he was close enough, he launched himself into the
air, planting a foot on the trunk of the limo as he pushed
himself forward. He sprawled across the top of the car,
feeling his body roll haphazardly as he gripped part of the
door frame on the passenger side.

An arm streaked through the window at the front of the
limo, which prompted Bolan to trigger a burst from the
Skorpion that almost amputated the limb. He pulled des-
perately, trying to maneuver himself over to the driver's
side. With the wheelman taken out, the limo had to eventually stop.

But as the limo fishtailed, Bolan lost his hold, rolling off to the side. He relaxed his body, knowing he'd be cushioned some by the sand, but that the impact would be stunning none the less.

He landed on his back and felt the breath whoosh from his lungs. Swaying with the effort, he got to his feet and brought the Skorpion up into target acquisition on the retreating rear of the limo. Before he could squeeze the trigger some of the onlookers stepped into his line of fire.

Spotting the Cherokee less than thirty yards away, he rushed toward it. Bolan pitched the Skorpion into the passenger seat and fired up the engine. He shoved the stick into first gear and locked it into four-wheel drive, knowing it would give him an advantage over the limo in the sand.

How much time was left? Bolan asked himself as he shifted gears. The transmission whined as he wound it out, redlining the tach each time before clutching.

Ahead, the limo had already gained the highway, swerving across both lanes of traffic as it raced back toward Diaz's mansion.

If it reached its goal nothing less than a tank would be able to penetrate the security system and defenses. And in the interim, time would run out.

When the limousine made the switchback to return up the hill leading to the estate Bolan knew he had only one chance to stop it. He slid the Skorpion to the floorboard on the passenger side. Then he locked the seat belt into place as he ignored the turning of the road and raced full tilt up the hill that the road was built on.

He felt the Cherokee bounce with the effort as the tires left the asphalt and bit into the rough terrain. The sharpness of the incline forced him back into the seat, and he held on to the steering wheel with both hands. Then he was airborne and weightless, with the engine roaring shrilly.

His stomach lurched when he started his descent.

The nose of the Cherokee dipped, and the black bulk of the limousine filled his windshield.

20

Abby had to force her way through the crowd that had gathered in front of the small café. Towing Jase behind didn't make things any easier. Frightened and confused voices rumbled around, some of them singling her out for special attention. She ignored them as she continued shoving through, occasionally standing on her toes as she tried to spot the Executioner.

By the time Abby reached the front of the crowd, both the limousine and the Jeep had disappeared from sight. She stood there feeling empty and scared. What if Bolan didn't have enough time to find out where the nerve gas was? How many people would die?

The downbeat of helicopter rotors drew her attention. Searching the sky, she spotted the chopper coming in low from the north, a splash of white against an azure sky. The pilot didn't try to land at the airport, hovering instead near the center of the beach before setting down.

Before the rotors had stopped spinning, Abby rushed to the helicopter, Jase at her side. The pilot was younger than she expected, with long blond hair and a face that showed the gray strain of controlled hurt. He wore a shoulder holster, and a rifle sat canted forward between the seats.

Abby opened the door and found herself staring down the barrel of a pistol. When the pilot saw the boy he put the gun away.

"Get in," he ordered.

Praying she was making the right decision, Abby shook her head. "There's no time. McKay needs you. The only way the nerve gas can be spread effectively is to release it offshore. You'll have to help him search for Ivanovitch.''

Chase Murphy stared at her from behind the mirrored sunglasses, not comprehending.

Abby pointed. ''They went back toward town. Mc-Kay's in a dark blue Jeep Cherokee, following a limousine.'' She slammed the door and stepped back.

A heartbeat later the rotors churned faster as the engine strained, lifting the helicopter up and away.

She felt tears on her face when she looked at Jase. Now, if anything went wrong, she had doomed them both.

THE SEAT BELT KEPT Bolan out of the windshield but felt like a vise across his chest. He went with the force, trying to find the path of least resistance as the Cherokee landed on the front of the limousine. But just living through the impact alone was resistance enough to warrant numbing pain.

He had to use the Ka-bar to cut himself free of the belt—the locking mechanism had jammed. The four-wheel drive shifted underneath him as he scooped up the machine pistol and slid through the open window on the driver's side. Holding the Skorpion straight up from his shoulder, Bolan rounded the front of the Jeep, looking for movement inside the big car.

Blood covered the windshield and the glass had starred from three different impact points. He stepped closer, hearing the broken radiators of both vehicles wheeze and drip water onto the highway. The front tires of the limousine had exploded at the time of impact, and the Cherokee's weight pushed the vehicle even farther down. The polarized windows made it impossible to see if anyone in the rear seat had survived.

Bolan reached for the front passenger door and jerked it open, stepping quickly away from the potential line of fire. A decapitated body slid off the seat and onto the ground, its feet trapped under the crumpled dash.

A single shot from inside the limo blew out the window of the rear door on Bolan's side, scattering black glass at his feet. Even as he dropped to the ground, the Executioner heard the door on the other side of the car pop open with a scream of wrenched metal. Peering under the chassis, the warrior brought the Skorpion in line and triggered a burst that cut the retreating man's feet from under him.

Then Bolan was up and opening the back door, Skorpion held at waist level. Ramon Diaz's eyes were wide and filled with fear. The drug king bled profusely from a scalp wound that slashed across half his forehead. He'd been seated between his guards and had escaped the brunt of the wreck. The man next to him was dead, his neck bent at an impossible angle as the dead stare absorbed nothing of what it saw.

Bolan lifted the muzzle of Skorpion as he pulled the dead man from the car. The body rolled brokenly to a halt against the rear tire. Then he turned to Diaz. "Where's Ivanovitch?"

The drug lord ran a bony hand through his hair, smoothing it back into a semblance of order as he stared at the weapon in Bolan's hand. "You'll kill me if I tell you."

"Ivanovitch will kill us all if you don't. This nerve gas isn't instant death. I've been told it takes several minutes of excruciating pain before the convulsions start, then several minutes more before you finally die. If you tell me where he is, at least you'll have a fighting chance of staying alive."

Diaz closed his eyes and took a deep breath. "First you have to promise me you won't shoot me if I tell you."

"How do you know I won't lie to you?"

"Because I know you. Vincent knew you in Key West. He told me about you. Don't shoot me and I'll go away from here. You'll never hear of me again."

"All right," Bolan said. "Where's Ivanovitch?"

"Northwest of the island. On my yacht. It's the *Serifano*, marked in gold and white."

The Executioner was convinced Diaz told the truth. If he wasn't, the man was just as dead as the rest of the island would be when Ivanovitch released the gas. He backed away from the vehicles, trying to figure out how to become mobile before the law arrived.

The sound of straining props drew him around to face back the way he'd come. As he watched, the helicopter made a beeline for him. Murphy sat it down only a few feet from the wrecks.

Bolan's first realization was that the pilot was alone. He jogged to the door and threw it open, feeling torn muscles tighten in response. "Where's the woman and boy?"

"She wouldn't come. She told me to come after you. She had that look in her eye, the one women get when they don't intend to change their minds. She seems like a hell of a lady."

A hell of a lady, Bolan agreed when he considered the sacrifice she'd made. He pulled himself into the chopper. "We're looking for a yacht, the *Serifano*. It's supposed to be northwest of the island."

Murphy nodded and started to power up.

Bolan glanced back at the wrecked limo, watching as Ramon Diaz struggled to get out of the back seat. He had tracked Diaz's operation for days, all the way from Atlanta. Memories played, of Rigaberto's daughter who had been dead for some time, of the fear in Abby's eyes when she realized her son might be dead within hours. Diaz didn't deserve to live. But the warrior had given his word, and that was one constant, one rule he had tried to abide by in every war he fought in. Diaz would live to face another day.

FYODOR IVANOVITCH sat in the rear of the yacht, staring at the twin cannisters. He could feel the eyes of his two guards as they maintained their vigilance from the helm, but he ignored them. Diaz hadn't seen fit to tell them of the exact nature of their assignment, and Ivanovitch could see no reason to enlighten them. They were expendable, just as he was committed. And they would all surely die.

He placed a hand on one of the petcocks, almost exerting enough pressure to turn it and release the gas. The sense of power the cannisters gave him was amazing. He had issued death before, but only a personal death. The thing he controlled now was a horror, unstoppable once the wind caught the gas and hurled it toward the unsuspecting masses that swarmed Carriacou's beaches.

It would be an international incident, the kind that would send the Americans and Russians spinning apart again, the way it had to be if Russia was going to be great once more. The way Lenin and Khrushchev had dreamed it would be. Not the Western clone Gorbachev would have it become.

In time, maybe the name of Fyodor Ivanovitch would become an important one in Russian history books. It was the kind of immortality that would be worth dying for.

Ivanovitch removed his hand from the petcock and stood, thinking he would wait a while longer and savor the feeling of power that flooded him. How many men could hold the lives of so many in their hands without constraint?

"Someone is coming," one of the guards shouted.

Ivanovitch looked up, noted the direction the man was pointing in, and climbed the stairs leading to the upper deck. Shielding his eyes against the sun, he located the craft. Smoke danced from the boats as they sped in his direction, and the gunfire crackled out of sync with the visual input.

Turning from the deck, Ivanovitch damned them, whoever they were, for spoiling the serenity of the moment and forcing his hand. He raced down the stairs two at a time, skidding across the deck until he reached the cannisters.

He gripped the first petcock, feeling adrenaline rush through his body. He twisted, holding his breath, hoping that his strength lasted long enough for him to open the second cannister as well.

The petcock remained immobile, refusing to budge even as Ivanovitch realized that the years immersed in seawater must have rusted it shut. He tried the second one, only to be faced with the same problem. Rage consumed him as he grabbed the first cannister and carried it across the deck to the stairs leading to the stateroom.

He would find a way, he promised himself. Even if he had to blow up the yacht to do it.

RECOVERING HIS BALANCE, Yuri Mikhailin spun the wheel and reversed the engines, heading the yacht out to sea. Was Kirov all right? Yuri was surprised to discover he cared about the old man as a human being instead of as the indestructible KGB agent he had seemed to be.

"Young Mikhailin."

Relief flooded Yuri's when he heard Kirov's voice. "I'm all right. How are you?"

"A little worse for wear, but still operable." The old man got to his feet, holding the big pistol under his captive's throat.

Back on the dock a handful of agents prowled among the moored boats, and Yuri realized they were looking for the right one to steal. He returned his attention to his steering, heading the yacht toward the open sea.

A sharp yell drew Yuri's attention. He turned his head toward Kirov, thinking the captive had somehow managed to turn the tables. Instead Kirov held the man supine on the deck, the muzzle of the pistol jammed against the man's chest. A short knife jutted from the old man's left fist, poised delicately over the captive's genitals. As Yuri watched, blood dripped from a shoulder wound on the old man and ran down Kirov's arm to mix with the blood of the man under him.

Without looking up, Kirov said, "I know what you're thinking, young Mikhailin, that only an animal would torture its prey and that maybe this man deserves mercy.

But had the situation been reversed and he been assigned to the Russian end of this operation, this man might very well be the one to take Natasha's and little Tanya's lives had they not been moved to safety.''

Yuri nodded and fought to maintain control of his stomach as it heaved threateningly, glad in a way that Kirov was there to extract the information. Hoping, too, that the man possessed it.

There were a few high-pitched screams before Kirov stood and put a bullet through the man's head. He refused to meet Yuri's gaze as he climbed the stairs, searching the instrument panel until he located the compass. He tapped it gently with bloodstained fingers.

''Chernetzsky and his men have found a boat. We go northwest to find the *Serifano*. There we will find Ivanovitch.''

The KGB agents were pulling out of the dock now, ranged across the stern of another yacht. Several of the men held assault rifles. Mikhailin and Kirov had the Galil, their automatics and the pistol that had belonged to the guard. Not nearly enough to take on the army that was following them. The best they seemed to be able to hope for was to somehow negate Ivanovitch and the nerve gas. Kulik's men wouldn't let them live.

More than anything else he wanted to see his family again, but that hope was dwindling fast.

Kirov had removed a folded handkerchief from his pocket and placed it under his shirt over the shoulder wound. Then he turned his attention to the Galil and began to fieldstrip it automatically.

''We have only sixty rounds for the rifle,'' Kirov told his companion. ''No more than that between us for our pistols, and perhaps another forty for the pistol we took from Chernetzsky's man. Our only hope to even partially succeed in this is to do as much damage as we possible can in a short time.'' He faced Yuri. ''It seems, young Mikhailin, that I have brought you thousands of miles from your home to have you die.''

Yuri was unsure of the emotions that coursed within him. Conflicting images of Kirov flashed through his mind: Kirov on the day he'd killed Petrovsky's son; Kirov when he'd played with little Tanya; Kirov as he'd been in the rest room at La Guardia Airport, taking out the men who pursued them; Kirov as he had been only moments ago, extracting the information about Ivanovitch. The man was deep, fathoms below the surface image Yuri had painted on Kirov.

Before he could say anything, a yacht swung into view, sitting lifeless in the placid waters. At the distance it was difficult to make out the name.

"The *Serifano*?" Kirov asked.

Yuri finally nodded, making course corrections that would bring them to the vessel.

Kirov raised the Galil, flipped up the L-shaped open sights. "I see two men. Is either of them Ivanovitch?"

"I can't tell."

Kirov sighed. He pressed his cheek into the stock of the rifle, melding mind and body with the rifle, so great was his concentration.

Yuri heard autofire crack behind them and risked a glance over his shoulder. Chernetzsky's team had donned their gas masks, looking inhuman in the black headgear. Bullets ripped into the lower deck as the bigger yacht started to catch them.

"Ram the *Serifano*," Kirov said, "then get aboard as quickly as possible. It will be our only chance against Chernetzsky's men. Aim for the stern and hopefully we can damage the engines and render them inoperable."

Hot brass ejected from the Galil as Kirov pumped the trigger. One of the two men standing on top of the *Serifano* pitched backward into the sea.

Something smacked into Yuri's leg, and the limb threatened to collapse under him. Grimly he hung on to the wheel as the vessel powered into the stern of the luxury yacht. For a moment he blacked out from the impact, recovering to find himself suspended in Kirov's grip.

"Move, young Mikhailin," the old man ordered as he pushed Yuri over the helm.

Yuri had to use both hands to prevent himself from sprawling onto the *Serifano*'s deck. He pushed to his feet, drawing his weapon as he pressed himself against the cabin wall. Kirov was at his heels, a silent wraith, despite age and wounds. The old man peered upward expectantly, watching for the remaining man on board.

The stolen yacht blocked Yuri's view of Chernetzsky's progress. He could tell from the way the deck moved sluggishly under his feet that the *Serifano* was taking on water, but not fast enough to end Ivanovitch's threat. Yuri wondered why the man hadn't already released the nerve gas.

Autofire drove him to the deck again as Chernetzsky's craft powered around the stern. The Galil barked behind him, and a form dropped from the attack boat.

Yuri fisted his 9 mm and streaked forward while the pursuit boat was out of position, intending to find the remaining guard and put him out of commission. He paused, watching Kirov climb to the steering section with the Galil draped over a shoulder.

A hand seemed to come from nowhere and knock his weapon away. Yuri tried to recover it, but a booted foot thudded into his midsection and forced the air from his lungs. He caught a fleeting glimpse of Fyodor Ivanovitch, his face a mask of rage, before the man gripped him in a painful hammerlock. He felt cold steel press against the back of his neck.

"Boris," Ivanovitch yelled, using Yuri as a shield by moving him from side to side, "Show yourself or I will kill him."

Yuri waited, tense with the sure knowledge that Kirov would let the threat go unanswered. His life didn't matter. The old man would do what he had to in order to achieve his objective.

Yuri waited for the bullet that would kill him, unsure if it would belong to Ivanovitch or to Kirov. He was totally unprepared to see the Galil come sliding into view and Kirov step into place behind it, his hands clasped behind his head.

BOLAN STRIPPED the telescopic lens from Chase Murphy's M-14. Hanging out the side of the helicopter and trying to fire through the scope would have proved almost impossible. The field of vision was too restricted.

Below, rocking gently in tandem with another yacht, the *Serifano* appeared abandoned. Smoke drifted from both vessels, creating disturbing patterns across the blue sea, like the breath of alien beasts.

Another boat circled the *Serifano*, and Bolan could see that a boarding crew was prepared to move in. He raised his binoculars and raked the mobile craft from one end to the other, wanting to identify the people on board. His combat sense told him these men were on the wrong side, and logic told him if they were connected with the law enforcement people on Carriacou, Ramon Diaz wouldn't have been running free this morning.

When they were less than forty feet off the deck of the boat, gunfire erupted from the men, ricocheting from the metal body of the chopper and ripping through the Plexiglas bubble.

"Do you know any *friendly* people?" Murphy asked as he banked to the left.

"Yeah," Bolan replied grimly, "and I'm trying to save a few of them now." He put the binoculars away and hefted the M-14 as the young pilot spun the chopper around for an engagement pass.

"I've got a little surprise for those guys down there," Murphy said. "Bobby Drake helped me get it set up right after you called. Which was why I was running late this morning. That man's a genius when it comes to getting his hands on black market materials. After palling around with you once and finding out the kind of company you keep, I figured I might need an ace up my sleeve."

The young pilot reached for an electric control bolted under the dash. The hand unit contained a toggle switch and a button. When Murphy flipped the toggle, a greenish target less than a palm's width lit up on the Plexiglas bubble.

"Fifty-caliber Browning machine gun," Murphy explained. "We concealed it behind a little new paint and a few pieces of fiberglass. Once I light this baby up, I got about a thousand rounds to use. That ain't much time in a firefight like this, because I'm not going to be able to get very close without taking a chance of being shot down. And a man with your record can't wait around for the local law to shake your hand and give you a big smile."

Murphy worked the stick, maneuvering the chopper into another pass.

"There won't be a reload on the machine gun. It's a onetime emergency set up. Everything's external except the hand control, and I didn't bring any extra ammunition. I'll try to get you on the *Serifano* and bird-dog those bastards while you nullify the nerve gas."

"Watch your tail," Bolan said as he checked his weapons. He had stripped out of the jacket and jammed into his pants pockets as many clips for the Desert Eagle and Beretta as he could. Murphy had only one extra clip for the M-14, and Bolan had already taped it to the butt of the first one for a quick reload. The Skorpion hung down his back by its sling, and the spare magazines for it were in an oilskin pouch at his side. "It might be a surprise the first time through, but they'll start firing earlier the next time you come over. The assault rifles they're using have a hell of a lot more range than what you're carrying."

Murphy grinned. "I believe in luck, McKay." He swung the copter wide, closing in on the yacht. "You're the one who's going to have to really watch his tail. I know who the bad guys are from up here, but how the hell are you going to tell friend from foe once you're down there?"

"Hopefully the good guys won't be shooting at me."

"You're a party crasher, guy, and open game. If you make it back off that boat, I'll be here." Reaching overhead, Murphy clicked on a cassette player and the music of Creedence Clearwater Revival filled the chopper.

Yeah, the storm clouds had definitely gathered on this one, Bolan reflected. He leaned out and felt the slipstream try to rip him from the helicopter. He pulled the M-14 to his shoulder as Murphy dogged the moving yacht, firing a 3-shot burst that knocked one of the gunners into the sea. He took another grip and sighted again, feeling tears being whipped from his open eye by the wind. The next burst went high and wide as a crosscurrent swept the aircraft up a few feet.

When the Browning cut loose, it sounded like the helicopter was vibrating to pieces, yammering a death song that scissored across the yacht from one end to the other.

"Son of a bitch." Murphy grimaced as he held his side. "You can feel the bastard beating the hell out of the underside."

"Are you going to make it?" Bolan asked.

Murphy headed toward the *Serifano*. "Do I got a goddamned choice? Get ready, we're going to do this right the first time without a net."

Bolan headed out the door, maneuvering onto the pontoon as Murphy reduced airspeed. He held the M-14 tightly in his left hand, then pushed himself off, dropping toward the deck, watching it rush up too fast.

"How DOES IT FEEL to be so helpless, Comrade?" Ivanovitch taunted.

Kirov remained silent.

"I didn't think you would come out of retirement, Boris, not even to stop me. When you walked away from the KGB, you said you'd had your fill of all the killing. Then one of my contacts said you'd killed one of Petrovsky's sons and were coming after me. I didn't doubt the man, but I couldn't guess why. Until I saw him." Ivanovitch lifted Yuri's head. "Then I understood."

"Where is the nerve gas, Fyodor?" Kirov asked in a flat voice.

"Below. It seems that the petcocks are rusted shut. I couldn't open them, so I carried them downstairs and set fire to the yacht. When it explodes, the gas will shoot into the air in an even bigger cloud than I had hoped for."

"And you would release this death on all those innocent unsuspecting people? Why?"

"To restore our country to the greatness it deserves. You walked away from the KGB when it started to go soft, Boris. You knew what would happen."

"I walked away from the KGB because I knew the era for men like me was over. There's a new world coming, and no matter how much you fight it, it will not resist being born."

"No, damn you," Ivanovitch yelled. "We will become the world leader again. We are destined to be a superpower."

Kirov managed a small smile. "So now you believe in Manifest Destiny, Fyodor? That is a Western concept. Maybe you aren't as flawless as you think."

The drone of helicopter rotors drowned out whatever reply Ivanovitch had. Yuri looked up and saw a man drop from one of the pontoons to the yacht's stern. Then he disappeared from view.

Moving suddenly, Yuri shifted in Ivanovitch's grip and felt the first shot from Ivanovitch's pistol burn across the back of his neck. He shoved an elbow into the agent's groin and broke free, leaping for the Galil, knowing he would never reach it in time.

Instead he felt Kirov's thin weight drop across him instantly, felt the old man jerk as bullets slammed into his frame. Yuri rolled from under Kirov, his weapon up and tracking. Ivanovitch was gone.

Hurriedly he examined Kirov and discovered that he was still breathing. Yuri rolled him over gently, noting the arterial flow coming from the old man's mouth. Kirov's breath was labored, ragged.

"Why did you save me?" Yuri asked as unexplained tears filled his eyes. "I know you have another gun. Why didn't you let him shoot me and kill him?"

Kirov smiled gently. He reached out to touch Yuri's hair. "I've wanted to talk to you since I had myself assigned as your partner." He coughed roughly, the pain closing his eyes for a moment. "A long time ago, when I was young, I married a woman I loved very much. Before she was killed, we had a child, a son. I named him Yuri, after my father who had been a farm laborer and a good man. After my wife's death, I arranged for the boy to be raised by the state without anyone knowing he was my son, not knowing he would follow in the same bloody footsteps I had made. But he was a man then, a chooser of his own path. Until I saw the machinations Vladimir Kulik had put into effect. I knew about the Israeli woman agent, and I knew that you were a good man, like my father, in a career you weren't totally cut out for. I knew you would be trapped between the forces Kulik had established, without anyone you could trust. I came to be with you."

Yuri's vocal cords had frozen; he could say nothing.

"I love you, Yuri. I'm glad I got to hold my granddaughter. She's very much the way your mother was. You are right to take pride in her." Kirov choked again and he could barely catch his breath.

"I love you too, Father." Yuri held Kirov until the man died, rocking him gently in his arms. Then he closed the old man's eyes and picked up the Galil.

BOLAN DIVED AND ROLLED, coming up in a combat crouch and raking autofire at a gunner who stepped from hiding. The 7.62 mm tumblers from the M-14 blew the guy over the side of the yacht. Fyodor Ivanovitch raced around the cabin from the other direction and hurled himself at the Executioner.

The KGB agent's weight slammed the breath from Bolan's lungs and knocked him across the deck. The railing caught him just above the knees, and he felt himself falling backward. He dropped the M-14 to the deck and grabbed Ivanovitch's shirt, pulling him over as well.

The water enveloped Bolan in its warm embrace, crystal and pure. Ivanovitch had gotten lost somewhere along the way, and he scanned the water as he swam for the surface.

"You're too late," Ivanovitch yelled in his ear.

Bolan attempted to turn, but the bigger man wrapped an arm around his throat and dragged him under again. Water filled the Executioner's ears, robbing him of his hearing. Oxygen bubbles spilled from his lips as Ivanovitch tightened his grip. He grabbed one of the Russian's ears and pulled hard, feeling the flesh tear.

Ivanovitch released him and fled.

Bolan opened his hand and let the ear float away, then angled to the surface in pursuit of Ivanovitch. When the Executioner surfaced, the Russian was hacking and struggling for air, holding one hand to the side of his head.

The ex-KGB agent struck without warning, a straight, off-the-shoulder right that caught Bolan full in the face.

The warrior staggered backward with the force, taking a deep breath. As his legs came up out of the water, he kicked the Russian in the temple. Ivanovitch's head rolled with the blow. Then the man was beneath the surface again, cutting through the water straight at the Executioner.

Bolan met him head-on, twisting his face to one side to evade the finger-thrust aimed for his eyes. They fought like wrestlers, fighting for holds that slid across wet skin, fighting against the clock that let their oxygen empty from their lungs.

Ivanovitch locked his hands around Bolan's neck, holding him from the front, until the Executioner managed to get a leg between them and force the bigger man away. They surfaced again, both of them gasping for air, swimming warily in a circle as they watched each other.

"Even if you kill me, American, you lose," Ivanovitch panted. "The nerve gas is on board, waiting for the yacht to explode and release it into the air. You cannot stop it. It will be recognized as being of American manufacture, and your country will experience yet another loss of face.''

Bolan glanced at the yacht and saw smoke curling up into the sky. If what the man said was true, there couldn't be much time left.

The sound of heavy-machine-gun fire signaled the return of the yacht circling the *Serifano*. As it powered into view, Bolan saw the helicopter in hot pursuit. There wasn't much time left for any of them. Murphy had probably exhausted his ammunition by this point and would soon be nothing more than a flying target for the assault rifles beneath.

The men aboard the yacht spotted him and directed their fire in his direction, making both of them dive to evade the bullets. Ivanovitch reached a hand to his calf and pulled a combat knife free of its sheath. The blade seemed to gleam with anticipation as Bolan drew his Ka-bar.

Ivanovitch lunged without warning, cutting through the water like a porpoise, the knife a sharp fang extended before him.

Bolan grabbed the man's wrist and let himself be turned, bringing his right hand up in a movement that raked across the Russian's throat, slitting it from ear to ear. A dark cloud of blood shot into the water and engulfed the Executioner. He ignored the lifeless body and swam for the surface, down to the stern section of the *Serifano*, where he could clamber onto the deck.

As he stood up, a coughing man stumbled from below deck carrying a stainless-steel cannister. He fell to his knees and looked at the Executioner, drawing a pistol from his waistband.

Bolan drew the Desert Eagle, bringing the .44 into target acquisition faster than the other man could line up his own weapon. The man didn't drop his gun, and Bolan knew he'd have to kill the guy to make him. But this man was carrying one of the cannisters from the fire, he reasoned, remembering Brognola had said there was a Russian team tracing Ivanovitch.

"I'm an American agent," Bolan said, never dropping the sights of the .44.

"Yuri Mikhailin, KGB," the man replied in English. "There's another cannister." He placed the weapon on the deck and picked up the cannister again, still coughing.

Holstering the .44, Bolan ripped a section from his shirt and tied it around his lower face. His wet clothes would protect him from the heat of the fire, and the cloth would protect his lungs, but there was nothing he could do for his eyes. He plunged down the stairs, barely able to make out the details of the cabin.

Bright yellow flames shone through the smoke, creating garish shadows on the walls. In the middle of the floor, he found the cannister, almost blistering hot, and seized it, ignoring the pain as he carried it back up the stairs.

He reached the top as Mikhailin threw the first one overboard. Bolan did the same. Now, even if the yacht blew, the islanders were safe from the deadly gas.

During Murphy's next pass over the *Serifano* Bolan waved him down. He and Mikhailin grabbed the pontoon only seconds before the pilot revved up the rotors and lifted them from the burning deck. Once inside the cockpit, Bolan made a note of the coordinates for transmission to Brognola and his special task force later. They'd be able to recover the nerve gas and put it somewhere safe— if there was a safe place for weapons like that.

"I don't suppose an American agent could resist turning in a member of the KGB?" Mikhailin asked from the back of the helicopter.

The *Serifano* exploded, the fireball enveloping the other two yachts. All three boats shot debris into the sky, rocking the helicopter with the concussive force.

"I didn't notice any KGB agents down there," the warrior said. "When I looked, we were wearing the same uniform and shared a common goal."

"I feel the same way." Mikhailin reached forward to take Bolan's hand.

The Executioner gazed down at the sea, aware of the winds of war and how they changed people. He glanced over his shoulder at Mikhailin, noting that the man had dropped into a deep sleep after attending to his leg wound. He knew Mikhailin had had to make his own way to Ivanovitch through soldiers of his own country, with little or no help. Knew, too, that the man would make a formidable opponent, even, perhaps, while hoping that day never came.

A warrior never knew his limits and capabilities until they were tested, exhausted. And the Executioner was determined to keep on giving of himself whenever and wherever he was needed. Until he was no longer needed.

Or until there was nothing left to give.

A secret consortium conspires to terrorize the world

DON PENDLETON's
MACK BOLAN

Tightrope

One by one, the top officials of international intelligence agencies are murdered, spearheading a new wave of terrorist atrocities throughout Western Europe. Mack Bolan's mission is compromised from the start. The line between good and evil is a tightrope no man should walk. Unless that man is the Executioner.

**Phoenix Force—bonded in secrecy to avenge the acts
of terrorists everywhere.**

Super Phoenix Force #2

American ''killer'' mercenaries are involved in a KGB plot to
overthrow the government of a South Pacific island. The American President, anxious to preserve his country's image and not
disturb the precarious position of the island nation's government, sends in the experts—Phoenix Force—to prevent a coup.

Out of the ruins of civilization emerges...

DEATHLANDS

The Deathlands saga—edge-of-the-seat adventure not to be missed!